ALL

OR

NOTHING

by

D. R. Evans

ANTE

MORTEM

Chapter 1

Pinetree, Colorado — Friday, August 12, 1994

Death stalked Matthew Chambers for twenty four years before finally catching up with him at the close of a summer day.

The clock stood at twenty minutes past nine as Matthew Chambers walked into his law office on the outskirts of Pinetree on the last morning of his life. Kathleen looked up from the copy machine where she was holding a mug from which drifted the odor of fresh coffee. Next to her, on a small wooden table, stood a yogurt from which a teaspoon protruded.

She smiled at him. Not for the first time, Matthew briefly wished that he was twenty four instead of forty four.

"Morning, Matthew."

"Morning, Kathleen. The first appointment is Jeremy Walters, at nine thirty, about a codicil, isn't it?"

"Yes, and then there's the minister at the Episcopal church, Reverend Allbright, at ten o'clock."

"Ah, yes," Matthew nodded. "That should take until noon, I expect."

"Then there's Rotary until two, and a couple of house closings this afternoon. One at Sutton and Dwight's at two fifteen with the Cavaliers, and one at Bolton and Smith's at three fifteen with the Allens."

He grinned mischievously. "So that's my day. And what about you? Anything special?"

Kathleen returned her employer's grin. She was lucky, and she knew it. She lived in a beautiful town, worked for an undemanding man who paid a very fair salary, and had a boyfriend who thought the world of her. Life could be a lot worse.

"Not really. I thought I might do a bit of typing, you know, just for form's sake; answer the phone, things like that, for which my expensive education trained me."

"Sounds fine to me. Let me know if it gets too much for you."

Matthew disappeared into his office, closing the door so that he could prepare himself for the arrival of Mr. Walters. As expected, Kathleen, for all the persiflage a remarkably efficient secretary-cum-receptionist, had placed Mr. Walters' file on his desk ready for perusal. His "In" basket contained the files that he would need later in the day.

He draped his jacket over the rear of his chair, loosened his tie, and opened the file labeled *Mr. Jeremy Walters.*

———————

Matthew Chambers returned to his office from Bolton and Smith as the clock in the reception area moved past four o'clock. As he walked in, Kathleen was seated at her desk, taking a telephone call.

He waited until the call was completed.

She said, "That was Mrs. Healy, calling to ask if you'd be willing to endorse her husband for mayor again this time around, and reminding you about supper this evening. I told her you were out and you'd get back to her when you were available."

A momentary frown creased Matthew's face.

"OK, I'll deal with it, thanks." His face cleared. "Now, Kathleen. It's past four o'clock on a beautiful summer day. What's more, it's a Friday. And to clinch the matter, your boyfriend will be in town within a couple of hours. Why don't you take the rest of the afternoon off? Just switch on the answering machine and get out of here. I have to be at the Healys' early and I need to go home first and get changed, so I'll be leaving in a couple of minutes myself. Have a nice weekend, and I'll see you nicely rested on Monday morning."

Kathleen scrutinized her boss. Presumably his comment about being "nicely rested" was a joke? But his face was a mask, so instead of laughing she threw him a muted smile and began to tidy her papers.

4

Matthew strode into his office and glanced around to check that there was nothing he had forgotten that needed his attention before the weekend. A minute later, the two of them left the building together.

Matthew drove his Cherokee back to his mountain hideaway with the window down, letting the breeze caress the side of his face. Already the sun was beginning to fall towards the mountains; in another hour parts of the town would be thrust into early-evening shadow.

He turned off the road and changed down for the climb up the long dirt driveway to his home.

Almost immediately, the openness of the valley was replaced by the packed boskage of the pine-studded slopes. Driving now in shadow, he was chilled by the sudden coolness, and shivered. He closed the window. Ninety seconds later, he pulled to a halt inside his garage. He discovered that he was whistling.

He showered, changed and recovered a bottle of wine from the refrigerator where it had lain for the past two days. As he had done several times earlier in the day, he exercised his right arm to make sure that there was still no pain from the shoulder where he had injured it playing racquetball on Wednesday. There was a slight twinge, but nothing serious; the anti-inflammatories Dr. Taylor had given him were doing their job.

He checked himself in the mirror one last time. Now that he had discarded his suit and replaced it with a long-sleeved cotton Oxford shirt and slacks, he looked every bit as relaxed as he felt. He checked his watch, performed a quick calculation, decided that he would arrive just about at the right time, and descended once more to the garage.

Matthew drove unhurriedly through Pinetree. Halfway through town, a quarter of a mile beyond his office, the sun ducked behind a mountain. Even in August, evening came early in Pinetree.

He arrived at the Healys' front door with a smile on his face and the bottle in his hand at five minutes to five.

Lucinda Healy greeted him at the door, while her husband hovered uncertainly behind her. Lucinda, almost the same age as Matthew, shared with him the happy characteristic of looking roughly ten years younger than her chronological age. Lucinda's hair, undyed and as firmly brunette as ever, hung past her shoulders as she held her head at its characteristic slightly-tipped angle. Her eyes shone, and the only lines on her face were placed there by her smile of greeting. She gave Matthew a quick hug and a kiss on the cheek.

5

"Good evening, Matthew. Glad you could make it."

She looked into his eyes a moment longer than was strictly necessary, and Matthew struggled to keep anything from showing in his face, fully aware that her husband was watching.

Lucinda stepped backwards, and Matthew took the opportunity to interpose the bottle between them.

"It's been in the refrigerator all day. It should be just about right after the drive over."

Lucinda took both the hint and the bottle, and turned toward the kitchen. Matthew stepped into the house and was greeted by Lucinda's husband.

Bill Healy was quite unlike his wife. Short and balding, he looked every day of his forty five years, and then some. He wore an open-necked shirt, exposing a mass of graying hairs on the upper part of his chest.

Despite his appearance, Bill Healy possessed a forceful personality that had served him well in local politics, culminating in his election as mayor of Pinetree four years ago. His reelection as council member and mayor this coming November was a foregone conclusion. Even Matthew intended to vote for him, although for reasons that had nothing to do with politics in the usual sense of the word.

Healy greeted him. "Come in, Matthew. I'm sorry we have to eat at such an ungodly hour, but Lucinda insisted that it had been much too long since we had you over and, as you know, she's going back east to visit her parents tomorrow. What with that and my work on the council and for Rotary, this was the only time we could fit you in."

"That's all right, don't apologize. I'm always happy to sample Lucinda's cooking. Makes a change from the usual bachelor fare."

"Well, I just hope you don't mind the early hour. The council meets at seven thirty and I have to leave by seven, you see."

"It's all right. Really. Don't worry about it."

"Well let me get you a drink, then. What'll it be? The usual? Vodka and orange for the first one and plain o.j. after that?"

"Yes, thank you. That would be fine."

They headed for the kitchen. Matthew hung back dutifully at the kitchen doorway, hesitating to enter Lucinda's domain. He watched while her husband extracted a nearly empty pitcher of juice from the refrigerator and poured the juice into a glass. Lucinda was putting the finishing touches to the salad.

She said, "You two go sit at the table, and we'll be ready to start in a few minutes. Oh, Bill, give me the pitcher; I'll make up some more juice for Matthew."

"What's for dessert?" Matthew asked.

"Pavlova. It's the most fattening thing I could think of," Lucinda said, a mischievous smile on her face. Her face suddenly became serious. "If that's all right," she added, a note of uncertainty in her voice.

"Fine, but I'll have to be excused for a couple of minutes."

"Be our guest." Bill Healy added ice and vodka to Matthew's drink and handed it to his guest.

Matthew walked to the dining table, put his drink down, and extracted a small device from his pocket. Placing it against his index finger, there was an audible click and he withdrew the device to reveal a maroon drop on the end of his finger. He took a small strip from his pocket and used it to sop up the blood.

Slowly, he returned to the kitchen, glancing every few seconds at his watch. He opened the faucet and thrust the strip into the stream of water. Without thought, he went through the thrice-daily motions, shaking the excess water from the strip, then drying it thoroughly on a towel. Walking back to the dining room, he withdrew a small machine from his pocket and inserted the strip. Within seconds, the liquid crystal display showed *100*.

Bill Healy crossed the room and stood at his shoulder, a half-empty glass in his hand. He looked enquiringly at his guest.

"Everything all right?"

"Fine. If you'll excuse me, I'll give myself a fix."

It was an old, tired joke, but it never ceased to amuse Healy. As always, he grinned with apparently genuine delight as Matthew went outside to his car. Matthew returned with his kit and locked himself in the guest bathroom.

He took the opportunity to urinate. He washed his hands; then, seating himself on the toilet, he opened his kit.

Extracting two small bottles, he rolled them in turn between his hands to mix the contents thoroughly. Taking an alcohol-soaked paper towelette, he cleaned the tops of both bottles then tossed the paper into the trash can. He removed a syringe from his bag, then stopped for a moment to consider the ramifications of the forthcoming pavlova.

He rarely varied his dosage, but the high sugar content of tonight's dessert convinced him that this evening it was a reasonable precaution, especially since he planned to drink two glasses of orange juice. Holding the syringe up to the light, he withdrew the plunger until it sat against the fiducial mark that signified 33 units — one unit more than his usual dose. He picked up one of the bottles. As always (his doctor twenty four years ago had stressed that he should always do things in the same order), the bottle of slower-acting NPH insulin came first.

Aligning his eyes with the syringe, he carefully injected twenty five units of air into the bottle. Then he withdrew the syringe and inserted it into the second bottle, into which he injected the remaining eight units of air. Then, slowly, he reversed the procedure: he turned the bottle upside down and extracted eight units of the regular insulin. Exchanging bottles, he drew twenty five units of NPH insulin into the syringe.

He looked down at his left leg, and searched for the last needle mark. There it was: a minute, red dot high on his thigh. He brought the needle so that its point rested against the skin about an inch farther down the leg. As always, he found himself — to his secret annoyance — holding his breath in readiness for the prick. Ow! Even after nearly a quarter of a century, it was still unpleasant. After all this time, he doubted that his reaction to the needle would ever change.

He injected the life-sustaining mixture.

The job done, he matter-of-factly withdrew the needle and threw the syringe in the trash can. The other materials he gathered together and replaced in his kit. Hitching his trousers, he flushed the toilet, washed his hands again, then unlocked the door and returned to what he always thought of as the land of the living, his ritual service to his chemical god complete.

The table in the dining room was set for the meal. He sat at his usual chair and looked out the mullioned window to the panoramic view of the slopes a mile away. He could just make out the ski lifts against the sunlit green of the forest background. One lift was operating, gondolas moving slowly up and down the mountainside, providing access to the restaurant at the top of the mountain.

He sipped his drink appreciatively.

"How's business?" asked Bill Healy as he seated himself, wresting Matthew's attention from the window.

They chatted politely about business and the weather until Lucinda joined them, carrying a wooden salad bowl filled with a colorful mixture of vegetables. She went back to the kitchen and returned a moment later with the bottle of wine.

Bill opened it and poured for himself and his wife. Matthew had already consumed the one alcoholic drink he allowed himself of an evening.

The meal began.

Lucinda was, as always, the perfect hostess; it was obvious to Matthew that she had expended her usual effort on the meal, and he relished it to the full. Even Bill seemed to be on good form, despite his occasional nervous glances at the clock on the wall. They talked easily — of Rotary, of business, of the glorious weather, of when the first snow might fall, of the prospects for the coming ski season — until the main course was concluded. Then they carried the dishes to the kitchen, where Matthew refilled his glass from the newly replenished pitcher of juice. The men returned to the dining room while Lucinda remained in the kitchen, attending to the pavlova.

For some minutes, Matthew had been fighting a sudden tiredness. He was finding it more and more difficult to concentrate on Healy's conversation. At first he had ascribed this simply to the entirely plausible possibility that Bill was being even more of a bore than usual. But now he was beginning to wonder if something was seriously wrong. He stood by his chair, holding it for support, hoping that the fatigue would pass.

Suddenly, he felt himself unequal to the battle. No longer able to keep his eyes open, he toppled gracelessly to the floor.

He woke as a sharp pain struck his face. He raised an arm to protect himself, but was too slow to ward off a second blow from Healy.

Matthew tried to remember how he had arrived in such a ridiculous position, slumped on the floor against his chair. His mind was foggy, and he could remember nothing after the sudden fatigue had overcome him.

"Are you all right? You took a fall there. You don't look very well."

It took Matthew a moment to realize that Bill was speaking to him.

"Unh... I guess I'm OK."

His voice sounded distant and disembodied. Bill helped him to his feet. He felt his strength returning. His head was sore just behind the hairline: he must have banged it against the table as he fell. He rubbed the soreness, feeling confused.

"Here, sit down. You spilt your juice. Lucinda has gone to get you some more; she'll be back in a moment."

Matthew nodded. Sitting on his chair, he rubbed his face, trying to clear the fog from his head.

Lucinda returned with a concerned look on her face. She placed a glass of orange juice on the table in front of him and handed him an ice pack, which he applied to his forehead and immediately wished that he hadn't. The cold hurt, but it cleared his head. Lucinda began mopping up the juice from the hardwood floor. After another couple of minutes of concern and confusion over what had happened, he began to feel himself once again.

Lucinda asked, "Can I get you something from the pharmacy, Matthew? It's only a couple of minutes away. Or do you want me to call Dr. Taylor?"

Matthew shook his head. The room span but then steadied itself.

"No. It's OK. I'll be fine. Maybe I've been working too hard. I think I'll just rest here for a few minutes and then go home and spend a quiet evening reading."

Healy laughed, too loudly.

"I wish I could spend a quiet evening reading, but duty calls. I'll have to be leaving shortly. Are you sure there's nothing we can do?"

"No, I'll be fine. Honest."

He caught sight of Lucinda, hovering nearby. He remembered the pavlova.

"What I need is a good dose of that dessert of yours, and then I'm sure I'll feel much better."

He smiled at her, trying to make light of the situation. She returned his smile, but the smile did little to mask the worry in her eyes.

They ate the dessert, but it was not the same group who had eaten the main course only a few minutes before. There was hardly any talk, and Lucinda and Bill kept sneaking glances at their guest, trying to assure themselves that he was not about to expire on them. As soon as the food was finished, and without waiting for coffee, Bill excused himself to change for the evening's council meeting.

Matthew looked at Lucinda.

"That was stupid of me. I'm sorry. I don't know what came over me. But I really do think that I'd better go home and take it easy for the rest of the evening. You probably need to finish your packing, anyway."

Lucinda nodded. "All right. But you take care of yourself. I might give you a call when I arrive, to make sure you're OK."

He tried to sound more positive than he felt. "All right, if you like. But I'll be fine. It was probably just hard work taking its toll, that's all."

Matthew got to his feet, using the back of the chair to hold himself steady. He was trembling. The idea of an evening relaxing at home was becoming more appealing by the minute.

"Say goodnight to Bill for me, won't you? Tell him he has my vote."

"I will. But you will take good care of yourself, won't you?"

"Of course. And thanks for the meal. It was great, as always."

"You're welcome. Any time."

She hugged him gently and gave him a peck of a kiss; then she escorted him to the front door.

"See you in a little over a week, Matthew. And I will call when I arrive."

"I'll talk to you then. Have a safe trip."

He made his way slowly to his car, where he forced himself to take five slow, deep breaths. What had come over him? That had never happened before.

He started the vehicle, turned around on the graveled area in front of the garage, and drove slowly away from the house and down the hill towards town.

By the time he reached his own home he had stopped shaking, but he had developed the grandfather of all headaches. He walked up the stairway from the garage, his head pounding with every step. Making straight for the bathroom, he swallowed a pair of extra-strength painkillers; then he lay down on the bed and closed his eyes. Within seconds, he was asleep.

When he awoke, he felt much better. The headache was nearly gone. The clock on the bedside table said 8:30. Half the evening had gone, but at least he was feeling like he was going to survive, which was a distinct improvement from earlier.

He stood up... and nearly fell over. He was light-headed, and he realized that his hands were trembling. For the first time, he began to feel truly worried. Maybe there was something seriously wrong after all. He should take something to help him sleep and then go back to bed. But there was one thing he had to do first. He made his way slowly out of the bedroom and into the living room.

11

Unsteadily, he crossed the room to where a chess set, a game in progress, stood on a coffee table. He needed to check his next move. He was due to call Henry Clarence before ten to give him the move. Normally he would wait until closer to the deadline, but tonight he would call in his move early. He looked at the board, trying to concentrate. Yes, rook to queen's knight four looked just fine. He had Henry Clarence on the run.

The board swam before his eyes.

He really did feel awful; perhaps he should call Dr. Taylor. He held out an arm and tried to steady himself against the table. It worked, for a few seconds; but then he began to see dark spots before his eyes; he felt hot, sweaty and nauseated; he was going to throw up; his lips tingled; he swallowed hard to keep from regurgitating his supper.

It was the tingling lips that warned him. Once before this had happened, twenty four years ago and under supervision in a doctor's office, only a few months after he had been diagnosed with adult-onset diabetes. That time it had been done on purpose, so that he would be able to recognize the signs should it ever happen again. Twenty four years rolled away, and his heart began to thud violently as he realized what was about to happen: he was about to go into a hypoglycemic coma. Despite the pavlova, his blood sugar level was dangerously low. How could that have happened? Surely he had not made a mistake when measuring his insulin dose?

He thrust his hand into his pocket for his roll of glucose candy, kept always within reach for just such an emergency.

He felt around in his pocket frantically. There were his keys, and a handkerchief. But *where was the candy?* Relief poured over him as his hand closed on a cylinder. But then he realized that these were not his candies, they were the anti-inflammatory capsules prescribed by his doctor for his racquetball injury. Irrelevantly, he realized that he had forgotten to take one with supper.

In desperation, he felt in his other pocket, but he already knew that there was something seriously amiss. The candies were always, *always* in his right-hand pocket. His left hand dived into a pocket to find nothing but a clean handkerchief. He began to move towards the kitchen. He had to get sugar inside him, *now*. He wanted desperately to vomit. Dark spots expanded and filled his vision. He stopped and closed his eyes to concentrate on the task of keeping his food down.

For about five seconds he stood there, shaking. Then his legs could support him no more.

They buckled, and he collapsed to the floor.

POST
MORTEM

Chapter 2

Outside, the day had already established the pattern to which it would cling for the remaining fifteen hours of daylight. Shortly after dawn, the gray mass overhead had coalesced and moved even closer to the ground. Shortly thereafter the first tentative raindrops had fallen. Another day in this record-setting summer had begun.

The surface of the thatch was by seven o'clock thoroughly soaked. Even so, there was no chance that the water would seep through the ten and a half inches of new thatch. The roof had been replaced only last year, in a summer as notable for sunshine as this one was for its cloud and rain.

The cottage had stood, weathering heat, cold, rain and occasional snow with equanimity, for over two hundred years. Originally built to house two families, it had been purchased by an ambitious local builder in the early seventies after nearly fifty years of decay and disuse. Two years later it had come on the market and was immediately snapped up by the first in a series of more or less successful young men who desired a retreat from the rat race of their weekday life in London.

The last time it changed hands was three years ago. The "For Sale" sign had been emplaced on the small grass verge some twenty feet in front of the cottage two days before being removed, its presence no longer necessary. Not that the sign itself had been in any way responsible for the sale; too few cars strayed along the narrow road for that.

Martin Salisbury had had a standing order with Mitchell and Stout, Oxford Real Estate Agents, that he was to be informed of any renovated cottages that came on the market. A telephone call was made by Mr. Stout to Mr. Salisbury, and a showing was agreed. Martin Salisbury, not a man accustomed to dilatoriness when a decision was called for, tendered an offer later that day. Two days later, he decisively extracted the sign from the clay soil by the side of the road and ceremoniously returned it to Mr. Stout.

Now, three years later, Martin Salisbury was still the sole owner of Birchwood Cottage. Ordinarily, however, he was not the cottage's sole occupant.

Six months ago he had met Davina Dawson — twenty eight years old, a bright, undeniably beautiful woman with long, auburn hair and the sexiest body it had ever been his privilege to behold, naked or clothed — while perusing the display racks of a video rental store in Oxford. He probably would not have noticed her, so intent was he on trying to find a video with which to relax and forget about the week's aggravations that Friday evening, except that as he reached out to pick up and read the box for *Out of Africa*, she had simultaneously done the same.

He had gallantly stood to one side to let her read first. It was, he noticed, the shop's last copy of the film. He also noticed — could hardly not notice — how attractive was the woman standing not three feet from him.

He wondered if she realized that he was appraising her.

It was a question that he finally mustered sufficient courage to ask three days later, to which she responded with a laugh. "Of course I knew you were looking, you twit. Do you think I've reached my age without understanding how a man's mind works? I'd been watching you for five minutes and it was obvious that I had to do *something* to make you aware of my existence."

The auburn-haired girl had passed the box over to him without comment. She remained standing next to him as he tried to concentrate on the words printed on the box. It was difficult. The smile she had flashed at him had had an almost physical intensity about it....

"It sounds good," he said after perhaps half a minute. He lifted his head to see her brown, green-flecked eyes smiling at him while simultaneously boring into and through him.

"Yes, I thought so too. But there's only one copy...."

18

He should, he supposed on later reflection, have simply offered the video to her. But he didn't.

Instead, he found himself saying, "Look, I live about ten miles out of town, but if you wouldn't mind the drive, I'd be happy to watch the film with you. I can probably rustle up some food, nothing fancy of course, and there's probably a bottle of wine somewhere in the house...."

And so it had started.

Two days later, Davina had permanently decamped from the flat that she shared with a girlfriend in the northwestern quadrant of the city and taken herself and her three suitcases and equal number of camera bags to cohabit (as her friends would have called it) with Martin Salisbury at Birchwood Cottage.

Davina had left England yesterday. After months of angling, she had finally landed what promised to be an exciting and lucrative contract.

Martin had tried not to influence her. He did not question Davina's apparent need to be engaged in gainful employment even though his income was more than enough for both of them. Besides which, after six months of living together he wondered if it might not be good to spend some time apart from one another.

It was not that his feelings for Davina were any less than they always had been, ever since that first meeting in the video rental store. In the intervening six months he had made a point of proposing at least once a month, each time to be turned down with the statement that she was "not sure yet" that she wanted to spend the rest of her life with Martin.

The last such occasion had been two days ago, on Thursday evening. Usually on these occasions he tried to impress her by taking her out to a swank restaurant in Oxford. This time he had tried a different tack, hoping that perhaps he would catch her off-guard. Knowing that she was nervous about flying to Kenya the next day, he had taken her down to the *Cotswold Arms*, given her two drinks and slyly slipped the proposal into an otherwise innocuous, although vaguely one-sided, conversation.

She had been quiet all evening: worried, she said, that she was going to leave behind some important piece of camera equipment, although it seemed to Martin that there must be more bothering her than such a trivial concern. Her eyes had unmistakably lit up momentarily at the proposal — or so Martin had thought at the time; the following morning he had been less certain — before her face reverted to its blank expression.

Her response had deviated a little from the norm for these occasions. "Oh, Martin. You're so good to keep asking. But I can't make up my mind right now. There's too much to think about getting ready for this trip. Ask me when I get back, OK?"

The following day he had taken the morning off work — after all, the press announcement was scheduled for three thirty in the afternoon and there was nothing he could do now to change anything that might be wrong with the product — and driven Davina, who looked uncharacteristically subdued but quite characteristically beautiful, to Heathrow.

He had dropped her at the curb outside the international terminal. Their farewells had been short, curtailed by the steady rain. He watched Davina push her trolley of bags through an automatic door. The door closed and she was lost to sight.

Martin remained looking at the place where she had disappeared for several seconds, his thoughts a tangled jungle. The window became opaque with the trails of raindrops. He turned, waited for a gap in the oncoming traffic, and joined the stream that would take him to the M4.

Seven o'clock on Saturday morning passed without anything occurring to mark the fact other than the changing numbers on the digital clocks throughout the cottage. Usually at this time, even on a Saturday, seven o'clock signaled the arrival of the new day, with the radio on the shelf beside Davina's head switching itself on in time for the final, long pip and the Radio 4 news. This morning Davina was thousands of miles away, and Martin had turned off the alarm before going to sleep last night.

Force of habit woke him before the red numbers indicated the passage of five more minutes. Groggily, he stretched out a hand under the bedclothes in Davina's direction. For a moment he was confused as his hand reached the edge of the bed without being blocked by her body. He opened his eyes and blinked several times. His view of the clock, usually hidden behind Davina's head, was unobstructed. He saw the last digit flicker from "4" to "5," and realized that he was alone, that his beloved Davina was by now wide awake in the tropical sun of equatorial Kenya, her first day on the photographic safari probably well under weigh.

He groaned.

He closed his eyes, trying to go back to sleep. But it was no good. After a couple of minutes he pulled the bedclothes back and, naked, got out of bed and made for the bathroom.

He glanced out the window on the way.

Since the cottage was a quarter of a mile from the nearest building, he had not bothered to close the curtains last night; now he was offered an unobstructed view of the bleak morning beyond the glass.

The rain was falling almost vertically beyond the thick thatch of the overhanging eaves. He produced a voiceless grunt of disapproval. Gray clouds hung low over the birch wood that abutted the bottom of the garden a hundred and fifty feet away. Closer, the grass of the lawn, which had needed cutting for over a week now, glistened here and there where puddles reflected the grayness overhead. He turned away.

As if he needed reminding, the first thing that struck him as he entered the bathroom was the absence of her things. Gone was her packet of oral contraceptives. He wondered vaguely if she was expecting to need them on the trip. Almost immediately he found himself intensely annoyed that the thought had even crossed his mind. This was not going to be a good day unless he stopped thinking like that. Certainly no way to begin a four-week break from work.

Next to where the pink packet of birth-control pills customarily lay, her spare diabetic kit was also gone, no doubt in a suitcase in some hot, unpronounceable village in Kenya, insurance against the loss or theft of the supplies that she carried with her at all times. Gone too were her toothbrush and the slim, mauve canister of powder with which she doused herself every morning after her shower. His eyes took in the absence of these things at a glance. It was going to be a long day.

He had missed the seven o'clock news, but he easily caught the eight o'clock edition. In the meantime he had retrieved the two newspapers from the hall floor, where they had fallen after being pushed through the letter box by the newsagent's son.

Scanning the headlines, he assured himself that there was no news of riots in Kenya; then he tossed Davina's *Guardian* to one side while he browsed his own copy of the *Daily Telegraph*. The business page indicated that stock in Smith Computers had jumped twelve percent on yesterday afternoon's announcement of their new Windows-compatible Graphical User Interface by Vice President for Software Development Mr. Martin Salisbury. He closed the paper and, his spirits somewhat higher, went in search of breakfast.

His meal consisted of corn flakes, toast and Cooper's, and the better part of a pint of milk, supped leisurely on the dining room table in front of the last page of the newspaper, on which he periodically entered — in ink — solutions to the crossword clues.

In the background, the voice of an interviewer on the radio alternated with the west-country tones of a farmer who was explaining that his cat, Ethelbert, had predicted two months ago that this would be the wettest summer on record, by virtue of the fact that he had curled up into a ball and remained indolent and uninterested in anything except the occasional plate of food and bowl of milk for a period of twelve full days. This, apparently, was a guaranteed harbinger of twenty four days of rain in August this year. So far, the cat and the weather seemed in complete agreement.

The pips sounded, and Martin listened to the headlines. Nothing of interest. He turned off the radio and returned his attention to the crossword.

Martin Salisbury, educated at Eton and Christ Church, Oxford, formerly a member of the Advanced Computer Research Group at the Royal Signals Establishment at Malvern and, for the past five years, Vice President for Software Development at Smith Computers had, at forty one, entered a singularly successful, happy and comfortable middle age. Six months ago, he had been merely successful and comfortable, but Davina had completed the troika. If only she would consent to be his wife, his happiness would be complete....

He forced himself to stop daydreaming, and looked at the ceiling, furrowing his brow as he searched the recesses of his mind for an eight letter word (something S something something something E something), an answer to the clue: *The uneasiness felt when Pluto isn't making a sound.*

At eight forty three, he completed the final word in the puzzle, filling in the blanks in 'something something E something something O something': *Reward the end of debate with regal lecturer.* Pleased to have finished, but vaguely dissatisfied with his performance, he strolled to the window and for some moments watched the rain.

The pathway that led to the black-painted wrought iron gate that gave access to the road — little more than a lane, really — sported a number of puddles. Through the gate he could just glimpse the road, along which no vehicle had passed for the better part of half an hour. Along the rest of the frontage, the road was obscured behind a tall beech hedge.

The hedge, always keen to outgrow its confines in the summer months, was looking positively bedraggled as the water weighed down its distended branches. The front lawn was in just as bad a shape as the rear one. But given Ethelbert the cat's prediction, it was likely to be a while before he would be given the opportunity to remedy that sorry situation.

He wondered what to do. The four weeks of vacation had been so nicely planned until the telephone call for Davina came from the BBC two weeks ago.

There was to have been a week of hiking for the two of them in Wales, ostensibly as a prelude to the more strenuous exercise of the following fortnight, but in reality, both of them knew, simply an excuse to spend an extended period alone together without fear of interruption. Then the flight to Colorado, followed by two weeks of more intensive backpacking in the Rockies with his cousin. After that, the return trip home and a week recuperating and working on all the things in the garden which would by then be almost beyond control.

But the telephone call had effectively destroyed their plans. For months, Davina had been trying to land an assignment. In the meantime, she had been remarkably domesticated, performing all the duties that were expected of a wife in a less enlightened age. She had uncomplainingly — indeed, voluntarily — taken Martin under her wing, ensuring that he was looked after properly at home.

Initially, her culinary talents had been more nascent than actual, and the first month or so of her residency had produced a series of unimaginative dishes in which macaroni and cheese and fish fingers had featured a little too prominently. Martin, though, had carefully refrained from comment and was pleasantly surprised to discover one weekend that Davina had taken it upon herself to purchase a thick cookery book with the intention, so she said, of "learning to cook at last."

She had been as good as her word; indeed Martin recently had begun to feel pangs of guilt at the amount of time Davina was spending in the kitchen.

Not that the rest of the house escaped her attention. Before Davina's arrival, the kindest statement that could have been made about Birchwood Cottage was that it was in no worse state than one might expect for a cottage inhabited by a bachelor just the wrong side of forty whose work week was full and exhausting and who refused on principle to hire a housekeeper. Now the house was spotless, a witness to Davina's countless hours of tidying, dusting and general chivvying that "now that it's tidy, let's keep it that way."

But she had continued to search for an assignment.

The urgency had gone out of her search since meeting Martin; Martin earned more than enough to keep the two of them in a style rather grander than either of them desired, but still she had not given up entirely. She told Martin that she did not want to feel entirely like a kept woman.

Then the telephone call had come from Roger Montmorency, offering her a berth as a combined still photographer and film camerawoman on a BBC-sponsored safari to East Africa.

Martin had not discouraged her from going. It was a pity that the two-week safari coincided almost exactly with the first two weeks of their planned vacation — with the all-but-certainty that the safari would be extended by at least a week — but on the whole Davina thought that this might be exactly what she needed to resurrect her career from the doldrums into which it had slipped.

Disappointed though Martin was about the change of plans, he was more concerned about Roger Montmorency. He broached the subject one evening in the kitchen as he helped prepare supper, although he could think of no tactful way of approaching the topic.

"This Roger Montmorency bloke: what's he like?" he asked, fighting back tears as he chopped an onion for the bolognese.

Davina did not look up from the pasta machine.

"Roger? Oh, I've known him for years. We've done a couple of assignments together. I think he's pretty good. He was in the Falklands right after the war, and did a great documentary on how life would never be the same for the people down there. That was what made his name.

"The first job we did together was pretty mundane, or so it seemed at the time. We did a combined film and still documentary on the wildlife of the New Forest. You wouldn't think that something like that would get much attention, but it won a couple of minor prizes and kept me in jobs for a couple of years.

"The other thing we did together was on the rain forest in Brazil. That was a disappointment really, after the New Forest thing. The subject was so much more exciting, you'd think we couldn't go wrong. It ended up being taken by Granada and used as an episode in one of their nature series, but it was nothing out of the ordinary. The stills were accepted by a couple of magazines, one in the States and one in Brazil, and used with some accompanying text in gallery articles, so I did rather better out of the project than Roger."

This was not really what Martin had been asking. He wondered if Davina was being deliberately obtuse, but she was still looking down, apparently absorbed in making the linguini, and he could not see the expression on her face.

"Good looking, is he?"

There was no response for a second, and then Davina's head jerked up and he found himself looking sheepishly into her laughing eyes.

"Martin Salisbury, I do believe you're jealous!"

"And why not, may I ask? Here you are, all ready to spend your holiday with me, and then, on the strength of a single phone call from an old flame, you drop me like a hot potato and tell me that you're going to go gallivanting half the world away with this Montmorency fellow. What kind of a name is Montmorency anyway? I bet he's loaded with money...." He knew that money could hardly be the issue, but at least it would put Davina on the defensive.

She threw back her head and roared with laughter. "Oh dear," was all he heard for about thirty seconds until she regained control of herself.

She wiped her eyes.

"You poor fish. Listen, Martin. Roger Montmorency is about thirty three years old, terribly, terribly gifted, six foot tall, dark haired, extremely dashing and handsome in a rather ostentatious way. He comes from a wealthy family, although at the moment I doubt that he has two pennies to rub together, but still, his prospects are sound. He's unmarried and would be a great catch for any woman... if it weren't for the fact that he's a raving poofter."

25

Relief poured over Martin, and he began to laugh, partly to express the relief, but mostly because he now realized that he had been stupid to distrust Davina.

They canceled the reservations for her flights to and from the States. After some discussion, he agreed with her that it would still be good for him to get away from the cottage. So, after a quick call to his cousin in Colorado, it was agreed that the two of them would go backpacking without Davina.

Perhaps it would be better that way, anyway, Davina had suggested. Matthew was probably a bit embarrassed about the prospect of being the odd-man-out. Now the two men could spend the week together indulging in all the macho, man-to-man, male bonding, man-against-nature stuff of which Martin had been deprived since she had come into his life.

Martin was unsure how much of what Davina said was in jest, but he knew that it would do him good to get away and clear his head after the stress of the last nine months. The product was out the door now and if he was ever going to take a break, now was the time. His reservation to Denver for next Saturday therefore remained intact. But what was he going to do with the week between now and then?

He peered through the gray rain, searching for inspiration. If the weather had been fine, he might still have gone hiking in Powys, alone; but with no early break in the weather predicted, he could think of few more unpleasant ways to spend a week. He glanced at his watch. Nine o'clock. He decided to put off the decision. He would take the Jag into Oxford to pick up some food to tide him over the weekend. Maybe the forecasters had got it wrong (again) and by Monday the weather would improve. Maybe.

Hurrying under the thatched eaves, he stepped out into the rain to unlock the garage. Behind him in the driveway, Davina's car, an old X registration yellow Volkswagen Polo that he longed to replace with something more stylish, stood underneath a soaked tarpaulin, drips falling from the corners every few seconds.

He got into the XJS and turned the ignition. The engine purred almost inaudibly underneath the gray-blue hood. He ejected the CD — Elgar's *Enigma Variations* — and replaced it with Billy Joel. He needed something a bit upbeat.

He backed the car carefully out of the narrow garage and out on to the road, hitting the horn twice to announce his presence against the unlikely event that there was traffic in the lane. He straightened the vehicle and headed in the direction of Oxford.

The telephones inside Birchwood Cottage began to ring. After thirty seconds, the ringing ceased.

Chapter 3

Judge Henry Clarence Madison pursed his lips. His brow, always deeply lined — matching the rest of his face — was even more furrowed than usual, the visible sign of the activity going on inside his skull. The light in the ceiling reflected off his glossy pate, a crescent of thin, gray hair guarding the bright reflection at its center.

He was standing in front of the telephone, which was one of two items occupying the surface of a table in one corner of the room. The other was a Rolodex card file open at the letter "C." In his right hand he held a glass one quarter full of amber liquid.

He was wondering what to do next. He counted up the hours once again to make sure that he had it right. It was two in the morning here, so yes, that meant it was nine a.m. in England. He wondered where Martin Salisbury could be so early on a Saturday morning. Well, there was nothing for it but to try again later.

He looked at the card he had taken from the Rolodex.

```
Matthew Chambers -- emergency
Martin Salisbury (cousin) 011-44-865-27496
Birchwood Cottage
Little Mereton
Oxfordshire  OX26 8PT
England
```

Turning the card over, he revealed a second name and address inscribed in his careful hand:

Joanna Baker (cousin) 011-61-3-274-9310
119 Riverwood Drive
Sutherland
New South Wales
Australia

He had no idea what time it was in Australia. Putting the card down, he walked to the bookcase that covered half the opposite wall. He bent down slowly, feeling his age, and removed a large book.

The world map was on page three, with time zones clearly marked. New South Wales, it seemed, was seven hours behind Colorado. Rather, it was seventeen hours ahead, since it was on the other side of the International Date Line, making it now about seven on Saturday evening. Except that Colorado was currently on Mountain Daylight Saving Time, and Australia would presumably be on standard time, it being the middle of the winter there. So the time in Sydney now must be about six in the evening. Something like that, anyway. Give or take an hour.

He wondered if he should call. He was less sure of his reception than he had been in Martin's case. Besides which, hadn't Matthew said something a couple of months ago about his female cousin being a party in a nasty divorce proceeding?

But the family had to be informed, it was the least he could do. He walked back to the telephone, picked up the card, and punched in the numbers.

The television was turned on, speaking to no one. The advertisement for Foster's — "The *real* Oz" — played to an empty room. The ad ended, replaced by one for Levi jeans.

Outside, the sun was below the horizon, but the sky was still bright as it percolated through the tangled, bare branches of the maple trees lining the street in the undistinguished middle-class suburban neighborhood.

There was clink from the kitchen; the sound of liquid being poured; the thud of a bottle being put down. A door was opened with a slight sucking sound, then there was the broken crack of ice cubes being removed from a tray. The tray was replaced and the door closed.

Finally, there were footsteps and Joanna Salisbury shakily entered the room.

She walked carefully, partly because her glass was nearly full, and partly because this was her fifth drink in ninety minutes.

The screen went blank for a moment and the advertisements were replaced by the sequence that introduced the six o'clock news. She slumped into the chair in front of the TV. Half a teaspoon of liquid sloshed over the side of the glass, wetting her cotton print dress. Joanna did not notice.

She took a large sip while the words and pictures flowed past without making an impression. The sky reflected glaringly off the screen, making it impossible to see clearly. She placed the glass roughly on the hardwood floor, misjudging the distance and spilling more of the drink. She wavered across the room and pulled the curtains closed, shutting out what remained of the northwestern winter evening light.

The television and the single chair in which she had been sitting were the only furniture in the room. They were all that Kevin had left her with. She stood next to the curtains, looking at the bare room. A single four-letter word escaped her lips. It sounded good; she repeated it half a dozen times before returning to her chair. Her first full day of freedom was drawing to a close.

Yesterday had been a strange day, and Joanna had spent the entire day being unsure how she was supposed to feel.

She had left the courtroom — a party on this occasion, not a witness — and returned to the police station just in time for lunch. The other female detective in the department, along with two female secretaries, had taken her out to one of their usual haunts, an unpretentious establishment on a slight rise from which a good view of the harbor could be had if one sat on the right side of the restaurant. They had been lucky, a table for four had been vacated just as they arrived, and Anne had promptly claimed it for them. Over the course of the next sixty minutes, all four had got sensibly drunk.

Joanna was the first of them to get divorced. (*How simple it sounds*, she thought: "*get divorced*"; *two words that hide a pain that lasts to the end of one's life.*) She wondered if she would be the last.

Somehow, it seemed unlikely; Karen's marriage had been shaky almost as long as her own, although its instability was due more to Karen's barely-hidden affair with her boss than any fault of her husband. But perhaps even affairs had their good points: if it hadn't been for Kevin's philandering, Joanna never would have got around to seeking a divorce. If he had been faithful, she would still be married to the son of a bitch, putting up with his drinking bouts, his verbal abuse, his violence.

So perhaps his three affairs (or at least, the three that she knew of) had not been without their mitigatory aspects. Until he told her about his lovers one night — in the middle of a screaming match that would have sent the neighbors to the telephone to call her colleagues in the department had they not heard its like many times before — she had still thought that deep down, somewhere, Kevin loved her. She had been prepared to excuse his behavior towards her on the grounds that it was the alcohol talking, not the Kevin with whom she had eloped, and with whom she had traveled half way around the world to marry "till death do us part."

But it had not been death; it had been the extramarital activities that had finally killed the dragging marriage.

And now, since late yesterday morning, she was free.

The settlement terms were simple. She got the house and the mortgage, he got everything else. Surprisingly, in the end it had all gone rather smoothly. Kevin had moved out two months ago and she had not seen him since. The moving truck had appeared yesterday afternoon and stripped the house of almost everything that could be moved. She had managed to hold on to the old armchair in the living room by the simple expedient of bribing the man in charge of the movers. But everything else had gone except the bed. Kevin, wherever he was living now, doubtless had little use for another one of those.

Last night had been the loneliest of her life.

Through lunch, her colleagues had joked about how Joanna was now free to spend her nights on the town.

"You'll be painting Sydney red tonight, Jo," Anne had joked, adding, "Need any help?"

But it was not like that at all. The end of a marriage, even one that stank as much as hers, was nothing to celebrate. It was a time to mourn, to take stock, to die a little inside.

Last night, she had stared at the painted walls of the living room for two hours, but afterwards could remember none of her thoughts. She had soaked in the bath and gone to bed early. This morning she had decided that she had to find something to occupy her evenings. She spent the morning comparing prices in electronics stores all over Sydney and, finally, she purchased a television set. She also bought a year's supply of alcohol. Tonight would not be like last night. Tonight's mistakes would be quite different.

She slumped in her chair, thirty five years old, her hair bedraggled and showing signs of graying, worry lines already beginning to etch themselves on her face. She had always, as long ago as she could remember, been called beautiful. They would stop calling her that soon.

On the television, advertisements came and went. Joanna realized that her glass was empty. She was past caring; her eyes remained glued unseeingly on the television set. The news began, accompanied by urgent, demanding music designed to exaggerate the importance of events that could have little or no impact on the vast majority of the viewers.

The announcer appeared. Good looking, perfectly groomed and immaculately coifed, he began to read the day's headlines from the TelePrompTer with an accent half Oz, quarter Yank and quarter Pom. Joanna vaguely noticed that he was about her own age and felt a twinge of resentment. No worry lines on his face.

Something about trade talks; a political scandal; a libel action; then pictures of gray rain filled the screen. A sequence of scenes followed, all dominated by a dismal haze of rain: rush hour in a city; green fields; empty beaches; a momentary shot of a weather vane; and, finally and staying on the screen, a forlorn covered cricket pitch. She began dully to listen to the reporter.

"...and so what passes for an English summer continues. Always the butt of jokes, this year the weather is having the last laugh. So far, this is set to be the coldest and wettest summer on record. The season is barely halfway over, and there's no letup in sight for the weary — and wet — Englishman.

"It has rained here in Manchester for twelve of the last fifteen days, with only an occasional break in the clouds to let the sun poke through to smile at her joke on the English. The beaches are empty, the farmers are worried about crops rotting in the fields and, worst of all from the Australian point of view, cricket has ground to a halt.

"Less than a third of the English league one-day games have been completed, and today should have marked the start of the third Test against Australia here at Old Trafford. The first two Tests, at Lord's and Trent Bridge, were abandoned as draws because of the weather. The Australian cricket team had been expecting to retain the Ashes this season, aided by the new fast bowling duo of Roberts and Benson. It looks like they may instead retain them without a single game being played to completion.

"The fourth Test is due to start twelve days from now. The weather forecast from the British Meteorological Office, courtesy of their supercomputers, calls for a 75% chance of rain. Most people I've spoken to think that's optimistic. This is Dennis Loveland for the Australian Broadcasting Corporation, the Old Trafford Cricket Ground, Manchester."

It was too much for Joanna. The shambles she had made of her life suddenly overwhelmed her and she began to cry. The studio newsreader returned to the screen and made a joke about the English weather, but she couldn't hear it through her sobs.

The telephone rang, intruding on her private hell. She made an effort to stop crying, prepared to make her way to the kitchen where the one remaining telephone was still plugged into the wall.

But why bother? she wondered. *If it's important they'll call back. Not that it is important. It never is.*

Eventually, the telephone stopped.

Henry Clarence Madison replaced the telephone on the hook. His hands were still shaking, and he wondered if he would be able to sleep. He drained his glass and headed for the bedroom. Perhaps things would look better in the morning.

The sun rose over the nearby summit of St. Valentine's Mountain and peeked down into the Pinetree valley. High above the town, the sun had already been visible for nearly an hour and the eagles were returning to their eyries with the first catches of the day. Now the town of Pinetree began to wake.

The first sunlight reached the clumps of condominiums scattered around the edge of town. The weekend visitors began to stir, opening their windows on the breathtaking views that the condominium

33

developers hoped would induce them to part with six-figure sums in exchange for the year-round use of one of the diminutive units.

In a twenty-five-acre parcel of undeveloped land adjacent to the Mountain View condominiums, the first of five hot air balloons left the ground, the roar of its propane burner clearly audible for several hundred feet in all directions. The huge multicolored canopy stretched high overhead, dwarfing everything save the brightly colored, slowly expanding fabrics of the other balloons and the solid pink and red mass of the Mountain View development.

In the bedroom of unit 312 of the pink and red structure, Henry Clarence Madison stirred as sunlight entered the room. He made a muffled noise and turned away from the light.

He dozed fitfully for another half hour, but eventually the brightness thwarted him. He gave up the battle and blearily sat up in bed. Out the window he could see three hot air balloons aloft. The weekend had begun. He rubbed his hands roughly over his lined faced, trying to coax some life into his body.

For Henry Clarence, the weekend had started late last night, and in an unforgettable and altogether unpleasant manner.

It had been an enjoyable party at the Crawfords', but even Henry Clarence, never one to be certain of his limits when it came to alcohol, was sure that he had broken them this time.

He had been planning to leave at nine thirty, to be home at ten to receive the call from Matthew Chambers. Matthew, he had to admit to himself, was going to win this game; but, according to their rules, if one of them did not make his move on time, he forfeited the match. Matthew might miss the deadline one day, which was Henry Clarence's only chance of winning this one.

He had checked his answering machine before leaving for the Crawfords' at six thirty, and there had been no message from Matthew then. So he had every reason to be home by ten; but half past nine came and went and he barely noticed.

He and Graham Crawford were by that time two and a half rubbers down. In more concrete terms, he was nearly two hundred dollars in the red for the evening. Graham's wife, Melissa, and their home-for-the-vacation daughter, Cassie, could barely hide their glee. They, it was quite clear, would be happy to play until dawn, given the cards that were coming their way.

Graham wanted his revenge. Henry Clarence tried to excuse himself, but Graham was having none of it.

"Come on, Henry. You got me into this, and you're just going to have to help get me out of it. We lost fifty dollars on that one hand when you just had to double their attempt at a small slam. And another fifty on that bid of three no trumps redoubled where we went down two. Come on, we have to extract some kind of revenge on these two, otherwise they'll be impossible to live with for the next week. Here, let me get you another Manhattan while you deal."

So Henry Clarence had stayed. Finally, just past midnight, when he had redeemed himself by making a doubled seven spades (and after he had taken at least two more drinks than was good for him) they released him. Only fifty dollars down for the night, he gave Melissa a barely-legible check, meandered unsteadily to his car, and tentatively began the drive down the mountainside.

It was late, but perhaps Matthew was still up: the thought came to him as the small track which led up to Matthew's house came into view around the corner. Without giving the matter any thought, he swung the car off the road, bounced over a couple of small rocks (which did the suspension of his Volvo no good at all) had a close but unnoticed brush with the lower branches of a pine tree, and began to make his way along the quarter-mile track to Matthew's house.

Yes, Matthew was awake: the lights were on in the living room. Henry Clarence pulled up outside the closed garage, got out, and climbed the steps up to the house. No need to prolong the agony; he'd just admit defeat so they could start a new game tomorrow.

He rang the doorbell and waited. The evening was chilly; he looked up to see a canopy of brilliant stars; almost overhead, one shone especially brightly. He breathed deeply of the pristine, chill mountain air. He rang the doorbell again.

He waited what seemed like a decent interval and opened the front door. It was not locked — he had not expected that it would be; Matthew never locked his house at night. He crossed the landing and walked down the two steps into the living room, on the far side of which was the table on which the chess game stood.

He was halfway across the room when he saw something out the corner of his eye, near the steps up to the kitchen.

He turned, his shoes pivoting on the hardwood floor.

For a fraction of a second he didn't move. Then he ran towards the kitchen.

On the floor, prone and slumped over the steps, lay Matthew Chambers. Henry Clarence bent down, but even before he touched Matthew's wrist to check for a pulse, he knew that he was too late. Matthew's face was drained of color, the natural paleness of his Caucasian skin no longer tinged with the pinkness of flowing blood.

Matthew's skin was cool to the touch. As Henry Clarence had expected, there was no pulse.

Henry Clarence looked the body over. There was no visible sign of what the police would term "foul play." He did not move the body; that was a job for professionals.

Sober now, he raised himself from his haunches and walked sedately to the telephone. There was no hurry; Matthew would not be going anywhere.

It vaguely crossed his mind that if Matthew had been attacked, his attacker might still be in the house, but he suppressed the thought as soon as it surfaced. It was obvious from the temperature of Matthew's body that he had been dead for some time. If his death had been the work of an intruder, that intruder would surely be long gone.

He stretched out his hand toward the telephone and then withdrew it. For a couple of moments he fumbled in his pocket, and then pulled out a handkerchief. Wrapping the handkerchief around the handset, and using a pencil from the table next to the telephone to punch the numbers, he called the dispatcher.

The conversation was over in two minutes. Waiting for the arrival of the police and the ambulance took considerably longer.

He approached the body and walked all the way around it, looking for anything unusual. There was nothing: no trace of blood, no sign of a struggle, no bruises or bumps on the visible parts of the body. Henry Clarence was forced to the conclusion that his friend had suffered a heart attack, unlikely though that seemed.

Of all the people he knew, none looked after himself — none *had* looked after himself — as well as Matthew Chambers. Still, a heart attack was the only conclusion he could come to, although he had read somewhere that heart attack victims rarely died quickly and usually betrayed the pain of their struggle on their face. Matthew's face, lolling over towards the table, looked completely expressionless, as if — if one could but ignore its pallor — he were merely asleep.

36

Henry Clarence turned from the body and crossed to the couch, where he lowered himself with a sigh to wait for the professionals to arrive.

Chapter 4

Martin jogged to reach the protection of the eaves, then fumbled quickly with his house key. Inside, the telephone was ringing. Normally, he would not have bothered to hurry, but perhaps it was Davina calling from Kenya; he did not want to take the chance of missing that call if he could help it.

He dashed into the house, dropping his shopping bag just inside the front door.

Grabbing the phone, he said, "Martin Salisbury."

For a moment there was silence. Then someone spoke.

"Er... yes. This is Henry Clarence Madison. You probably don't remember me; I live in Pinetree, Colorado."

Martin tried to place the name. After a moment, he recalled a series of impressions from his one visit to Pinetree, twenty one months before. A short, black man; getting on in years, perhaps in his middle sixties, a narrow arc of white hair running around the back of his head; a wrinkled face that smiled frequently. Plays good chess; keeps a running one-move-per-day game with Matthew. A district court judge. "Pinetree's token professional black," he had called himself on the one occasion they had met. Drinks and gambles too much, Matthew had said, but other than that the finest human being that walked the Earth, or at the very least, the finest human being in Pinetree.

Martin said, "Yes, I remember you. Judge Madison. What may I do for you?"

"Mr. Salisbury, I'm afraid I have some bad news for you. Your cousin is dead."

Henry Clarence continued talking, but for several seconds Martin was unable to comprehend what he was saying. Random memories ran through his head: images of Matthew's beautiful house, snow falling and making it worthy of a picture postcard; Matthew challenging him to a skiing race down the mountainside; sitting together in the living room with Judge Madison, drinks in their hands, warming themselves with the alcohol and the fire that roared in the huge open grate.

He dragged his mind back to the present.

"...late last night. I found the body myself. It looks like it was a massive heart attack, but there will have to be an autopsy to confirm that. I'm awfully sorry to have to be the bearer of such bad news. I know he was looking forward to his backpacking trip with you next week; he's been talking about nothing else for the past few days." There was silence for several seconds. "Hello, Mr. Salisbury, are you still there?"

"Yes, yes. I'm sorry. I was just trying to take it in. It's such a shock. Matthew seemed so healthy last time I saw him. I would never have thought of him as a candidate for a heart attack."

"No, neither did I. He was always so careful with his health. Still, it can happen to anyone, I suppose. It came as a complete shock to me, I assure you. I saw him only yesterday at lunch, and he seemed fine then. He had bruised his shoulder playing racquetball earlier in the week, but that seemed to be getting better. Apart from that he was his usual self. Anyway, I'll be sure to ask the county coroner on Monday about the cause of death; he's a good friend of mine. I'll let you know what he says."

Strange thoughts and emotions were running through Martin Salisbury's mind.

He had worked himself to the point of exhaustion over the past nine months, getting the new software finished in time for its scheduled debut. Part of the incentive had been that as soon as it was all over, he and Davina were going to put as much distance as possible between them and civilization. Then had come Davina's trip to Kenya. And now *this*.

Only a few hours ago, Martin had been wondering what to do for the next week. Now he had nothing to do for the rest of the month. Dammit! He had to do something, had to get away, otherwise he would go crazy.

An idea took root and grew.

"No need, Judge," he said. "I'll ask him myself. I'll change my flight. Instead of coming out next week, I'll get on a plane tomorrow. I'll stay at a motel or something. I need to get away from here, so I might as well come over straight away. Maybe I'll rent a car and drive around the mountains for a few days. I don't know."

Henry Clarence did not speak for several seconds. When he did, there was doubt in his voice.

"Well..., if you're sure. I'd offer to have you stay with me, but there's not a lot of room in my condominium. I don't know who Matthew's heirs may be, so I don't know who the house belongs to now. I'm sure that as soon as the cause of death has been established the police won't mind if you were to stay in the house if it's OK with his heirs."

Matthew's heirs. Martin had not thought about that. As far as he knew, Matthew's only living relatives were himself and Jo. And that brought up another point.

"Have you talked to anyone else, Judge? Matthew has... had another cousin, my sister, who lives in Australia."

"I know. I tried to reach both of you earlier, but I couldn't get through to either of you. Now that I've contacted you I was hoping that you might be willing to call her."

Martin considered that proposition.

He had been putting it off for months, but it was, he supposed, inevitable that he would have to talk to Jo sometime. Another burden to bear.

There was an audible sigh in his voice as he said, "OK. I'll talk to her. It's probably best coming from me anyway."

He wondered if Matthew had left Jo anything. Not that it mattered one way or the other; she'd only fritter it away on some mirage or other.

The judge said, "Look, let me know when you'll be arriving, won't you? Maybe once you've settled in at a motel we can meet and I'll fill you in on the details."

Martin could almost see the judge's kindly, wrinkled smile; his eagerness to help was almost palpable.

"Sure. I'll ring the airline in a few minutes and then call you back to let you know when I'll be arriving in Denver. It's a couple of hours from there to Pinetree, if I remember rightly."

"More like three and a half, once you include the time it'll take to rent a car and drive the extra distance. Last time you were here you probably flew into Stapleton. That airport's closed now, and the new Denver International is quite a bit farther away, so it'll take rather longer than you remember."

Martin thanked Henry Clarence for the information, noted his phone number, and, after a few parting words, put the telephone down.

Monday, August 15

Martin was tired, but it would be several hours yet before he could sleep.

The day had started fifteen hours and five thousand miles ago, when he had given up trying to sleep and got out of bed to face the long day ahead. He had spent the first hour and a half puttering around the cottage, checking that he was ready for the flight. At seven thirty a taxi took him to Oxford station, whence the train had trundled through Oxfordshire and Berkshire to Reading. Then the coach carried him to Heathrow.

He purchased the most recent *Daily Telegraph* book of crossword puzzles from a bookstore in the departure lounge.

That kept him occupied while he waited for the plane and for the first hour or so of the flight. Then he began to be bored, and twice he hurried to start a new puzzle without first finishing the one before. He watched the in-flight movie.

The last several hours of the flight he had rotated between trying (unsuccessfully) to doze, looking mindlessly out of the window at the ground crawling by below, reading the in-flight magazine, and mulling over the clues to the unfinished crosswords that had stumped him earlier in the day.

He started another puzzle, and pondered the first clue with his eyes closed. (*"Burke's Peerage"?*; two words, ten letters and five letters.) He dozed. The answer came to him and, drowsily, he sat up, aware suddenly that the sound from the airplane's engines had changed and that the plane was now descending.

Looking out the window he saw a confusion of lights.

The cabin's public address system crackled into life, informing the passengers that they would be on the ground in ten minutes and telling them to prepare for landing.

The lights came closer. The new airport looked immense. The main terminal building was roofed by grand manmade mountains that glowed translucently. He'd read somewhere that for two years Denver International had been the largest construction site on the planet. He could believe it.

Five minutes later the plane banked to enter the glide corridor. It flashed over the airport's perimeter fence and, moments later, touched down.

Half an hour later, Martin walked out of the immigration hall and looked around to get his bearings. Someone stepped out of a small crowd. For a moment, Martin ignored the, vaguely registering only that he was short and black.

"Mr. Salisbury?"

Martin recognized Judge Madison.

"Good evening, Judge. I didn't expect to see you here."

"Well, a three-hour drive is no fun for someone who has just arrived from London. And it's just as easy to rent a car in Pinetree as it is here. So I thought I'd come down and pick you up."

"Well, thank you. It's very kind of you. I *am* rather tired and I must say that I really wasn't looking forward to driving all that way on the wrong side of the road."

The two men rode an elevator down to the parking area and were soon ensconced inside the judge's Volvo. Henry Clarence edged his way out the parking structure and on to Peña Boulevard, heading for the interstate and away from the simulated mountain peaks of the terminal building. Within minutes they were heading west on I-70 towards the real mountains somewhere ahead of them, hidden by the darkness.

Martin tried to nap, but found that after a ten minute doze he could sleep no more. He contented himself with looking out the window as they drove through Denver. They left the city behind and began to climb steadily.

They drove for an hour, the judge assiduously holding to the speed limit, his passenger gazing at the landscape through sleepy eyes. They left the interstate and crossed the continental divide, dropping into a dark valley.

"About halfway there now," said Henry Clarence.

They had spoken no more than a few dozen words since Martin had stepped off the plane, none of them about Matthew. Now Martin opened a conversation.

"I suppose the coroner's finished his report by now? It was a heart attack, I assume?"

The judge said nothing for several seconds. When he replied, he spoke slowly, as if he were choosing his words carefully.

"Yes, well, that was the other reason I came to collect you. They've performed an autopsy. The official report isn't available yet, but I had a quiet word with Dean Halliwell, the county coroner, early this afternoon. It wasn't a heart attack. According to Dean, it was hypoglycemia."

Martin processed this in silence. A heart attack had been surprising; hypoglycemia was nothing short of astonishing.

"Hypoglycemia? Low blood sugar? But Matthew was always so careful about that. He wouldn't even go backpacking alone. He tested his sugar at every meal. How did he let it get out of control?"

"We don't know; but the police are already looking into his movements in the last few hours before he died. The coroner also said that there was something puzzling that doesn't immediately seem to make sense."

"Oh?"

"It seems that there were traces of a couple of drugs in Matthew's blood."

"Drugs? You mean illicit ones?"

Martin was having difficulty picturing his health-nut cousin taking illegal drugs; but, he supposed, in a place like Pinetree with its smattering of "rich and famous," anything was possible.

The judge clarified, "No, nothing like that. There's residue of an anti-inflammatory, I forget its name, and also traces of a sleeping pill, a hypnotic I guess is the correct medical terminology, but certainly not enough to kill him. He was on medication for a sore shoulder, which seems to be the source of the anti-inflammatory, but the hypnotic is a bit of a mystery. But the coroner says that he is 100 percent positive that there was nothing in his blood that could have killed him. Apart from the lack of sugar, that is."

"So we conclude that for some unknown reason, he let his blood sugar get too low?"

"Seems like it. The police have his blood sugar meter and they're checking its accuracy. There was no sign of foul play when I found the body, and both the police and the coroner confirm that there were no bruises or contusions anywhere on his body. In fact, Dean told me that you'd have to go a long way to find a forty-four-year-old body in such good condition. So for now we don't really know what happened."

There was silence while the car covered another mile.

Martin asked: "What about candy? My girlfriend's a diabetic, and she says that one of the rules is always to have a roll of glucose candy within reach just in case of a hypoglycemic attack. Didn't Matthew have candy on him when he died?"

"I don't know. I didn't search the pockets myself, and I didn't watch the police do it either, although one assumes that they must have done so."

Martin thought for a while.

"Not a very satisfactory conclusion to a life, is it? I mean, at least we ought to be able to figure out *why* he died. Maybe, like you suggest, his meter was acting up."

"Maybe." Henry Clarence sounded dubious.

"What's this coroner like? Is he any good?"

"Dean? Oh, yes. Pinetree County is quite forward-looking in that regard. You'd be surprised how many Colorado counties still use morticians as their county coroners. Dean is a medical pathologist; in real life he works at the Pinetree County Hospital. He may not be the world's best, but I'm sure he would have noticed anything suspicious. He says he's having a second sample of the blood analyzed by another lab in Denver to see if it matches the first report. But he thinks it's very unlikely there'll be any difference."

Martin lapsed into thought.

"What about that sore shoulder? Did he get that playing racquetball like you thought when you rang me?"

"Oh, yes, no mystery there. He banged his shoulder playing racquetball last Wednesday. I guess it hurt rather badly, so he took it to his doctor, who prescribed an anti-inflammatory. Nothing odd there at all.

"The police department has a detective working on the case. He'll probably be up at Matthew's house tomorrow. You should probably make an effort to meet him; he'll be able to tell you more than I can. He'll have the house off-limits at first in the morning, but I expect he'll've finished with it by noon, and you can probably talk to him then."

The road became narrower. They encountered little traffic as they made their way around the tortuous curves, climbing toward another pass. They reached the top and dropped into a long valley.

An hour later, the car crawled up the side of another mountain. They passed a wooden sign, barely visible in the darkness, announcing Pinetree Pass — elevation 10,413 feet — and began to drop down the northwestern side of the pass.

There was a grunt from the passenger seat and Martin opened his eyes. He had been dozing for a while. Blinking, he looked around, but could see little in the quasidarkness. A gibbous moon was trying to light the scene, but its efforts were thwarted by thin clouds.

"We'll be there in about ten minutes. Just around this corner and you should be able to see Pinetree," said the judge.

They turned the corner. Yellow and white lights slid silently into view in the middle distance.

The lights were below the level of the car, but they seemed to rise up to meet them as the minutes ticked by and the car dropped into Pinetree Valley. They disappeared momentarily as the vehicle navigated a severe bend in the road, only to reappear brighter and more nearly at the same level as the car.

Two minutes later, they drove past a well-lit sign that declaimed the entrance to "Ski Country USA — Pinetree — Pop. 7362 — Elev. 7521." Another three minutes and the car came to a halt in the parking lot of the Downhiller Motel. In the light from the motel's reception area, Martin glanced at his watch: it was a quarter past midnight.

It took a couple of minutes to rouse the duty receptionist, even with several sharp taps of the bell on the counter. When the receptionist appeared, bleary eyed, he made short work of checking Martin in to Room 245. Henry Clarence helped Martin with his baggage and instructed the latter to call him in the morning. The judge left, and Martin undressed quickly and went to bed.

Tuesday, August 16

Martin awoke at seven the next morning. At least, that was what the clock on the bedside table indicated, although his body was considerably less sure.

It was shortly after midnight when he had got to bed. Seven hours' sleep, not bad in the circumstances, he supposed.

There was a choice of morning news shows. He selected the one with the prettiest anchorwoman and paid the show a modicum of attention while he went about unpacking. He showered, and leisurely donned fresh clothes.

He soon became annoyed with the program, which presented slight "human-interest" stories as if they were news. He became positively angry with the frequent interruptions for commercials. He snapped the television off. Now he remembered why he never watched TV when visiting the States on business.

He opened the drab curtains, and revealed a sight that almost took his breath away.

In the foreground were the usual paraphernalia of humanity: a tarmaced parking lot with a smattering of cars; beyond that a wide street, with two shops clearly visible: *The Mountaineer — Ski Equipment Rentals*, and *Harriet's Clothiery*. But beyond these was a simply gorgeous view of Pinetree Mountain. Martin forgot his annoyance with the television and stood in awe, drinking in the view.

He had been to Pinetree once before, twenty one months ago, but then it was ski season, and the view before him was unrecognizable from what he remembered.

Then, everything had been covered by an integument of snow, augmented by the six inches of new powder that had fallen during his visit. The town itself had been trapped under a white shroud, but the mountains had looked magnificent, the snow juxtaposed with the greenery in a visual perfection. Dividing the forest that clung to the slopes were wide corridors of white, down which moved little dots — the skiers who had come to escape their quotidian cares in the exhilaration of speeding down the mountainside.

Now, as he looked out on the mountain in its summer garb, he decided that he had been mistaken: the mountains were made for summer, not winter. The sunlight shone off the trees with a vividness that almost assaulted his eyes. The wide swaths of the downhill ski trails were no longer white scars on the mountain, but simply part of the background, the lighter green of the grass variegated amongst the darker green of the evergreens. He stood, looking, and understanding how a person could easily be seduced to live in such a place as this.

Martin shook himself, only partly breaking the spell. He opened the door and stepped out into the morning. Sucking in his breath, the unanticipated sharpness of the early-morning air slapped him with an almost physical intensity.

He went in search of breakfast.

He found it in the lobby of the motel: thick orange juice from concentrate that had been insufficiently diluted, and a waxy pastry surmounted with glaze and sugar. It was hardly what his stomach needed, but he supposed it would do for now.

He eyed the tea bags and hot water suspiciously. Who could guess how stale the tea was? And in any case, he now remembered, it was impossible to make a decent cup of tea at this altitude: water boiled at a mere 199 degrees Fahrenheit, so the tea did not steep properly. He poured two bitter cups of coffee into his stomach while he thumbed through the morning's edition of the *Denver Post*. The coffee helped, slightly.

A female receptionist appeared and busied herself behind the counter. She studiously ignored Martin as he searched the newspaper for a decent crossword puzzle. He gave it up as a bad job. He pushed the paper away, and gave himself over to fuzzy memories of his conversation with Henry Clarence Madison.

So there was as yet no real explanation for Matthew's death. That seemed rather strange.

Hypoglycemia, of course, was a diabetic's continual concern. If he had not known it simply by watching Matthew on his last visit to Pinetree, he certainly knew it after living with Davina for six months. But because they lived so close to the edge, diabetics always seemed to take great care to maintain their blood sugar within strict limits. If they didn't, they died; it was as simple as that.

It was inconceivable that Matthew had allowed himself to slide into coma voluntarily. The thought of suicide flashed into his mind, only to be rebutted instantly by the words of Matthew's last letter, written barely three months ago: "Never felt better in my entire life, and looking forward to our vacation." No, something here wasn't quite right. He shrugged and stood; perhaps it would all become clear when the second lab report arrived.

He asked the receptionist where he could rent a car. She was short and dark, with a swarthy skin. Hispanic, probably. Twenty five or thereabouts. She replied in a heavy accent, and with some embarrassment he was forced to ask her to repeat her answer several times before he was sure he understood it.

Mumbling *graciase*s, he edged his way out the lobby and into the parking lot.

Turning right, he walked along the sidewalk of the main thoroughfare through town. He breathed deeply and strode briskly in the sharp morning air.

He found the sign two hundred yards down the road: Hertz Rent-A-Car; but according to the notice in the window the travel agency that acted as the local Hertz agent would not open its doors for another half hour.

Martin idled away the time by walking. Pinetree was long and narrow, a single strip of habitation along a paved artery fed by lesser capillaries that edged up the mountains. He began to remember landmarks from his previous visit, vastly changed though they all were without their winter garb of white.

There was the Episcopal Church, the only concession to religion (other than Mammon) that he remembered seeing, standing on the north side, partway up a mountainside and slightly above most of the town. On the southern side of the valley was the four-seat gondola, which in winter whisked skiers to the top of Pinetree Mountain. Farther along the valley, he could make out the smaller chair lift that reached chillily halfway up Mount Devonshire.

He passed a cinema, two small shopping malls and a number of little motels not noticeably different from the Downhiller.

Martin glanced at his watch, turned, and ambled back to the car rental agency.

They were ten minutes late opening their doors. Even when they finally did open — courtesy of a slip of a girl no more than twenty years old who seemed to be entirely alone — it was several more minutes before she was ready to process his request.

Still, once she got down to it the girl was efficient enough. And in any case she was only just short of beautiful, and from a pretty girl Martin could forgive much.

He selected a comfortable-looking gray Camry. Another five minutes and the paperwork was complete.

He drove the short distance back to the motel. Returning to his room, he dialed the number that Henry Clarence had given him last night.

"Judge Madison's chambers," said a male voice.

"This is Mr. Martin Salisbury. Judge Madison gave me this number and said I might reach him this morning...."

"Let me look at his docket for the morning."

There was a shuffle of papers.

"His docket looks pretty short today. I expect he'll only be another half hour or so, unless something unexpected comes up. Can I get your number, Mr. Salisbury? I'll tell the judge you called as soon as he's available."

Martin left his number and replaced the telephone. Taking out his book of crossword puzzles, he was soon engrossed in a world of his own.

Chapter 5

Martin whiled away the next hour completing several puzzles that had defeated him on the flight. He was puzzling over a particularly difficult clue (*Dickens's traveller was so unbusinesslike* — he was sure that the answer was "uncommercial," but he could not see *why* that was the answer) when the telephone rang. It was Judge Madison.

"Good morning, Martin. I trust you slept well?"

"Yes, thank you, Judge. By the way, I have a car now."

"Ah, good. Listen, something's come up and I'm afraid it looks like I'll be stuck here in court all morning. I'm in a recess right now. Why don't you take a drive up to Matthew's house and you could see if it's OK for you to take a look around. The police should be up there. I'll be free here about midday, I expect, and we could meet for lunch if you like. Do you remember how to get to Matthew's house?"

"Yes, I think so. The west end of town and then south up the big mountain?"

"Yes, that's right. You'll pass the county courthouse on the way. It's a sandstone building, three storeys high, on the south side of the valley, maybe a quarter of a mile before the turnoff for Matthew's place. I'll be in my chambers as soon as I've finished with the docket this morning. Just come by when you're free and we'll have lunch together."

Martin thanked the judge and put the phone down.

He was in no hurry. After all, as he reminded himself, he was on holiday. So he picked up the book and spent another half hour completing clues.

Around ten, he went outside. The slopes on the south side of town were darker now, the sun casting them in shadow. The four-person gondola on Pinetree Mountain was moving, the cabins inching their way up and down the mountainside.

The sky was almost cloudless, with only a pair of high, fluffy cumuli moving from west to east. The air was still cool. He breathed deeply. At this altitude, the air was distinctly thin.

He well remembered how, on his last visit, he had nearly blacked out just as he reached the foot of the ski slope on one of the early runs of the day. Matthew had been just behind him, chaperoning him until he became used to the blue-coded intermediate slopes at the Pinetree ski resort. Matthew himself was a decidedly able skier, quite capable of conquering the black advanced slopes, but more than willing to look after his guest while Martin tried to remember the nuances of skiing.

Martin had suddenly felt dizzy, just as he completed a run. He heard a *swoosh* and found himself being propped up by his cousin.

"Are you OK?" There was obvious concern in Matthew's voice.

"I don't know. I suddenly felt faint."

"Here, bend down a minute and you'll feel better. It's the altitude. It's much harder work than you realize, concentrating on getting down these slopes when you aren't used to it. The lack of oxygen makes it easy to overdo things. You should take it easy for at least half a day until you've got some confidence in your ability to ski at this altitude. Slow down and relax and you'll enjoy the day a lot more.

"Don't be afraid to stop and take a few deep breaths. We don't want you plowing into a tree and ending up in the hospital or the mortuary, do we? It happens, you know: once or twice every year someone flies up here from sea-level, hits the slopes and kills himself by running into a tree in the first hour or two."

Now Martin gazed at the slopes. It was hard to imagine that the green inclines on the southern side of town would be filled with skiers in less than three months. Harder still to comprehend that Matthew would not be among them.

He got lost just once trying to find Matthew's house.

He found the turnoff from the highway, but the road looked very different from the way he remembered it — covered in snow, with two-foot drifts hiding the details — and he missed the narrow turning which was Matthew's quarter-mile-long driveway.

51

He retraced his steps, and this time noticed Matthew's mailbox next to the narrow dirt driveway. He drove slowly along the single-lane track; pine and aspen branches reached within inches of the car. The car lurched over a little rise and he found himself in a level clearing in front of Matthew's house. He braked just in time to stop himself from running into a car which was parked immediately in front of the garage, directly in his path. A battery of lights was spread across the roof of the car. On its trunk a seal bore the legend "Pinetree Police Department" arched over the top half and the motto "Serving the People" in an arc around the lower half.

Martin got out and closed the door noisily, alerting the unseen officer to his presence. He waited for the officer to appear.

Matthew's house towered above him. It was built into the slope of the mountain, and the trees nestled within feet of the building, in many places overhanging the redwood deck that almost completely surrounded the house. The lowest floor of the house comprised an enormous garage-cum-workshop whose overhead door was now closed. Above that was the single living floor of the house, supported partly by the garage beneath and partly by stilts that obtruded from the rock of the mountain itself.

The eastern half of the house had high cathedral ceilings, the western part, even though it had an attic, was somewhat lower. The house was liberally windowed, which made it light and airy inside even though, because it was on a northern slope, it spent most of its time in shadow. The elevation afforded the house by the garage and the stilts lifted it sufficiently high that from the windows one could see across the valley to the slopes on the far side of Pinetree. It must have been like moving to another planet when Matthew had moved here from Chicago.

The front door swung open and a man in plain clothes stepped out on to the deck. He looked down at Martin.

"Good morning, may I help you?" asked the policeman.

"My name is Martin Salisbury. I'm from England, a cousin of Matthew's. Judge Madison drove me up from Denver last night. He said that maybe I could look around Matthew's house, if it's all right with you?"

The man beckoned, and Martin climbed the winding steps to the deck. They shook hands.

"How do you do?" asked Martin — "How are you?" asked the policeman at the same time.

They both grinned.

The policeman was younger than Martin, in his early or perhaps mid thirties. He was cleanshaven, about five feet eight, with bright blue eyes that seemed almost translucent. His hair was light blond and slightly longer than seemed appropriate for a policeman. His handshake was firm; his smile appeared genuine.

"Good morning, Mr. Salisbury. I'm Detective Harry Jones, with the Pinetree PD. I'm investigating Mr. Chambers' death. The judge told you, I suppose, about what happened?"

Martin nodded. "Yes, he called me the night it happened. I was planning on flying over this coming weekend to spend a couple of weeks with Matthew, you know...."

Harry raised a hand to interrupt. "If you'll just wait a minute, sir. My notebook is inside, and I'd like to get your statement down. If you'd follow me?"

Martin was momentarily taken aback. He had not thought of himself as providing a "statement" to the police. Not that it mattered, of course. In a way, he supposed he was glad; it showed that the police were seriously concerned about what might have caused Matthew's death. Even so, it was somewhat unnerving.

He followed Detective Jones into the house.

Martin stopped for a moment just inside the door. He was standing on a small landing. Directly in front of him, on the far side of the massive living room, he could see part of the kitchen at the rear of the house. The bedrooms were to his right. Between the bedrooms and the kitchen was a bathroom that was recessed out of his view. He descended the two steps to the living room.

Windows filled one wall. There were several chairs and a sofa spread around. A piano stood in one corner, a green cloth draped over it as protection from the sun. Near the easternmost window was a small table on which stood a chess board, the position of the pieces reflecting a game in progress.

Martin crossed the hardwood floor to the chess game. He pondered it for a few seconds, oblivious to the presence of the policeman who was standing behind him.

Black was in deep trouble.

"Who was winning?" Martin asked.

"Don't know, sir. I don't play. Mr. Chambers was white, so Judge Madison says. Seems they used to make one move every day. In fact, this chess game is the reason that the body was discovered when it was. But you must know that, sir."

Martin shook his head. "No, I didn't know. And for what it's worth, white is going to win in about eight moves, I would say."

The detective began to write in his notebook. Martin quickly qualified his statement. "Don't hold me to that exact number, of course. But white is definitely in a winning position. Black really should have resigned already."

"Play much chess yourself, do you, sir?"

"Not any more. I used to, in school and at college. I was the school champion three years in a row. But I don't have enough time for it these days. Matthew and I played a few games when I stayed with him, but I'm afraid that I wasn't really in his class, so it probably wasn't much fun for him."

The detective raised a light brown eyebrow. "So you've been here before, sir?"

"Oh, yes. Didn't the judge tell you? I was here, let's see, it was early December of 1992, just for a couple of days. I stopped off on my way back to England after attending Comdex in Las Vegas. That's a computer trade show. I'm in computers: software, with Smith Computers. You probably haven't heard of us, but we're a pretty big outfit in the U.K."

Detective Jones scribbled down the information. He looked up. "Now, sir; what was this about coming to stay with Mr. Chambers this weekend?"

Martin sat on the sofa to make himself comfortable, and explained about the planned backpacking trip. He told the detective about Davina, and how her sudden safari to Africa had put, as he said, "a spanner in the works." Then he explained how Judge Madison had called him with the news of Matthew's death. The detective seemed particularly interested about this conversation.

"Can you remember the exact words?" he asked.

Martin shook his head. "No, not really. I mean, I can give you the gist of things all right. He just said that Matthew was dead, he was the one who found the body, and it looked like a heart attack."

Yesterday, Martin now remembered, the judge had told him exactly where he had found the body, and now his eyes fixed on the steps to the kitchen, as if he expected Matthew's body suddenly to materialize in front of him.

"I was out the first time he called, because it was early morning in England and I went out shopping that day. So he didn't get through to me until afternoon my time to tell me what had happened."

Martin told him about Jo, too, because she was Matthew's only other relative. Not too much; nothing about her private life, nor what she did for a living. "But she doesn't know Judge Madison, and she hasn't spoken to him or anyone else directly. She only knows about this whole thing through phone conversations with me."

The detective asked about Martin's prior visit to Pinetree, and Martin tried to be as straightforward as possible.

It had been a pleasant two-day break from work after the stress of the exhibition in Las Vegas. At that time, it had been somewhat more than two years since he had seen Matthew, the last time being the occasion of a visit by Matthew to England when the two of them had joined a party of Martin's friends to go longboating on the English canals. Matthew had been living in Chicago then, and had seemed only too happy to exchange the stress of his job in a large law practice in the big city for two weeks of indolence on the English waterways.

"And the move from Chicago to Pinetree? Do you have any idea what caused that?"

"Not for sure. You might ask the judge about it. He might know more. But it happened shortly after Matthew came longboating with us, and I can tell you that he was pretty eaten up at the time. In Chicago I guess Matthew was thought of as something of a hot shot, an up-and-coming high flier.

"He used to do a lot of criminal trial work; I really don't know the details. But I remember that he had just finished a case that went badly. I think there was a white teenager who had been mown down by a car that turned out to have a couple of black kids in it. One of them was stoned out of his mind on pot and one was way over the legal alcohol limit.

"Martin worked for a big law firm — I don't remember the name, but I'm sure Judge Madison could give it to you — anyway, I guess that one of these two black kids had an important real estate executive for a father, and he gave the defense to Matthew's law firm. Matthew landed the job of trying to get them off. They were as guilty as hell, you understand. Well, Matthew got the kids off, scot-free. The police had made some kind of a technical error when they collected the evidence. I'm sorry I don't know the details, I'm not very conversant with American law. You might try asking Judge Madison about details. He might know."

"I thought you said the case went badly."

"Yes. Sorry. He won the case, but he felt worse about it than if he'd lost. You understand?"

"Yes, I think so."

"Like I say, Judge Madison probably knows a lot more about it."

The policeman nodded, and Martin was left with the impression that the detective had, in fact, already spoken with the judge and that Martin was merely confirming what the judge had already told him.

Martin tried to change the direction of the conversation. "So, how is the investigation going? Have you discovered the reason for my cousin's death yet?"

The young detective looked at him for a moment before answering.

"No, sir. We are still waiting for some lab tests and the final coroner's report. I'm afraid I'm not at liberty to disclose any more than that at the moment. And, unless there's something else I can do for you, I'll have to ask you to leave now. I'm still collecting physical evidence here. As soon as I'm finished I'll let you know, and you'll be free to visit the house then. Could you give me an address and phone number where I might reach you, sir?"

"I'm staying at the Downhiller Motel. I don't remember the telephone number, but it must be in the book." He fished in his pocket for the room key. "I'm in room 245."

The detective made an annotation in his notebook. Martin turned to leave just as the telephone rang — a long, insistent electronic noise from the corner of the room where a cordless telephone stood in its charger on the wall.

The detective answered the phone. After a moment, he offered the instrument to Martin.

"It's for you."

The caller was Judge Madison — it could hardly have been anyone else — with news about the findings from the second blood test. They confirmed the results from the first lab: low blood sugar; anti-inflammatory; hypnotic. Martin acknowledged the information, and accepted the judge's offer to meet him in his chambers in half an hour for lunch. He glanced at his watch. It was now eleven o'clock. He remembered that Americans, at least in this part of the country, seemed to eat lunch much earlier than he was used to. He replaced the phone and took his leave of Detective Jones.

Harry Jones stood on the deck and and watched the retreating car. He found himself wondering about Martin Salisbury.

It was always difficult to understand the motives and priorities of other people, especially people whose thought processes were quite different from one's own. Martin was a successful English businessman, vice president of a large computer company, someone who understood the intricacies of both people and computers, according to Jonathan Smith, president and founder of Smith Computers, with whom Detective Jones had spoken within the past hour.

It was unlikely that Martin Salisbury had anything to do with Mr. Chambers' death, of course, but it was comforting that everything Martin had said confirmed — and was confirmed by — Judge Madison's version of the facts. Not that the judge was much of a suspect either, but one could never be too careful when investigating an unexplained death. Although it wasn't as if there was anything exactly suspicious about Matthew Chambers' death. But it was a bit of a puzzle.

Detective Jones shook his head to clear it, breathed deeply a couple of times, and went back inside.

Chapter 6

Lunch was a congenial meal, eaten in a small restaurant two blocks from the county courthouse.

The coroner, the judge informed Martin, had received the result of the tests on the second blood sample that morning and would issue the final report by mid afternoon. The second series of tests confirmed the first series.

"So," the judge said as Matthew chewed a mouthful of Philadelphia sandwich, "it looks like we have a bit of a mystery on our hands. Unless, that is, Detective Jones has found something that he hasn't told us about yet. By the way, what did you make of him?"

The judge sipped expectantly on a tall glass of some kind of herb tea while waiting for Martin to answer.

"I don't know," Martin eventually said. "He seems to play his cards close to his chest. He grilled me for information that he would have been much better off getting from you, but told me almost nothing in return."

"What sort of information?"

"Oh, just background. Like why Matthew had left Chicago, what relatives he had, that sort of thing."

"And he didn't tell you how his investigation is going?"

"No. He said that he was waiting for the final report from the coroner. It wasn't even clear to me if there is any investigation *per se*; although he did say that he was examining the house for physical evidence."

"I wonder what he'll do when he reads the report."

"Who knows? Will he be kept on the case looking for some sort of cause of death, or will the police just drop it?"

"Oh, he'll probably spend another day or two on it unless they have just cause to believe it was a homicide. It'll just fade away, I expect. They'll keep the case open, of course, but they'll probably assign Jones to another case before the end of the week, and that, for all practical purposes, will be that."

The two ate for a while in silence.

Eventually, Martin said, "So, what do you think happened? You must have formed some sort of an opinion."

The judge shook his head. "I don't know. I honestly don't know. It seems melodramatic even to suggest that he didn't die naturally."

"You don't think...?"

The judge shrugged. "I knew Matthew well, probably better than anyone else. I have a hard time believing he would have allowed himself to lapse into a coma. On the other hand, it's not as if Matthew had any obvious enemies or anything. So I don't know. Maybe I am being melodramatic.

"He kept himself pretty much to himself, you know. He joined the Rotary club shortly after he arrived in town, mostly to help business, I think. That was how I met him. I sat next to him shortly after he joined, and we discovered that we both enjoyed playing chess and contract bridge.

"He and I formed a bridge pair, you know, and we've cleaned up at the local tournament for each of the past three years." Martin didn't know. "And we always had a game of chess going on.

"That was how I found the body. We played a game where one move had to be made each day, by 10 p.m., otherwise the game was forfeited. Normally, we would just call one another in the evening just before ten, but last Friday I was playing bridge with some friends up the mountain beyond Matthew's place. On the way back, rather late I must admit, I thought I would drop by and look at the board one more time. I was losing rather badly, you see, and I couldn't quite decide whether to continue in the hope that he would make a catastrophic mistake or whether I should simply resign.

"It was Matthew's move. By the way, we know that he almost certainly died before ten o'clock, because there was no message from him on my answering machine when I got home. Anyway, I arrived at Matthew's place around midnight and let myself in — he didn't lock the house at night. The light was on, so I knew he was awake. I walked into the living room and as I was crossing to the chess game, I saw his body on the floor, on the steps to the kitchen. He must have been going to the kitchen when he died."

"And there was no sign of a struggle or anything?"

"No, nothing like that. The game pieces were still standing. If there had been any kind of a struggle, I'm sure that at the very least the table and chess pieces would have been upset."

"Was he face up or face down?"

"Down. Well, more sideways, really."

"And there wasn't any sign of a pulse?"

"No. Nothing at all. He was cold, though. The coroner put the time of death as somewhere between eight and nine, so he'd been dead maybe three and a half hours by the time I found him."

"And his face: was there any expression on it? Any sign of pain or anything?"

"No. He looked quite peaceful and relaxed, really, as if he had just collapsed on the spot with no warning. I had pretty much decided that it must have been a massive heart attack or maybe a brain aneurysm or something like that: you know, one of those things that give no warning and can kill in a few seconds. But the coroner says that there's no chance it was any kind of physical failure in his body. That's what he thought at first too, so he was especially careful to look for it."

Martin leaned back in his chair and pondered for a moment.

"He'd had some sort of shoulder trouble, you said?"

"Yes. You'd need to talk to Felix Taylor, Matthew's doctor, if you want to know the details. I just knew about it because when Matthew and I sat together at Rotary on Friday, he popped a capsule from one of those small plastic bottles that pills come in, you know, and I asked him about it. 'Something Felix gave me yesterday for a shoulder problem. They seem to be working. I'm feeling much better. Serves me right for playing racquetball at my age' was all he said, if I remember rightly."

Martin nodded. He had finished his meal and sipped his iced water thoughtfully.

The judge asked, "Any sign of a will yet? There must be one. After all, that was pretty much how he made his living, writing wills for other people, so he must have had one himself."

Martin had not given the matter any thought. He shook his head. "I don't know of one. But, as you say, there must be one somewhere. Tell you what, I should probably drop in at his office this afternoon. I'll ask around there. Does he have any partners or anything?"

"No, no partners. He had a secretary, though. I don't remember her name. I'll ask my clerk if you'd like. He probably knows. One of the advantages of living in a small town: if you don't know someone personally, you're sure to know someone else who does. I'll call you at the motel. I'll leave a message if you're not there."

The two men rose and said goodbye. Martin headed for his car, the judge for the courthouse.

Martin Salisbury made three visits in the course of the afternoon, with a short break between the second and third to make an international telephone call.

First, he drove to Matthew Chambers' law practice, whose address he found in the telephone directory.

The door was, unsurprisingly, locked. Matthew had shared the small log building with an insurance agency. Martin went into the agency. A middle-aged, gray-haired secretary looked up from her computer.

"Good afternoon. May I help you?"

Martin began to explain who he was but the secretary soon interrupted.

"Such a shame. Mr. Chambers was a real gentleman, you know. I feel real sorry for Kathleen, that's his legal secretary, you know. He was so kind to her. Let her leave early whenever she wanted. She'll be out looking for a job, I suppose, as soon as she's gotten over the shock of it all. But she'll be lucky to get a boss like Mr. Chambers. And he paid her above the going rate, too, you know. Such a nice man. Kathleen must be pretty shook up about it all."

She paused for breath, and Martin seized the opportunity to interrupt the flow.

"I'm trying to find Kathleen. Has she been to the office since Friday?"

"Not that I know of. Not that I would necessarily have seen her, of course. I mean, she might have come into the office over the weekend, and I wouldn't have seen her then, you know. Or she might just have

61

dropped in for a few minutes; I might not hear her then. But I expect she would have come over to see me if she'd done that."

Martin thanked her and withdrew. Just before he closed the door he heard the woman say, "You're welcome," and then, almost inaudibly, "you dishy man."

He grinned all the way back to his car.

His second stop was at 124 Columbine Way, an address acquired from the phone book under "Kathleen Freeman," the name that Judge Madison's clerk had provided him.

He got lost twice, but eventually located Columbine Way on the northwest side of town, hidden from the main highway and running parallel to it at the foot of the slopes.

It was his first introduction to life for the less-than-prosperous in Pinetree.

Until now, and throughout his prior visit, he had seen no evidence to refute the proposition that everyone in Pinetree was wealthy and lived in what, back home in England, would have been regarded as almost palatial luxury. Had he stopped to consider, he would, of course, have realized that this could not be the true state of affairs, but this was the first time that he had come face to face with the proof.

He parked in the shadow of a large cottonwood tree, one of a series planted long ago along a verge between the road and the sidewalk. The sidewalk slabs were now cracked and uneven, broken and tilted by the roots of the trees. He sat in his car and examined the neighborhood.

There were three cars parked in the road. One was just in front of him: an ancient, dented green Datsun B210 whose paint was faded and peeling from exposure to the sun. The tires were worn almost bare. The license plates had expired two months ago.

On the opposite side of the street, perhaps a hundred feet away, was a beige Volkswagen Beetle — Bug, he quickly corrected himself, remembering the American name. The Bug was covered with a patina of dirt and did not look like it had moved for some considerable period of time.

Parked opposite him was a nondescript red two-door Subaru of somewhat less ancient vintage than the other vehicles. It was parked in front of 124 Columbine Way.

His eyes surveyed the houses. The reason why the cars were parked on the street was immediately evident: the small wooden houses were uniformly devoid of garages or even of driveways in which cars could be parked. All along the street were patches where oil had leaked from aging engines.

124 Columbine Way was essentially identical to all the other houses. It was a small, single-storey wooden structure, once painted what was probably a cheerful yellow, but now peeling and faded to a fulvous, splotchy oatmeal. It was approximately square, possibly as much as thirty feet on a side. The roof, of wooden shakes that curled where they were not nailed down, was stained and in need of repair. The house was surrounded by grass that had been recently cut. A low fence, white but desperately in need of a new coat of paint, separated the grass from the crooked, fractured paving stones of the sidewalk.

Martin crossed the road and, to the sound of protesting hinges, pushed open the gate. He walked five steps up the narrow path, on to the house's cramped porch.

There was no doorbell, merely a large brass knocker. Martin raised the knocker and dropped it heavily.

He did not know what exactly he had been expecting — if, indeed, he had had any expectations at all — but in any case he was momentarily surprised by the girl who opened the door. If he had been expecting anyone, it was a woman along the lines of the receptionist at the insurance agent's. This girl was certainly nothing like her.

Kathleen Freeman — he assumed this was she — was in her early twenties, little more than five feet tall, with a tanned, unblemished skin and dark hair with random flecks of color somewhere between auburn and blond. Her hair was long, so long that it disappeared down her back, with no indication of where it might end. Her eyes were deep, brown, languid and fixed on him. She looked up at Martin with a hesitant smile that revealed two rows of nearly perfect teeth (but they were not quite perfect: one canine was slightly crooked, which only added to her charm, suggesting as it did that everything about her was natural).

He recovered himself, hoping that she hadn't noticed her effect on him. Or maybe she was used to it.

"Excuse me, I'm looking for Kathleen?"

"Yes?"

"My name is Martin Salisbury. I'm a cousin of Matthew Chambers, her employer. I was supposed to fly over from England next weekend to go on a backpacking trip with Matthew, but when I heard what had happened, I felt that I had to come at once and see if there was anything I could do."

"I'm Kathleen Freeman." She stepped back from the door. "Please come in."

She led Martin to a small, homely living room, where he accepted a seat in a comfortable armchair.

The house was cramped but tidy. For a moment the tidiness jarred with what he had seen outside, but then he remembered the recently mown grass. He deduced that the house was rented and the external appearance was the landlord's responsibility, while the interior decoration and the lawn maintenance were in the care of the tenant.

Kathleen offered him a drink: "Water, Coke or something stronger?"

Martin accepted the water. While Kathleen went to the kitchen, Martin examined the shelves of the tall oak bookcase that filled half of one wall.

The books were an eclectic mixture, as were the records standing on the bottom shelf of the bookcase. Many, indeed most, of the books were protected by a shiny lamination of transparent plastic; at the base of their spines were circular stickers indicating that these books had once resided in a public library.

He removed a volume at random: *To Serve Them All My Days*, a novel by the English author R. F. Delderfield. He opened the book. Stamped across the flyleaf was the legend "Pinetree Public Library." Overlaying these words was the single uppercase word: "WITHDRAWN," stamped in red. He replaced the novel and extracted a second one, Tom Clancy's *Clear and Present Danger*. It was stamped identically.

"What are you looking at?" the voice pleasantly inquired, surprising him. He had not heard her re-enter the room.

He lifted the book so that Kathleen might read the title.

"That's a good one, one of his best. Have you read it?" she asked.

"No. I don't get much time to read."

"Borrow it if you like."

Feeling guilty for no reason that he could immediately ascertain, he shook his head and replaced the book.

"You have quite a collection there," he said, accepting a glass of iced water.

"Not all of it's mine, but most of it is. Some of the books belong to my housemate. Same with the records. Mine are mostly the classical ones and hers are mostly the pop. I can put one on if you'd like."

Martin was no great fan of music of any kind, although he could tolerate some of the better type of rock and most classical music, especially Ravel's *Bolero*, which he and Davina sometimes played to the accompaniment of other activities. For a fleeting moment he wondered how Kathleen would perform in the same circumstance. He wrenched his mind on to other subjects.

They talked for over an hour. At first, Martin was reticent about discussing Matthew's death, worried that it would upset Kathleen, but he quickly discovered that she herself displayed no such reluctance.

"Of course, it was a terrible shock. I didn't hear about it until Sunday evening. I spent most of the weekend with my fiancé; he drove over from Steamboat Springs on Friday evening and the two of us went camping a few miles up the river. We didn't get back into town until late on Sunday.

"I should have seen the note on the kitchen table right away, but I went to have a soak in the tub first. When I came out, Sylvia — my housemate — was back from evening Mass and she asked me if I had seen the message. I said I hadn't, and she told me that Matthew had been found dead on Friday evening.

"It was an awful shock. Apparently, the police had been calling all weekend, wanting to talk to me. Eventually they had given up and simply asked Sylvia to have me call them when I returned. I phoned them and they told me all about it. It's awful, isn't it? Such a horrid shock for everyone. He was such a nice man. Such a nice man."

She sat shaking her head, her eyes far away.

Martin prompted her to continue.

She had spent a harrowing morning with the police on Monday. They told her that there was no sign of foul play, and it looked like Matthew had died quickly and suddenly, possibly from hypoglycemia.

"The problem is not the cause of death," the policeman had said, "the coroner was fairly sure of that — but rather how someone as careful and experienced as Mr. Chambers could have let his blood sugar get so low. So to be on the safe side, I must ask you to treat this as we are doing, at least for now, as if it were a homicide. If you think of anything that might be relevant — anything — I must ask you to let us know immediately."

Kathleen did not seriously believe that someone could have killed her employer, and she could not really believe that the police thought so either. But still, the word "homicide" had a chill to it, and she found herself shaking uncontrollably by the time the interview was over.

She did not think that she had been able to help them very much.

Yes, Matthew had appeared perfectly normal on Friday. He had gone to Rotary as usual at noon and returned briefly to the office afterwards, gathering papers for two house closings that afternoon, one at Sutton and Dwight, and one with Bolton and Smith.

Yes, his shoulder had been bothering him some on Thursday after he had collided with a wall while playing racquetball on Wednesday afternoon. He had had an appointment with Dr. Taylor on Thursday morning and was taking some anti-inflammatory medication which seemed to be doing the job. She had specifically asked about his shoulder on Friday morning and he had told her that it was feeling much better. "The pain will be completely gone by tomorrow at this rate," he had said.

The pain had been gone by tomorrow, she thought, but bit her lip painfully to stop herself from voicing that thought.

The police had asked her for a key to the office. She had tried to refuse, but the detective had insisted, saying that there was no need for her to be present, but they must have a key. She did not know if they had been to the office yet; Kathleen herself had been feeling too shaken to go to the office herself on Monday.

Martin asked, "What about today? Now? Do you think you'd be up to taking me there? I'd really like to take a look around."

For a moment Martin felt guilty about imposing on her. Kathleen's eyes watered, but no tears came. She looked vacantly at the wall; then, with a slight sniff, she straightened and said, "Of course. Life must go on, mustn't it?"

He rose and held out a hand.

"Yes, it must. Come on, let's go to the office and see if there isn't something there that might shed some light on things."

He helped her out of her chair.

"Excuse me a moment. I feel so silly...," Kathleen said, trying to sniffle back tears. She hurried from the room. He heard the sound of running water. She returned a minute or so later looking considerably more self-composed.

Martin drove them in his car. The little building that housed the law office was as he had left it earlier, except that there was now a white, recently washed two-door Toyota parked outside the insurance agent's half of the building.

Kathleen disappeared around the back of the building and returned carrying a key. Martin followed her inside.

The reception area was about twelve by ten. Across from the doorway was Kathleen's desk, two piles of paper neatly stacked on the left and right sides. When seated at the desk, Kathleen would face the door through which he had just walked.

As well as the papers were two small trays, one empty, one containing three manila folders. A telephone, a large spiral-bound book and a small, cylindrical holder filled with a miscellany of pencils and pens completed the adornment of the desk.

To the left of the desk (as he looked at it) was a window that looked southward across the gravel parking lot towards the main road through town. The window was covered with a net curtain, permitting those inside to see out, but rendering it almost impossible to see into the office from outside.

To the right of the desk, perpendicular against a wall, was a small computer table on which sat the beige shapes of a computer, a keyboard and a monitor, all protected by translucent dust covers.

Kathleen walked between the desk and the computer table, and took her seat in the old-fashioned wooden chair behind her desk. She looked rather lost.

"Oh! The mail!" she exclaimed.

She went outside. There was the tinny noise of metal on metal and she returned carrying a handful of envelopes, looking at them intently. She returned to her desk.

"Anything interesting?" asked Martin.

"No."

She let the mail fall on to her desk. For a moment she looked close to tears.

"This Matthew's office?" Martin asked, nodding to the only other doorway, in the center of one wall.

She nodded, not trusting herself to speak.

Martin walked through into Matthew's office. It appeared to be about the same size as Kathleen's. It was darker, though, to the point of gloominess. Beyond the net curtain covering the north-facing window were the lower slopes of Pinetree Mountain, not more than a couple of hundred yards distant. A smattering of buildings similar to this one ranged over the lower slope, with grit-covered roads like lengths of dirty spaghetti linking them. The mountain reared up out of sight beyond the top of the window.

He switched on the light.

There was a single desk, larger and more impressive than Kathleen's. A couple of files were on the desk. Half a dozen filing cabinets lined the wall to his left.

The walls were covered with panels that were designed to look like oak, although Martin suspected that they were just chipboard covered with cheap facing. Several paintings hung on the walls. There was no theme that he could discern. All were oils, signed with names that he did not recognize. A seascape showed a storm beating against cliffs, an island in the middle distance supporting a dimly visible lighthouse from which a light shone on the cliff face, adding a man-made intensity to the natural eeriness of the lightning that flashed across the sky. A second: a forest scene, tranquil, with no single point of focus, just trees from foreground to background, the sun filtering through the uppermost branches in a way that seemed to Martin to be not quite natural. A third: a herd of zebra, heads down, taking refreshment at a small watering hole, two of the herd standing guard to one side.

The African scene made him think of Davina, and he realized guiltily that he had barely thought of her since his arrival in Pinetree. He wondered what she was doing right now. He glanced at his watch. Half past three. That would make it what? sometime in the late evening, towards midnight, in Kenya. She'd be sleeping, then, after a day of chasing animals across the veldt. He wondered how her assignment was working out.

There was a noise behind him: Kathleen slitting open the mail. He dragged his thoughts from Kenya to Colorado.

He examined the last picture in the room, affixed to the western wall: a snow scene which could be any one of a thousand places in Colorado. A single peak stood forth against an intense blue sky. The painting was so bright that it could have been a photograph were it not for the brush marks in the bright, white snow. The sky behind the mountain turned almost to white near the left hand side of the picture, suggesting the presence of the sun just off the edge of the canvas. There was something a little unsettling about the mountain itself: there were no rocks, no trees, nothing to give a sense of scale or perspective.

Turning around to survey the room, he realized now that this room was slightly shorter than the other.

Now why would a lawyer have a smaller office than his receptionist? Of course!

He lifted the picture of the mountain away from the wall. Behind it, embedded in the east-facing wall, was the numbered dial and sheened metal handle of a wall safe. He placed the painting on the desk.

"Kathleen, do you know the combination to Matthew's safe?" he called.

Before she could answer, there was another sound from the outer office — the sound of a door opening.

From where he was standing, he could see part of Kathleen's office, including the outside door. Through it stepped Harry Jones. The detective looked around and his eyes landed on Martin. From where he was standing he would not be able to see the safe.

"Good afternoon, Miss Freeman. Good afternoon, Mr. Salisbury. Didn't expect to see you two here. But I'm glad to find you anyway."

Martin moved forward, standing in the doorway and blocking the policeman's view of Matthew's office.

"Mr. Salisbury, I thought I ought to tell you that it is now official: the cause of your cousin's death was hypoglycemia. The coroner's final report is now in."

Martin shrugged.

"You know," the detective continued, "I'd have appreciated it if you or Miss Freeman here had called me before coming to the office. There might be evidence here, you know, and you could easily destroy it unknowingly." He said it good-naturedly, like a parent scolding a child for a minor infraction. But he left Martin in no doubt that a second transgression would not be so easily overlooked.

Martin said, "So, what is it then. Accident, suicide or murder?"

"Sir?"

"How could a long-term diabetic ever let himself fall into a hypo-glycemic coma? Remember, I've stayed with Matthew and saw how careful he was. Why didn't he take his glucose?"

"Glucose?"

"He kept a roll of glucose sweets... candy within reach at all times. It's common practice with diabetics, so they can get sugar into their bodies quickly if they need to. Matthew kept a roll in his pocket."

"I didn't know about that. But there was no candy in his pockets when he died."

"You're sure?"

"I'm sure. I was the one who made the inventory. There was nothing edible in his pockets when we went through them."

The statement hung in the air.

Not really believing it, Kathleen offered: "Perhaps they fell out of his pocket?"

"Not into his car, nor on to the floor anywhere in his house."

She said, "He had dinner with the Healys that evening. Have you checked there?"

"Not yet. We didn't know we should have been looking. But I will now. Thank you. Now, sir, what is that I see in the wall behind you?"

While he had been speaking, the detective had moved closer to Martin, and he was now in a position to see the safe.

Martin turned and gestured. "Matthew's safe. We haven't opened it yet."

The detective entered Matthew's office and looked at the safe.

"Have either of you been here since Friday?"

"No."

"And have either of you touched this safe at all?"

"No," again.

"Miss Freeman, do you know the combination to the safe?"

"No. But Matthew told me where to find it. Hang on a moment."

She walked to the file cabinets in Matthew's office and opened a drawer. She rifled through the folders and withdrew a sheet of paper.

"Here it is, filed under a fictitious client, Mr. Ardmore."

She handed the paper to the detective.

He placed it on the table. "If you'll be so good as to wait here. We must be careful to check for prints." He left the room.

Martin asked Kathleen, "What kinds of things did he keep in the safe? Any idea?"

She shook her head. "No. Private papers, I assume. As far as I know he had no business secrets from me. Of course, I suppose if they were secret, I wouldn't have known about them...." She smiled at her half-joke.

Detective Jones returned carrying a black case. He placed it on Matthew's desk and opened it. Out came a bottle of white powder and a small shaving brush. He dusted down the front surface of the safe, its knob and handle. He removed a Polaroid camera with a macro lens from the case and photographed the dust. The detective placed the photographs inside a folder.

"Now, to open it."

The safe opened easily. It was much smaller inside than outside, and contained only a single large yellow envelope. The detective carefully removed it and went through the procedure of dusting and photographing it.

Attached to the envelope was a bright yellow Post-It, with the message "Duplicate in safety deposit box" scrawled on it.

Martin read the note over the detective's shoulder. "Safety deposit box. That's somewhere else you need to look."

Harry Jones smiled and looked up into Martin's eyes. "No, sir. I've already done that. This, I expect you'll find, is Mr. Chambers' last will and testament."

Martin felt suitably deflated. "*Touché*, Detective Jones. So what does it say?"

The detective pressed the sides of the envelope so as to open its mouth, and peered inside.

"I'll have to check it back at the office, to make sure it doesn't have any prints, and also to make sure that it's identical to the other copy, but it looks the same."

He dropped the envelope into his case. "Mr. Chambers' will was quite simple, especially when you consider that he was a lawyer. It breaks down as follows: $10,000 in cash to Miss Freeman 'in appreciation of her services as my legal secretary,' $10,000 to Judge Henry Clarence Madison 'in appreciation of countless convivial evenings,' $2,000 to St. Peter's Episcopal Church, and the remainder of the estate to be split equally between 'Mr. Martin Salisbury, my cousin, of Oxford, England, and Mrs. Joanna Baker, *née* Salisbury, my cousin, of Sutherland, Australia.'

"Now, I wonder if there's anything else in here that might tell us anything. If you two would be so good as to leave the room and close the door, I would appreciate it."

Martin said, "Come on, Kathleen. I'll take you home. It looks like Detective Jones wants us out of the way."

He held out his hand to the detective, who accepted the gesture with a friendly smile. The two shook.

"See you later," Martin said.

As Martin drove Kathleen back to her house, tiredness began to overcome him. Jet lag was kicking in. She offered him a cup of coffee when he stopped to let her out of the car, and under other circumstances he would have accepted with alacrity, but he still wanted to make one more stop before crashing. And he needed to make a phone call.

"Thanks, but I need to catch up on my sleep. I'll try to catch you tomorrow sometime, OK?"

"OK," Kathleen agreed.

She slammed the car door out of custom.

He drove back to the Downhiller Motel. In his room he paused for a moment to think, then he picked up the phone.

In the suburban house in Sutherland, the new day was just beginning. The sole occupant was busying herself in the kitchen, preparing breakfast. From the new stereo system in the living room, rock music blared forth, the invisible binary digits on the iridescent disc converted by some sort of technological magic to a wall of sound.

All the windows were closed, not because it was cold outside but because this way she could turn up the volume without any chance of a complaint being filed by the neighbors. Not that it was really very likely that anyone would file a complaint against a police officer.

Joanna Salisbury was singing loudly along with the Beatles. The first stages of the trauma of the divorce were now firmly behind her. She had made a big mistake when she was too young to know better, but now she was determined not to dwell on the past and to get on with her life. She had a lot of catching up to do.

She was thirty five, and not getting any younger. She had to move on. If she didn't do that, she was likely to slide into a pit of despair and self-pity — what was that phrase she half-remembered from literature classes at school? a slough of despond, that was it — and spend much of the next ten years in psychiatrist's offices. Worse, there were other ways of escape that might tempt her, and she had too often seen the results of following after those mirages.

Monday morning, she had driven to the electronics showroom off Victoria Street and purchased a magnificent stereo system, along with a dozen compact discs. She had winced at the cost, but, damn it all, she had promised herself a present and a present she was going to have.

The music faded and she heard the sound of the telephone ringing harshly in the silence.

How long had it been ringing? She would never have heard it above the sound of the disc and her own singing.

She cursorily wiped her hands on the towel draped through the handle of the fridge and lifted the telephone, just as the music of the next track began. She pressed her right ear tightly against the instrument and the index finger of her left hand into her other ear.

It sounded — amazingly — like Martin.

"Hang on a mo, let me turn the music down."

She dropped the telephone on the counter without waiting for a response, hurried into the living room and, after a moment's searching, hit the button displaying two thick vertical lines that, for reasons that were a complete mystery to Joanna, represented "Pause" in the international iconic language that adorned electronic equipment these days. The music stopped in the middle of a chord. Joanna hurried back to the kitchen and lifted the phone.

"Hello. Sorry about that; I bought myself a new present and I guess I was playing it a bit too loud."

"Hello, Jo. This is Martin and I just wanted to let you know that I arrived in Pinetree OK, and also to let you know that there's something a bit strange here. But first, how are things with you?"

Joanna was suddenly attentive, wondering what could have been sufficiently "strange" to cause Martin to make the international phone call. Martin was possibly the most logical person she had ever known. If he said something was strange, it was generally worth taking notice. She ignored his question.

"Strange?"

"Well... yes. Just a bit. It'll probably come to nothing. But I was met at the airport yesterday by a friend of Matthew's, a judge here in town. In fact, he was the man who found the body. Anyway, I don't remember it too well because I was too tired after the flight. But it seems like Matthew died from an attack of hypoglycemia. Matthew was a diabetic, you know" — she didn't — "but he was very careful and so far they don't seem to know how he could have let his blood sugar get so low. Anyway, I've just got back from talking to the detective who's handling the case, and there're a couple of things that might interest you."

"Tell me more."

"In the first place, he left the bulk of his considerable estate to the two of us, so that, among other things, you now own one half of a rather nice house on the outskirts of Pinetree."

Joanna was speechless. Matthew had sent a photo one Christmas. The house was simply gorgeous.

"But in the second place, there's a bit of a puzzle about Matthew's death. Like most diabetics, he always kept sugar with him so it was readily available in an emergency. But the sugar wasn't in his pockets when he died."

"Sugar? Like you get in packets in restaurants?"

"No. Glucose sweets. I guess it's absorbed more quickly or something. Anyway, he wasn't carrying them when he died."

"He must have dropped them."

"Doesn't seem like it. They haven't been found yet."

"Perhaps he simply forgot them."

"Not likely. Anyway, they'd have been in the house. They weren't."

"You aren't suggesting foul play?"

"Well, that's probably going a bit far. But there's definitely something a bit odd about it all."

"What about having a second coroner look at the body? Maybe this one is just missing something very obvious? It wouldn't be the first time."

"Well, I don't know. I'll suggest that to the judge of course and see if it can be arranged."

"What about the detective? If this one's like that Columbo fellow on television..."

Martin had to laugh. "He certainly doesn't dress the part. He seems like an ordinary, plodding kind of guy who'll just do his best. Quite young, but seems competent enough."

Joanna gave voice to an idea that had just come to her. It seemed ridiculous. But why not? She hadn't seen Martin for seventeen years....

"You know, I have two weeks of vacation due. And I haven't seen you for an awfully long time...."

Suddenly, she wanted to cry.

This was not how the idea had seemed in her head, but it was too late to stop now. Fighting back tears, she continued.

"Oh, Martin; I've made such a mess of my life. We were so close when we were young, and I just walked away from you all. And then when Mum and Dad died, and I couldn't even get away for the funeral. I felt so terrible about that. I... I'd really like to see you again. I don't have much money, but I have a credit card and if you'd like to see me, I'm sure I could get away in a day or so. I don't have any big cases or anything, just a lot of paperwork, and I'd really like very much to see you...."

Martin was unprepared for this. He was exhausted, and the raw emotion flooding down the telephone line caught him off-guard.

Seventeen years ago he had been dumbfounded when his younger sister had, without warning, eloped half a world away to marry a good-for-nothing adventure seeker. In the intervening years, his shock had frozen into a solid anger at the way his sister had maintained so little contact with the family. Then, when their parents had died in that awful crash, Jo had simply sent a letter of regret that she would be unable to attend the funeral and the anger had hardened into fury. From that time until he had called her to tell her about Matthew's death, there had been no direct communication between the two.

And now, here was Jo admitting her mistakes and, apparently, wanting to see him again.

He remembered her as a child, then as a beautiful teenager, sought by all the boys in town, enjoying their company but never, as far as he could tell, becoming seriously involved with any of them. *Why didn't we understand then how happy we were?* he wondered.

He remembered her pride when she had won a scholarship to Cambridge, only to throw it away four months later when she eloped.

There were holidays in Cornwall, playing in the sand on the golden, seemingly endless beaches, swimming through the waves together to reach the calm water beyond the surf. He remembered with a mixture of emotion the time that Joanna's bikini top had come loose and disappeared into the white surf and he had surfaced from a dive to see his sister, utterly embarrassed, looking desperately around in the creamy water for some sign of her lost garment, her teenage breasts glistening in the sunlight.

He realized he was grinning, and he knew what he had to say.

"Jo, don't worry about the money. That's one concern I don't have any more. If you want to, just get on a flight and come on over. I've rented a car and I'll pick you up at the airport. Denver is the closest big city; I'm sure you'd be able to get a flight there with no trouble. I'll give you the money to cover the flight when you arrive. We've been apart too long, Jo. Maybe some good can come from Matthew's death...."

Joanna sniffed back her tears. She had been so afraid of rejection that she was shaking. She knew that she didn't deserve to be forgiven this easily. But she should have known better. Martin had never been one to put justice before love; he had always put people first. Perhaps, the thought now occurred to her, that was why he had been so successful in the business world. He was, when you got right down to it, simply a nice guy.

"Yes, yes. I'll do that, Martin. I really do have some paperwork that I need to get finished, but I'm sure they'll let me go once that's done. I'll give you a ring as soon as I've sorted things out at this end. Give me your number and I'll be in touch."

Martin read his number off the phone, and also gave her the judge's number at his chambers.

"Thank you, Martin."

"That's all right, Jo. I love you."

When was the last time that she had heard those words? Too long. Much too long. She nearly burst into tears again, but held them back just long enough to say, "Me too, Martin. Bye." She put the phone down.

Then the tears began to flow.

Martin Salisbury entered the county courthouse.

The building had many uses, as he discovered when he looked over the directory. Building Department, Assessor's Office, County Clerk — but there was no mention of Henry Clarence Madison. He wandered the corridors for a while before poking his head into a random office and asking his way.

"Oh, there's a separate entrance to the chambers and courtrooms, on the western side of the building," a middle-aged woman said, barely looking up from a stack of papers on her desk.

He made his way around to the western side, where there was an entrance with the legend "County Courtrooms — 1904" engraved in the sandstone above the lintel. Entering through the glass swing doors, he was stopped by a uniformed officer who was standing next to an X-ray machine and metal-detector portal. The officer's holster, like that of his companion seated several steps away and eyeing Martin warily, was prominently open. Martin passed nervously through the detector and asked for directions to Judge Madison's chambers.

"Up the stairs, then to the right; his name is on the outside of the door," said the officer next to the metal detector.

Martin climbed the stairs wearily. He glanced at his watch. 4:30; 11:30 p.m. in England. Not very late, but late enough, given his disturbed pattern of sleep.

Chambers of Judge Henry Clarence Madison, the sign on the bare wooden door declared. *Not a very prestigious office for a judge*, thought Martin as he paused outside. A simple wooden door on a none-too-wide and vaguely musty corridor. The wood appeared to be pine.

He knocked.

Someone said, "Come in."

He walked into a smallish anteroom that contained a set of filing cabinets, several chairs, a desk behind which sat a young man who looked up at him as he entered the room, and little else.

"May I help you?" asked the young man.

"My name is Martin Salisbury. I'd like to see Judge Madison if it's convenient."

"Certainly. Please wait a minute."

The man opened a door on the opposite side of the room. "Mr. Salisbury to see you," he said, leaning through the doorway into the room beyond.

"Good. Send him in, George." Martin recognized the judge's voice.

George ushered him into the judge's chambers. Only marginally larger than the clerk's office, although with the added luxury of a window that overlooked the grassed area in front of the courthouse, the room struck Martin as meager in the extreme for one whom society had chosen to dispense justice.

He stifled a yawn as he took a seat opposite the judge. Henry Clarence held out a thin sheaf of stapled papers.

"I thought you might want to see this. It's a copy of the coroner's final report. The police should have received their copy a couple of hours ago. As I told you, the conclusion is that Matthew died of extreme hypoglycemia. His blood sugar level dropped so low that he lost consciousness. He never woke up."

Martin glanced through the papers. Most of the report was filled with dense medical jargon at whose meaning he could only guess. But the conclusion was clear enough: "the subject died from coma induced by a blood sugar level of 10 milligrams or less per deciliter of blood."

He looked up to see the judge's eyes on him.

"So what are you going to do now?" asked the judge.

Martin stifled another yawn.

"Right now, I'm going to go back to the motel and get some sleep. Jet lag is catching up on me, I'm afraid. I should be OK by tomorrow. Let me sleep on this, if it's all right to keep this copy, and I'll let you know tomorrow if I come up with anything."

"Sure, that's your copy. Don't bandy it around, though. It's not really for public eyes; at least, not yet. I'll be here most of tomorrow. I have a light docket for the first hour or so in the morning, and then I'll be writing opinions for the rest of the day."

Martin drove back to the motel. Letting himself into his room, he saw the red message light on his telephone blinking urgently.

He swore quietly, considered for a moment, then decided it would keep. He threw the report on to the table next to the window, stretched out on the bed and in seconds was asleep.

Once made, it had been an easy decision to put into practice. Joanna had expected more than token opposition to her declaration that she was taking her vacation without notice, but she was pleasantly surprised when the Chief Inspector supported her.

"Glad to hear it," he had said. "You need to get away from everything for a while. Go away and do something completely different for a couple of weeks. Get the beast out of your life, put it all behind you and start again. We all support you, you know, and we want to do anything we can to help."

Joanna had not realized — had not even guessed — that her colleagues cared. The Chief Inspector's words boosted her self-confidence more than she would have thought possible. She cleared her desk of urgent paperwork and left the office early to pack. On her way home, she turned her car radio 20 decibels louder than usual and sang along with the 1970s rock music. By the time she arrived home, she almost felt young again.

Chapter 7

Martin woke. It was dark, although a hint of light filtered through the curtains. The red LED digits by his head informed him that it was a couple of minutes past five.

He groaned and raised himself to a sitting position. Slowly, his brain began to function. A light on the telephone pulsed redly. He ignored it. He crossed the room, and peeked through the curtains. Artificial lights were still bright against the night outside, but away to the east he could see a lightening of the sky, the first hint of the false dawn of the coming day. He let the curtain fall.

He stripped and made his way to the bathroom. Somewhat guiltily, afraid that he would wake other guests, he filled the tub with hot water and lowered himself into it.

Martin soaked for nearly half an hour. When he finally pulled himself out of the tub, he felt refreshed and invigorated, ready for the day ahead.

He selected a set of clean clothes and dressed. The coroner's report was where he had dropped it yesterday evening, but he decided against re-reading it. Instead he retrieved the crossword puzzle book from its place on the bedside table and opened it to the next empty puzzle.

He read the first clue — 3 across: *Racehorse going backwards for means of death (6)*. Grimly he entered the answer and closed the book. He wondered if it was a portent.

He looked at the light on the telephone, stretched, and made his way down to the lobby.

There were two messages. The first had been taken yesterday afternoon. From a Reverend Steven Allbright, the message gave a local telephone number but no indication of the reason behind the minister's call.

The second had been taken at 2:30 in the morning. "I no want wake you" was the explanation offered by the Hispanic woman behind the desk. "I tell lady you sleep. I take message," she elaborated.

Martin accepted the piece of paper. He smiled pleasantly and thanked the receptionist, inwardly wanting to strangle her as soon as he saw what she had written. "Continentul flit 244 from LA arrive Denver Wensday 9:30 p.m." The message was from "Joennah."

He hurried back to his room and tried to call his sister in Australia, but predictably there was no answer. Presumably, Jo was already in the air.

He pressed the hook to clear the line and dialed directory enquiries. They gave him the number he sought. On the third attempt, he finally succeeded in reaching a Continental agent who confirmed that flight 244 was scheduled to arrive at Denver International from Los Angeles at 9:30 p.m. The agent refused to divulge whether Joanna Baker — or possibly Joanna Salisbury — was on the flight.

He put the phone down.

He began to mull over Matthew's death. He opened several drawers until he came across one that contained some sheets of writing paper and a cheap pen. He began to make notes.

By the time he had finished, it was half past seven. He laid the pen down, crossed the room and opened the curtains. Daylight flooded in.

His stomach rumbled. He briefly considered breakfast in the motel lobby, then dismissed the thought. Once was enough. He'd find somewhere better. There must be somewhere not too far away that served a real breakfast.

He found the restaurant about half an hour later. "*La Pattisserie: petit déjeuner, déjeuner et dîner,*" the sign pretentiously announced. Through the window he could see that most of the tables were occupied by breakfasting patrons. He went inside

The omelets were good, the orange juice better, and the coffee best of all. He left satiated and glad of the walk back to the motel, which would at least assuage his conscience for having eaten such a self-indulgent meal.

At seven and half thousand feet, even a brisk walk can be strenuous exercise, and he was short of breath by the time he arrived back at the motel. He checked at the office; there were no more messages. Back in his room, he dialed the Reverend Steven Allbright's number.

"St. Peter's Episcopal Church," a female voice answered.

"Yes. Reverend Allbright left me a message yesterday, and I'm trying to return his call. This is Mr. Martin Salisbury."

"Certainly, sir. Please hold."

The sound of a local radio station filled his ear as he waited to be connected. A voice broke in.

"Steve Allbright."

"Yes. This is Martin Salisbury. You tried to reach me yesterday?"

"Oh, yes, Mr. Salisbury. I wanted to contact you about the arrangements concerning the funeral of Matthew Chambers. You are his next of kin, I understand?"

"Well, yes, I suppose so. I'm a cousin; he had no siblings and his parents are both dead."

"Well, the coroner has finished his examination and the body has been released from his care. Mr. Chambers was a member of our church and it seems appropriate for us to hold the funeral here. Unless you had other plans, of course. I understand that as a stranger to our community you might be reluctant to make the arrangements yourself, but I'd be more than willing to take care of them for you. Mr. Chambers was quite generous to our church, and it seems like the least we could do."

Martin cynically wondered if the news of Matthew's bequest might have reached the pastor's ears.

"Yes, certainly. That's very kind of you. If you would make whatever arrangements are necessary I would be grateful. If you need to contact me, I'll be out of town this evening, but I should be available again in the morning."

"If it would be convenient for you, I'll try to arrange a brief service for tomorrow afternoon, then. That would give us time to get the word out to our congregation and put something in the morning newspaper. I'll leave you a message at your motel later, if that would be all right."

"Yes, thank you. Oh, and Mr. Allbright, just in case Matthew didn't tell you, I understand that he left your church a sum of money in his will."

"Oh. Well. How kind. Matthew did say that he would remember us, and we are, of course, most grateful. But we would much rather have had him still with us, you understand. Such a shock, and so sudden. It just goes to show, doesn't it, how every day is in the hands of the Lord?"

"Yes; yes indeed it does."

Martin tried to sound sincere as he disengaged himself from the conversation.

Replacing the telephone, his thoughts turned to the coming evening. He would meet Jo at the airport — but what then? Would they be able to put the past behind them? Or was it a big mistake to think that they could ignore all that?

Joanna Salisbury looked down at the island falling away behind the airplane.

Her emotions were finally beginning to reach some sort of equilibrium. And she found, to her surprise, that the feeling that was uppermost was excitement.

Not elation, which would have been understandable given her new freedom; nor sadness at the destruction of a relationship with a man that had lasted half her lifetime; but instead the faint tingle in her stomach betrayed a definite excitement.

Fiji disappeared behind the starboard wing of the Qantas 747. She smiled to herself. Why shouldn't she feel excited? She was on a journey half way around the world; a journey that was completely unexpected; a journey at the end of which she would see her brother for the first time in seventeen years.

She wondered if they would recognize one another at the airport. *Has he received my message?* she wondered. There had been no time to wait for a reply. She had left her office at two thirty and within the hour her seat on the plane was reserved. Three hours after that she had presented herself at the airport, where she had had time to make only a single unsuccessful attempt to contact Martin.

She had been more than slightly embarrassed at the difficulty she had experienced trying to communicate with the woman at the motel. She knew that Americans spoke strangely, but the woman had spoken in a peculiar, thick, almost Spanish accent and the two had barely been able to understand each other. Joanna had repeated the important information several times, but had been unable to make the girl understand her request to read the numbers back to her. If she had time, she would call again from Los Angeles. There was nearly an hour between the arrival of the Qantas flight and the departure of the Continental flight to Denver, so there might be time to try to get through to Martin again.

The "Fasten Seat Belts" sign went out, and Joanna settled herself more comfortably in her seat. What would it be like to see Martin again after all this time? Then, vaguely, she wondered, what would America be like? She gave no thought to the other question: what had caused Matthew Chambers' death?

Martin's day passed uneventfully.

He spent the morning at Matthew's house (Harry Jones having provided him with a key now that his own work there was complete). He tidied the kitchen, discarding fruit and vegetables that were spoiling, and began making an inventory of the contents of the house. He supposed that he and Jo would have to see about disposing of the contents and selling the house.

He drove into town and ate lunch at an uninteresting restaurant which provided a peculiarly bland genus of food — in this he must have been unfortunate, for a glance at the yellow pages had shown him that Pinetree was unusually endowed with eating establishments of all kinds. After lunch, he returned to his motel where he napped for an hour, spent half an hour filling in crosswords, then made his way to the police department, where Harry Jones informed him of the latest non-developments.

"I've been talking with Mr. Chambers' acquaintances. The only interesting information came from Mr. Healy, the mayor — his wife is out of town, but she's made arrangements to come back for the funeral tomorrow. If you remember, your cousin ate his last meal with the Healys.

"Mr. Healy says that Mr. Chambers was perfectly normal, except that he seemed somewhat groggy over the meal, shortly after he had given himself an insulin shot. At one point he actually passed out.

Mrs. Healy was in the kitchen when that happened; she brought him some juice and an ice pack to help him recover. Mr. Healy says that Mr. Chambers seemed a bit confused and tired after that, but neither he nor his wife, nor Mr. Chambers himself, had any real qualms about Mr. Chambers' ability to drive himself home."

"What about the candy? Any luck finding that?"

"No. Mr. Healy didn't know anything about it, and he says that he hasn't found anything in the house. I went up there myself and spent half an hour looking. Nothing. I've thoroughly retraced Matthew's footsteps on that last day, and the candy seems to have simply disappeared. If it ever existed. Perhaps he just wasn't carrying any."

Martin shrugged and made a sound of dubious assent.

"One more thing. Before the meal, Mr. Chambers gave himself a shot of insulin in the guest bathroom at the Healys'. Apparently, he took insulin twice a day, at breakfast time and again in the early evening. The syringe and its contents are being tested now. Perhaps his insulin was tainted. I've sent in his entire kit: meter, strips, insulin, for testing. Perhaps they'll give us the answer."

"Perhaps."

Martin was not convinced.

Joanna's heart was thumping rapidly. Adrenalin coursed through her system. In a few minutes she would be on the ground. And a few minutes after that, she would see Martin again.

Joanna had tried to sleep on the leg from Fiji, but without success. The last time she had slept had been before the refueling stop in Fiji. Soon her lack of sleep would begin to catch up with her, but for now she just stared at the mountains slipping past beneath the airplane.

She had almost missed the connection. The fifty minutes between flights in Los Angeles had been barely enough. The line at immigration had been longer and more glacial than she had expected. Then customs had similarly been unpleasantly unlike her usual experience.

On her occasional visits to New Zealand, customs in New Zealand and Australia had never been more than a cursory formality. Never had she been stopped, let alone had her luggage searched. But the Los Angeles customs inspectors seemed to have stopped every person on the flight and forced each person to open at least one bag. Joanna must have looked hurried, because her inspector had been particularly thorough, forcing her to open her suitcase and her carry-on bag, and then requiring a detailed explanation of the reason for her visit to the United States.

Eventually, she had escaped, only to find that the Denver flight was due to leave from a completely different building. She had been the last passenger to board, sweat dribbling down her cheeks as she took her seat. It was not until she was safely settled and the plane was taxiing for take-off that she realized that she hadn't called Martin to confirm that he would be at the Denver airport to meet her.

The flight from Los Angeles to Denver took nearly three hours. At first, as soon as the metropolis was left behind, she was surprised to see that she was flying over desert, very similar to the terrain that filled the interior of her adopted homeland.

The captain pointed out Las Vegas: a verdant oasis surrounded by barren aridity. They flew over deep rutted canyons until suddenly the brown of the arid canyons gave way to the viridity of pine forests and then the snow-capped peaks of the Rocky Mountains.

About half an hour out of Denver the plane began its descent to the Mile High City. The last of the snowy peaks dropped behind as the plane descended in the lee of the mountains. The ride became turbulent; out of the window she could see the plane's wingtips bouncing up and down. The "Fasten Seat Belts" sign came on, and the captain warned that the ride would be bumpy for the next few minutes.

Denver spread out below the plane, huge like Los Angeles even though it was home to only a tenth as many people. The swimming pools that had dotted the landscape of the western city were nearly absent here. As the plane came lower, she could see that the houses were spaced farther apart, and there was more greenery than in the City of the Angels.

Denver dropped behind as the plane made a wide circle around the airport. The peaked roof of the main terminal glowed white, looking like bright snowy mountains. Planes were gathered around three concourses, like so many newborn animals suckling at a mother's multitude of teats.

The plane turned sharply and began its final approach. As they touched down, she felt a frisson of uncertainty, wondering if her brother would be here to meet her and what he would say when they met. Would there be recriminations and "I told you so"s? Would she regret coming all this way?

The plane taxied to a gate with the admonition from the captain that "anyone who moves out of his or her seat before the plane taxis to a complete halt will be laughed at by all the other passengers."

The plane stopped with a slight jerk and in a second all was bustle and noise as eager passengers freed themselves from their belts, collected their hand luggage, and lined up to disembark.

Joanna undid her lap belt and sat quietly without moving, allowing the rush of people to leave the plane. As the crowd began to thin, she retrieved her carry-on bag from beneath the seat in front. She stretched her legs, then squeezed through to the aisle and made her way to the front of the plane. She was one of the last passengers to leave.

She strode up the jetway... towards what? A brother? A stranger? Forgiveness? Recriminations?

And what if he wasn't there?

She stopped as she walked out of the jetway and on to the concourse, momentarily disoriented. Then she saw him. His hair was graying now at the temples, and he was dressed more expensively than he could have afforded twenty years ago. But most important of all, he was smiling broadly. He rushed forward.

They embraced. Joanna fought to keep tears out of her eyes. Then she surrendered. Standing in the entrance to the jetway, the tears flowed as she hugged her brother for the first time in seventeen years.

Martin had expected that they would recover his sister's luggage and then make straight for Pinetree, but he quickly realized that that plan was infeasible. They did retrieve her single suitcase, but then they wheeled it with them across the enormous bridge — the only airport bridge in the world under which 747s routinely passed, according to a small sign attached to the wall — to the main terminal building. They found a restaurant, ordered coffee to keep the waitress happy, and began to catch up on the last seventeen years.

They left forty five minutes later. Martin wheeled Joanna's suitcase, while she insisted on carrying her own bag to the parking structure below the terminal. Within ten minutes they were on I-70, heading west towards the mountains.

The three-hour journey was anything but lonely; brother and sister had plenty to talk about.

Chapter 8

Detective Harry Jones looked at his watch. One minute to go. Reluctantly, he gathered the sheaf of papers and knocked them square on what passed for his desk. The large room was balkanized by inexpensive dividers that stood five and a half feet high, leaving him an 8×8 space that was the late-twentieth-century version of an office.

Harry detested the cubicle; it gave neither him nor his neighbors the privacy that was essential to investigative police work. Every time a neighbor's telephone rang, he had to force himself not to eavesdrop. He supposed he was fortunate that he spent so little time in his so-called office; most of his days were spent in the real world.

Even so, there was the inevitable paperwork that came with being a police detective, made more burdensome, it seemed to him, every year as the courts required increasingly detailed paperwork to back up criminal cases. As if criminals, especially those who could afford a good lawyer, did not already have the scales of justice tipped far enough in their favor. He had lost count of the number of times he had taken a case — usually a theft or mid-level drugs charge — to the district attorney only to have it fall apart in the following weeks after the defendant hired a good attorney.

He shook his head at the irony. For how many years had he wanted to be involved in a good old-fashioned simple murder inquiry, with clues to be found, evidence to be sifted and, finally, an arrest to be made? Now he had his wish at last — or did he? Was this a murder?

Or was he just fooling himself? — and he was making no progress at all.

The chief had given him until ten o'clock this morning to make substantial progress in the Matthew Chambers case and here it was, 9:59, and he was as puzzled as ever.

No, since the faxed report from the toxicologists in Grand Junction had arrived an hour ago, he was *more* puzzled. All his thoughts and ideas would have to be revised in light of the report. Maybe it would buy him more time with his boss, but what good would that do? He was out of ideas.

The digits on his watch flicked silently to 10:00, and with a last look to make sure that he had all he needed, he left his cubicle, walked through the swing doors and down the corridor, and knocked on the frosted glass panel in the door of Chief of Detectives Salter's honest-to-goodness office.

"Enter."

He always felt uncomfortable in Salter's office, and not merely because it was cramped and dark — the one window looked out on the brick of the sheriff's wing fifteen feet away. The chief's office was fastidious, almost compulsively neat. Nothing was out of place. The desk behind which the chief sat supported three short stacks of paper: one in the "In" tray, one in the "Out" tray, and a thin pile in front of the chief.

Harry Jones took the seat that was wordlessly offered. He waited while the chief finished writing on one of the sheets.

The chief looked up. Chief Salter was some fifteen years Harry's senior, a refugee from Houston five years earlier; someone, so it was rumored, who had sat one too many times at the bedside of a dying colleague who had been shot while attempting an arrest. John Salter had relinquished all hope of advancement by transplanting himself to the small community of Pinetree, where he had immediately been appointed to the vacant position of Chief of Detectives, with all of five officers — grown to seven in the intervening years — reporting to him. It was a different world from the one he had left behind.

Harry Jones had to admit to himself that, if anything, his boss looked younger now than he had done in those early days. Then he had appeared an easy sixty five; now he looked closer to fifty. His hair, what remained of it, was a thick white arc around his otherwise bald dome, and wrinkles were etched permanently into his visage, but no longer was there the constant look of tension in the eyes and around the mouth. Sometimes, it was said, Chief Salter had been known actually to laugh, although Harry Jones had never witnessed this phenomenon himself.

More relaxed he might be, but the chief's voice was still somewhere between gravel and flint, and the eyes were hard and unblinking as he straightened and looked at his junior officer.

"So, Harry, any progress on the Chambers case?"

Harry took a deep breath and verbally laid out the happenings of the past five days. It was smooth going; his boss did not interrupt, although he made copious notes in shorthand — which Harry could not decipher — as Harry told his story.

After fifteen minutes, Harry reached the events of this morning. "And here's the toxicology report on the capsules, sir."

He made no attempt to summarize the contents of the report; he merely handed the stapled sheets across the desk. Chief Salter placed his pencil on his desk so that it was parallel to the sides of the notepad on which he had been writing, adjusted his reading glasses, leaned back, and began to read.

Harry watched the chief's expression. It did not change until the middle of the third page. Harry knew exactly what the chief was reading:

> Despite the identical external appearance of the three capsules, their contents differed substantially. Two of the capsules, samples number PDP-9408001 and PDP-9408003, contained essentially identical contents. The third capsule, sample PDP-9408002, contained different ingredients.

> The contents of sample PDP-9408001 weighed a total of 482.3 milligrams. Of this total, 24.8 milligrams comprised the active ingredient indomethacin (an anti-inflammatory drug) and the remaining 457.5 milligrams was inactive filler (for a breakdown of the chemical composition of this inactive ingredient, see the detailed report below).

> The contents of sample PDP-9408003 weighed a total of 491.0 milligrams. Of this total, 24.9 milligrams comprised indomethacin and the remaining 466.1 milligrams was filler.

> The contents of sample PDP-9408002 weighed a total of 503.6 milligrams. The entirety of this total was potassium cyanide.

Chief Salter looked at Harry with wide eyes. After several seconds, he asked: "How much potassium cyanide to kill a man, Harry?"

Harry was unsure if the chief genuinely wanted to know the answer or if he was merely testing his officer to see if *he* knew. He did. He'd looked it up in the department's library half an hour before coming to the chief's office.

"A dose of between a hundred and two hundred milligrams is typically regarded as potentially lethal, sir."

"How quickly does it act, and what are the symptoms?"

Harry reeled off: "Very quickly; usually within seconds, sometimes as long as a minute. The usual symptoms are dizziness, nausea and loss of consciousness."

The chief nodded and returned to the report. Harry could see, even behind the reading glasses, that his eyes were narrower now. He completed the report without further comment, then returned it to his subordinate.

"I want a copy of your complete file, Harry, as soon as possible."

"Yes, sir." Harry nodded.

There was a long silence. The chief stared at the wall behind Harry, his brow creased in concentration. Eventually, he spoke.

"So..., what do we do now, Harry? Where do we go from here?"

Harry had spent much of the hour before the meeting pondering exactly that question. Walking to the chief's office, he had concluded that only a fool does not know when he is beaten; and that's more or less how he felt right now. Not beaten exactly, but completely unsure what to do next.

Honesty, he decided, mentally mixing his clichés, was perhaps the better part of valor.

He shook his head. "I don't know, sir. It seems like we have three options, but none of them seems very attractive."

The chief nodded encouragingly. "Go on. What do you think are our options?"

He removed his reading glasses, leaned back in his chair and steepled his hands, giving Harry his undivided attention.

"Well, sir. We could do nothing; that's always an option. Or I could go over Chambers' house again and see if there's anything I've missed. Honestly, I doubt it; and Detective Jordan was with me part of that first day up at the house, so it's not like I haven't had help. If there's anything there that might help us, it sure isn't obvious."

"But of course you didn't know about the cyanide then."

"True. I suppose I need to look at his medicines more carefully. Although we can't possibly test everything."

"And the third possibility?"

"Well, you're not going to like this, sir...."

"Try me."

"We could have Dr. Taylor in and talk with him about the capsules. After all, we're pretty sure they came from his office, even though there's no indication to that effect on the bottle itself. It looks like a sample bottle, the kind that doctors hand out. His receptionist confirmed the doctor's statement that Matthew Chambers was there on Thursday for an appointment, and the anti-inflammatory in the capsules is indomethacin, something that could easily have been prescribed for Mr. Chambers' aching shoulder.

"And then there's the statement from Mr. Chambers' receptionist, Kathleen Freeman. When she asked after his health after the appointment, Mr. Chambers said: 'He gave me some pills. They should do the job in a day or so.'"

"How much have you spoken with Dr. Taylor?"

"Not much. Only by telephone, to confirm that Mr. Chambers visited him. There didn't seem any need to bother him until now."

"OK. I suggest that you interview him. Make it seem unimportant. Do it at his office; it'll be less threatening that way. But watch his face, particularly the eyes. See how he reacts. Don't let him know what we've found. Make it seem like a routine follow-up. He's not a fool; he isn't going to say anything if he is involved somehow, and he's certainly not going to give us anything we can use in court, but if you watch him carefully, you might get a feel for whether he knows more than he's saying."

Harry got up to leave.

"One more thing, sir. You said I was on this case only until ten o'clock this morning...."

"If it weren't for this toxicology report, I'd be inclined to pull you off it right now. We need an extra officer on the Carson drug case. But interview Taylor and report back to me when you've done so. I'll make a decision then, but I don't think we can just leave this now that this has come up. A diabetic dying of hypoglycemic coma is one thing; a capsule containing a lethal dose of cyanide is something else entirely."

Harry left.

Chief Salter drummed his fingers together in front of his face. For thirty seconds he sat thus, his brow furrowed in concentration.

It wouldn't do any harm to check, he thought, and picked up the telephone. He dialed the number from memory. A receptionist answered.

"Good afternoon. This is Chief of Detectives Salter with the Pinetree PD. I'd like to speak with Dr. Halliwell."

He was put on hold and, a minute later, the voice of the county coroner came on the line: "Halliwell."

"Dean, it's John Salter here. Say, I apologize if one of my detectives has already asked you this, and I'm kind of reluctant to bring it up. Don't take this personally, but it's about the Chambers body...."

"Yes...," Halliwell's voice was guarded.

"I've seen your report, and it's about as unambiguous as they come. But I was wondering if there's any chance, any chance at all, that you might have a made a mistake. Is it at all possible, even remotely, that death could have been caused by ingestion of a lethal dose of cyanide?"

There was silence for several seconds. Halliwell, as the detective knew, was not a man to dismiss the possibility without giving it at least some consideration, no matter how far-fetched his question was.

But the answer came quickly enough. "No, John, there's no chance of that at all. Pathological findings are not particularly characteristic in cyanide poisonings, but there was no trace of it in the blood. We had two independent labs test two blood samples, and both of them came up negative for anything like that. Mr. Chambers did not die as a result of ingesting cyanide. I can make that statement unequivocally. In court if you'd like."

"OK. Well, thanks, Dean. And please don't mention to anyone that I called you about this, OK?"

"Sure, John. Is there anything else I can do for you?"

"No. Thanks for your help."

"You're welcome."

Salter hung up the phone. His fingers began once more to drum in front of his face.

Chapter 9

The waiting room was like ten thousand others: an undistinguished room with chairs surrounding low tables and hugging walls painted a neutral beige-ish color. On the tables lay a scattered assortment of magazines designed to appeal to any reasonable taste, with publication dates going back three months. Detective Harry Jones glanced over the titles: *Sports Illustrated, Time, National Geographic, People, U.S. News & World Report.* All very predictable.

Five feet of wall space near one corner was occupied by a brightly lit aquarium. A few tropical fish swam aimlessly around their watery cage.

No one else was waiting. Harry Jones was seated facing the receptionist.

A couple of minutes passed, and a woman and a child about four years old emerged into the reception area in the company of a female nurse. His eyes rested on the nurse as she laid a manila folder on the counter in front of the receptionist.

Harry Jones, thirty five years old and the survivor of numerous amorous entanglements but currently unattached, wondered about the nurse's status. She was not what Harry would call beautiful, but she was certainly attractive. He appreciated the slim, bronzed legs that were visible between the hem of her white coat and her dark, sensible shoes. Her legs were the color that most women attain by the simple expedient of wearing hose, but the color of the nurse's face, now turned three quarters away from him as she spoke to the receptionist — fifty five if she was a day — was the same color: what used to be called, before its dangers were understood, "a healthy tan."

The nurse turned unexpectedly, and she looked squarely at Harry in what he thought — although perhaps he was imagining things — a faintly accusing manner.

His vaguely sexual thoughts evaporated as she said in a decidedly businesslike manner, "Dr. Taylor will see you now, Mr. Jones. If you'll follow me."

They went down a short passage. She stopped before an unmarked door and opened it for Harry.

"Dr. Taylor will be with you in just a moment. Please have a seat."

She pulled the door to, but not entirely closed. The detective looked around the office in which he found himself.

It was a doctor's office not substantially different from any other. One wall was covered in bookcases, filled with medical texts covering a wide range of disciplines. He wondered if Dr. Taylor ever read any of them. He raised his hand and ran it along the tops of a pair of volumes on diabetes that stood at eye level. Removing his finger he was faintly disappointed to see that his fingertip was gray with dust.

The wall behind the obligatory desk was almost filled by a large window, the view beyond hidden by a venetian blind whose slats were angled to let in the sun but not the view. The wall behind the detective and the one to his immediate right were partially obscured by paintings of golf courses and several certificates attesting to Dr. Taylor's medical credentials. In front of the doctor's desk were two chairs, silver and black affairs that completely failed to harmonize with the rest of the room.

He seated himself and was almost immediately interrupted by the sound of the door behind him opening. He arose and turned in an uncomfortable maneuver to greet the owner of the office. He extended his hand to meet the one that was outstretched towards him.

Dr. Felix Taylor was in his mid to late fifties, his hair thoroughly gray but as thick as it had ever been. The doctor was tall, six feet or a little more. He was dressed casually, the white coat of his trade unbuttoned to reveal a white shirt with narrow blue stripes and the monogram "FLT" on the pocket. From the shirt pocket extruded a pair of tongue depressors and two pens.

Harry looked directly into the doctor's face. The doctor's eyes, gray in a way that matched his hair and added to his aura of command, met his with neither a smile nor a blink.

The hands clasped and pumped and separated, and the doctor moved around the desk to his chair. Harry tried to watch every movement without being too obvious, looking for any telltale sign of stress. There was none. Dr. Taylor moved fluidly, with a relaxed quasi-smile on his lips. If he was worried, there was no sign of it.

This, Harry realized, was not going to be easy.

The dance began with the usual preliminaries. The doctor took the lead.

"Good Morning, Mr. Jones. I think we spoke on the phone a few days ago about the death of one of my patients, Mr. Matthew Chambers, who died unexpectedly last week?"

The detective nodded. "Yes. I'm sorry to bother you. If it's possible, I'd like to obtain a copy of his medical file before I leave today. Also, I'd like to ask a few questions about Mr. Chambers."

"Certainly. I anticipated you might. I've already instructed my receptionist to provide you with Mr. Chambers' file. You will have to sign for it, of course, and I would ask that you not copy any part of it without checking with me first. The file will be waiting for you when you leave."

Harry Jones thanked the doctor, then asked: "Could you please tell me something of Mr. Chambers' medical history? Just informally. I realize that all the details will be in the file."

"Certainly, although there really isn't much to tell. Apart from the usual minor problems that inflict all of us from time to time, the only thing really worth mentioning is Mr. Chambers' diabetes. Do you know much about diabetes, Detective Jones?"

A week ago, the detective could have answered honestly in the negative. Since Matthew Chambers' death, he had checked two books on the subject out of the public library and he now considered himself more than averagely knowledgeable on the subject.

He prevaricated. "Only what I read, Dr. Taylor."

The doctor, as the detective had intended, took this as an invitation to enlighten. The detective removed a notepad and pen from his pocket and opened the pad, ready to take notes. The doctor removed one of the tongue depressors from his pocket and fiddled with it for the remainder of the interview.

"Mr. Chambers suffered from what is commonly known as adult-onset diabetes. He'd had it for about twenty four years.

"Diabetes is a disease in which the pancreas produces insufficient insulin. Insulin is a chemical which permits a body to absorb sugar from food so that it may be used as fuel. Without the correct amount of insulin in the system, sugar is not extracted properly and the body can no longer function."

"It's a dangerous disease, then?"

"Deadly. Fortunately, although it is both deadly and incurable, it is also treatable; and the treatment, while inconvenient, is quite simple. The body simply needs to be supplied with the insulin that it cannot manufacture. Generally, it has to be supplied intravenously. The insulin then acts as if it were the body's own and permits the sugar from food to be processed properly."

"You said it's incurable. So the condition is permanent?"

"Yes. Once a diabetic, always a diabetic."

"What happens if one takes too little insulin? Or too much?"

"If it's only a little too little or too much, probably nothing very drastic. The patient would feel unwell if it continued, and generally a physician would advise an appropriate change of dose."

"But if it was a lot?"

"Ultimately, coma and death. Too much insulin is much more dangerous than too little, though. Without going into detail, too much insulin would mean that the blood sugar level would drop precipitously, the brain would be starved of energy, and coma and death would quickly occur. That's what we call hypoglycemia.

"Too little insulin means that the body begins to use fat instead of sugar as an energy source. This precipitates the formation of ketones, which are poisonous substances, in the body. Coma occurs, but usually the coma can be relatively long-lived before permanent damage occurs. By contrast, in hypoglycemia permanent damage can occur after only a few tens of seconds of coma."

"And what about Matthew Chambers? Tell me about his diabetic history."

"Well, it's all in the file, of course. Briefly, he was diagnosed with diabetes mellitus about twenty four years ago, when he was twenty and serving in Vietnam. He was discharged for health reasons. In my experience, he was an excellent, conscientious patient. He was on about 64 units of insulin per day, which is pretty typical. He never missed a checkup, and, as far as I know, he always took his insulin on schedule. He was careful about what he ate and drank. I don't know what else to say; what more do you want?"

"He was a model patient, then?"

"I would say so, yes."

"How long had he been your patient?"

"Not long. Maybe eighteen months. Perhaps less. It'll be in the file."

"And before that?"

"He was with Dr. Henry, who was also with this practice. Dr. Henry passed away unexpectedly — he was only in his mid forties — and Mr. Chambers transferred to me."

"So he stayed with the same practice?"

"Yes."

"How does the practice work exactly? Do you ever see other doctors' patients?"

"Yes, frequently. Each of our patients has a principal doctor, the one whom they prefer to see. A few patients will see only that doctor, but most are willing to see another one if their own doctor is unavailable for some reason."

"How many doctors are in the practice?"

"Three."

"And had you ever seen Mr. Chambers before you became his doctor?"

"I don't recall. It'll be in the file."

Harry looked over his notes. "You said he was a model patient. What do you mean by that?"

"He didn't miss a check-up. He looked after himself."

"I see. Did he come to see you for any reason other than a check-up?"

"Not that I recall... except that he did see me the day before he died...."

Harry interrupted. "I'll get to that in a minute. Returning for a moment to his diabetes. I understand that many diabetics carry some form of sugar with them. Did Mr. Chambers do that?"

"Well, I don't know for a fact, but I imagine he did. I advise all my diabetic patients to do so. It's standard practice, so I'm sure he did, yes."

"But you never actually saw anything?"

"No; but there's no reason why I would have."

"Now, it is our understanding that Mr. Chambers visited you on Thursday of last week; that is, some thirty six hours before his death. We were wondering if you could shed some light on the reason for that visit."

The doctor leaned back in his chair and looked thoughtful for a moment.

He replied, "Mr. Chambers called the practice early on Thursday morning. That would be, let me see, the eleventh, I think. We don't keep a record of the time of each telephone call, but I've talked it over with my receptionist and she thinks it was one of the first calls of the day. You'll have to ask her for corroboration, of course.

"Anyway, Mr. Chambers called, probably between eight thirty and nine, complaining of an extremely sore shoulder. He must have impressed the receptionist with the severity of his pain, because she interrupted a consultation with a patient to ask me how soon I could fit in Mr. Chambers. I told her that I could probably squeeze in one more patient before lunchtime, so if he would not mind the possibility of waiting, I'd try to see him around twelve thirty.

"The appointment was made and I thought no more about it until the time for the appointment arrived and I saw Mr. Chambers in one of my consulting rooms."

"How many consulting rooms do you have, Dr. Taylor?"

"Two. They are identical. I have two so that my nurse can prepare one patient while I'm seeing another. I'll be happy to show you the room in which I saw Mr. Chambers before you leave, if you like."

"If you would be so kind. But if you would continue, please...."

"Mr. Chambers was stripped to the waist, and my nurse had taken his vitals — temperature, blood pressure and pulse — and noted them on his chart by the time I arrived to see him. That's standard procedure. The numbers will be on his chart, but they were entirely normal.

"His temperature was slightly elevated, about 99.4, I think, which is normal for him during the summer months. His blood pressure I don't remember exactly, but it was somewhere around 110 over 60, and his resting heart rate was 52, which would usually be regarded as abnormally low, but is actually not all that unusual for healthy, fit residents of Pinetree."

"Would you say then that, in general, Mr. Chambers was physically fit?"

"Oh yes, most definitely. He could probably have run farther and faster than yourself, for instance, even though ten or more years your senior, and if I were you I certainly wouldn't have challenged him to a game of racquetball. Mr. Chambers was in many ways an ideal patient. He ate right and lived right. That was one reason why I was willing to see him at such short notice. Matthew never needed to see me except for his diabetes checkups. If he had taken the trouble to call me, it seemed likely he needed medical attention."

"And was there, in fact, a medical problem?"

The doctor leaned forward in his chair, his eyebrows slightly raised.

"Yes, but as it turned out it was nothing very important. Matthew had played racquetball on Wednesday evening. During the game, he banged his shoulder rather badly against a wall. On Thursday morning, he awoke in considerable pain and wondered if he had seriously damaged himself."

"And had he?"

"No. His shoulder was bruised and inflamed from the injury, that's all. Nothing serious."

The detective kept writing, although he had little interest in Matthew Chambers' shoulder condition. The autopsy had made it clear that the shoulder injury had nothing directly to do with his death. But he continued to write and to ask questions.

"A racquetball game... do you know who he was playing?"

"No, sorry; I don't think he said."

"OK. Please carry on."

"Well, there was definitely a problem with the shoulder, you could see it if you looked carefully. The area of his right shoulder blade was swollen and inflamed. I advised Mr. Chambers that I was going to put him on some anti-inflammatory medication for a few days to see if they would make him more comfortable."

"I see. So, you prescribed an anti-inflammatory?"

"Well, yes and no. I wrote a prescription for indomethacin. Its effect is similar to ibuprofen, but stronger. I also gave him three days' worth of capsules. It was a sample bottle. We get them for most drugs, and hand them out to patients. I instructed him to take the capsules until he had finished them. Then he should go off the anti-inflammatory for a day or so. If the pain returned, then he could get the prescription filled and continue taking the medication. I asked him to call me if he found that necessary. I gave the matter no more thought until I spoke to you over the weekend."

"Why did you want him to call?"

"I expected the pills I had given him to be enough. If he felt the need for more I wanted to talk to him to see if things were getting worse, in which case I would have wanted to see him again. We would probably have scanned the shoulder if that had happened."

"I see. Now, about the weekend. How did you spend it? If you don't mind my asking, that is...."

"Oh, that's fine. Beautiful though Pinetree is, I often get out of town on summer weekends when travel is easy. I was here Saturday morning, playing golf at the Country Club with Bill Healy. I had an early lunch at the club and then drove to Denver. I stayed with Dr. Kuykendall, an orthopedic surgeon in Cherry Hills, for the rest of the weekend. We played a couple of rounds at the Cherry Hills Country Club in Denver, one on Saturday in the early evening, one at lunchtime on Sunday, so I was completely unaware of what had happened to Mr. Chambers until I received your message on my answering machine on Sunday evening."

"And the drug that you gave Mr. Chambers. Could you describe that for me?"

"It was indomethacin, 25-milligram capsules, the same strength I prescribed for him. As I'm sure you are aware, doctors are continually bombarded with free samples from the various drug manufacturers. It happened that I had some indomethacin left. It's a common drug, often used to ease minor swellings which are a little too much for aspirin or ibuprofen. I gave him six capsules, enough for three full days."

"He was to take two a day, then?"

"Yes; with meals so as not to upset his stomach. One at breakfast, one with his evening meal."

"And the physical description of these capsules. What did they look like?"

"Oh, fairly typical. The gelatin coating is half green, half white, marked 'MSD 25' and with the name of the drug."

The detective nodded; the description matched the capsules that had been the subject of yesterday's toxicology report.

"And the bottle, what did that look like?"

"Oh, you know, just a small plastic bottle. Brown, I think. It was unlabeled, of course, which I suppose was a little naughty of me, these things are always supposed to be labeled carefully. But indomethacin is not a dangerous drug, and I couldn't foresee that there was any problem in giving him an unlabeled bottle." The doctor's expression changed, as if a thought had struck him. "Why? The indomethacin wasn't somehow connected to his death, was it?"

The detective closed his notebook. "Just checking facts. Nothing to worry about. I'm sure you understand. Now, if you'll just show me the consulting room, I can be on my way. Thank your for your assistance, Dr. Taylor."

The doctor stood, a little flustered by the sudden end of the interview, and asked the detective to follow him.

The consulting room was next to the office. It was as undistinguished as the rest of the practice. The walls were painted in clinical white; an expensive-looking couch/table combination on which patients would sit or lie as necessary was covered in cheap-looking black plastic; a glass-fronted cupboard held an assortment of instruments and charts; next to that, a certificate attested to Dr. Taylor's degree; a small wooden table and a pair of quasi-comfortable chairs of the type which Harry Jones had just vacated completed the furnishings.

"Thank you," the detective said. "I'll let you know if we need anything else."

Bidding the doctor an abrupt goodbye, he made his own way to the receptionist's desk where he recovered the slim manila folder containing Matthew Chambers' medical history.

Sixty seconds later, he pushed open the door of the building and halted, standing in the sunshine. *Now what*, he wondered, *would Dr. Felix Taylor make of that?*

Joanna awoke at eight o'clock. For a few seconds she wondered where she was. Then she remembered the long journey of the day before.

She lay in a nightgown on the bed. Her clothes were piled haphazardly on the floor beside her open suitcase. The sun filtered through the curtains.

She tried to gather her wits — she barely remembered getting changed for bed; tiredness had overtaken her before she had been able to pull back the covers. What day was it? She puzzled for several seconds before giving it up as a bad job. Thursday, she thought, but with nothing approaching certainty. She would find out when she saw Martin.

Joanna caught sight of a piece of paper standing on the bedside table, propped up against the lamp. Even after all these years she recognized the handwriting. "Room 245," it said.

She sat up in bed and adjusted her watch to correspond to the figures on the clock next to Martin's note. She crossed to the door to make sure that it was locked, flicking on a light as she went. Then she stripped and went in search of the shower.

She knocked on Martin's door at half past eight. He was inside, working at the small round table which was the closest thing to a desk in the cheap motel rooms. He looked up, saw her, smiled, and hurried to open the door. They stood for a moment, unsure of themselves, and then embraced in greeting.

They breakfasted leisurely in the restaurant down the street. Breakfast was in danger of turning into lunch before they left.

Seventeen years of Martin's life had been covered more or less thoroughly by the time the meal was concluded. As for her life, Joanna summarized it by saying: "You don't want to know about it, Martin, you really don't. It's over now, and now I'm just going to get on with my life as if Kevin never happened."

Martin probed once or twice, but she resisted his efforts, and finally he gave up, deciding that if she really wanted to keep it private, it was not his place to try to force any information from her.

He asked about her future and she shrugged.

"I don't know, Martin. I've tried to avoid giving it much thought these past few days. I have a good job, you know, and everyone seems to think that I'm good at it. There aren't many female detective sergeants in Australia, and there's a good chance I'll make senior sergeant within the year, so I could probably move anywhere and get a job. But I haven't decided yet. Maybe I'll stay in Sydney. Maybe I'll move out of the area. Maybe even move out of Australia altogether. I just don't know yet. One of the reasons I came here was to get away from everything I'm familiar with and try to put my life into some sort of perspective."

She shrugged again.

At first, Martin had been reticent about bringing up the subject of Matthew, unsure whether she would want to be bothered with the confusing details of his death. After all, as she had just said, she was supposed to be getting away from her job.

But Joanna could not resist her professional training. She wanted to know about Matthew.

Martin told her, briefly, of Matthew's career as a successful litigating attorney with a large Chicago law firm; of his disillusionment with the judicial system when he succeeded in freeing a wealthy client's son who was guilty of the crime as charged; and of his move four years ago to Pinetree, where he had set up a successful one-man law firm specializing in what Matthew himself had called "small-town law."

Joanna asked if any progress had been made in determining how Matthew had allowed his blood sugar level to fall to a fatal level.

"No, not yet. The police are checking his insulin kit, but they don't seem to think it will tell them much. It's a puzzle, I agree. But it's not as if someone killed him."

They finished eating. Martin picked up the check, looked at his watch, and said: "Come on, we should be going. The funeral is this afternoon, and I don't have anything appropriate to wear. Neither, I suspect, do you. So let's get going and see if we can't find somewhere that will outfit us in clothes suitable both to the occasion and to the weather."

He bustled her out of the restaurant, stopping only to pay for the meal on his credit card. Joanna felt a pang of envy when she saw the gold card — she had enough trouble making the monthly payments on her ordinary multicolored plastic card. The little piece of gold-colored plastic spoke more to Joanna about her brother's success than anything he had told her. Firmly, she pushed her jealousy aside. They were together again. That was what mattered. As they ambled to the car, Martin suddenly gave her hand a squeeze. Like the card, it said more than any words.

They purchased clothes that the saleswoman insisted were entirely appropriate for a funeral. Both Joanna and Martin wondered if she was pulling their legs. Neither his casual shirt and slacks nor her cotton print frock would have been remotely appropriate for a funeral in England or Australia. But, as the clerk reminded them, "This is the West. We're a bit more casual here than in other places, I guess."

So they had made their purchases, returned to the motel by way of a stop at McDonald's for a bite of lunch, changed into their new purchases and then, still unsure of their attire, drove the few blocks to the church.

As they got out of the car, Joanna spontaneously embraced her brother. A thought flitted through her mind and was immediately gone: she was grateful for Matthew's death, because in a sense it had brought her life once more.

She squeezed Martin's hand before falling into step beside him. Together they made their way to the graveside.

It was a subdued gathering.

The sun glowed liquidly in the sky, the afternoon clouds just beginning to form. Harry Jones looked up and judged that within two hours the sky would be cloud-covered and quite possibly Pinetree would be experiencing one of its frequent summer afternoon soakings.

But for now the sun was warm on the small gathering at the graveside.

The service was due to begin in two minutes. There were few mourners.

Next to the detective stood Kathleen Freeman. Her presence was a distraction, but she was either unaware of her effect on him or, more likely, unconcerned.

Kathleen was standing by his side for no other reason than that, having arrived early, she craved the closeness of another human being. She had been unable to summon sufficient courage to look into the oblong hole in the ground. She had arrived determined not to cry, but she found herself sniffling into her handkerchief even before the service had begun.

She was surprised at the intensity of her emotions. Even though he had already been dead nearly a week, this was the final acknowledgment that she would never again laugh at his jokes, offer him a bite of a doughnut knowing that he would refuse with a quip about "saturated fat pills," make him an early-morning cup of coffee. She had spent the morning clearing out her desk, leaving Martin Salisbury to look after the details of closing the business. Cleaning her desk had been easier than Kathleen had expected; attending the funeral was going to be much more difficult.

Harry Jones stood next to her, trying to keep his eyes off the legal secretary and his mind away from salacious thoughts. The sound of a footfall brought him back to reality. Martin Salisbury had arrived, clad in slacks and a dark long-sleeved shirt and accompanied by a woman who must be the sister he had mentioned yesterday.

Joanna Salisbury, her life as Joanna Baker being pushed more firmly behind her with each passing hour, felt better than she could remember feeling for many years. Her state of mind was readily apparent on her face despite the somberness of the occasion.

Her mind, bruised and battered no less than her body through seventeen years of marriage, was quickly pushing Kevin firmly into the past, concentrating instead on the positives of the here and now.

As if her reunion with Martin were not enough, she was becoming intrigued by the puzzling circumstances surrounding her cousin's death.

She had never met Matthew Chambers. He had visited England several times, but never before she had left for Australia. As far as she knew, he had never visited her adopted homeland; or, if he had, then he had made no attempt to contact her. Indeed, it had come as something of a surprise when Martin had told her that her name and telephone number were in Matthew's card file. The fact that she was a beneficiary of his will was even more surprising. Perhaps he was unaware of what a mess she had made of her life. She stopped and breathed deeply of the mountain air. Enough of that. It was over. Over. Things were going to be different from now on.

The service started on time and was completed ten minutes later.

There were fewer mourners than Harry Jones had expected. Apart from the minister, the detective, the Salisburys and Kathleen Freeman, Harry Jones noted the presence of the Healys — Mrs. Healy had returned early from visiting her folks back east — Henry Clarence Madison, the Gardeners and the Smiths. No real surprises. All knew Matthew well and indeed he might have been more surprised had they not been present, especially if subsequent investigation showed that they had no other commitments that afternoon.

Dr. Felix Taylor was not present. Harry wondered whether to make anything of that. Probably not. He was a doctor with a busy practice, and undoubtedly had patients needing his attention all afternoon. As like as not it had not even crossed his mind to attend.

As far as Harry had been able to determine, the only connections between Taylor and Chambers had been that they were doctor and patient and they were both members of the town's small and rather elitist Rotary Club. Bill Healy, Felix Taylor, Robb Gardener and

Henry Smith were all members of the Rotary Club and of St. Peter's church. Judge Madison was a member only of the former. No obvious deduction could be made from the presence of any of them at the service.

He surveyed the gathering as the minister gave his concluding monologue — a discourse spiked, it seemed to Harry, with an unjustifiable hope for the future.

Everyone around the gaping grave looked suitably mournful. Mrs. Healy had even gone so far as to wear a veil: her face was hidden behind impenetrable dark netting, although it was obvious that she was sobbing.

The others were all more casual in their attire. Most of them, after all, were interrupting a working day to be here, and would have to face customers or clients later in the afternoon. As the minister spoke about "the certainty of new life" Harry gave up trying to make any deductions. His mind began to wander back to the absent Dr. Felix Taylor, trying to find a motive and a method to fit his suspicions.

The service ended and people began to disperse. One by one, those who desired stepped forward, lifted a handful of the freshly dug earth, and dropped it on to the coffin at their feet.

Martin wondered, illogically, how the noise of the soil striking the wood must sound inside the coffin.

He stepped forward, picked up a small handful of soil, and opened his hand over the coffin. He saw that he had picked up only the barest scraping of earth, and there was merely a faint skitter as the dark grains bounced on the top of the coffin.

He paused for a respectful moment, his mind blank, then turned away.

Joanna did not move forward; she had never met Matthew Chambers and it would be hypocrisy to go through the motions of saying goodbye. It was meaningless anyway, wasn't it?

She and Martin walked wordlessly back to the car.

Harry Jones was the last to leave. As the service came to an end, he had pushed thoughts of Felix Taylor away, to concentrate on those who had attended the service, watching hopefully for anomalies, discrepancies, unexpected behavior. There were none of these things.

The mourners, some after briefly acknowledging the detective's presence, had turned away, returning to their own lives. Within two minutes he was alone apart from the gravediggers who were standing as unobtrusively as possible beneath a large cottonwood that provided the only shade in the graveyard. Well, he had not really expected to learn much from the service anyway. He began to make his way to his car.

Martin looked up and saw Harry approaching as he unlocked the car. Quietly, he asked his sister: "Do you want to meet the detective on the case? That's him in the blue shirt with the gray slacks, coming this way."

"Yes, please. He looks like he's coming over to see you anyway."

The detective was indeed walking across the parking lot towards them. He held out his hand and greeted Joanna as Martin introduced them.

"Any news?" Martin asked.

"Yes. And a real shock it is, too. You shouldn't let this get about, of course, but I thought you ought to know."

He proceeded to relate the contents of the toxicology report that had arrived that morning. As he spoke, he found that what seemed like every few seconds he had to drag his eyes from the Englishman's sister, who was regarding him raptly, apparently drinking in his every word. He would force himself to look at Martin, the car, the church, anything; and then, seconds later, he would find that he was once more looking at Joanna's open-eyed face. It was most disconcerting.

What with Kathleen and now Joanna, it was getting difficult to keep his mind on the case.

Martin and Joanna received his news in silence. Suddenly things had become a lot more serious. Was it really possible that someone could have killed Matthew? Missing candy was one thing; a cyanide capsule was something else entirely.

Harry left.

"Do you have a pen and paper in the car?," Joanna asked as Harry drove away. "I need to make some notes."

"Good God! You don't waste much time, do you?" Martin grinned. "OK, Detective Sergeant, you can tell me who did it and why on the way back to the motel."

He squeezed her hand, more like a young husband than a forty-one-year-old brother, and with a distracted air they got into the car. A minute later they departed the earthly remains of Matthew Chambers.

Chapter 10

Joanna wrote as Martin drove. Her notes were in shorthand, and incomprehensible to him. She numbered the people standing at the graveside sequentially, and asked for names to match the numbers only when she seemed satisfied that she had completed her cryptic descriptions of the graveside numerals. Martin could identify with certainty only Harry Jones and Judge Madison — and the Reverend Steven Allbright, of course. She would need to ask one of them to identify the others.

He looked at his watch as they arrived back at the motel. It was not yet three o'clock, and he vaguely wondered how they should spend the remainder of the day. Joanna intruded on his thoughts and settled the matter as they got out of the car.

"The judge," she said. "He was the one who discovered the body, wasn't he?"

Martin could not miss the change that had come over his sister. As soon as Harry Jones had told them about the cyanide, she had become a different person. She was now unmistakably Detective Sergeant Joanna Salisbury of the New South Wales police; and she was was, however unofficially, on a case. Even her speech was different. Before it had always been "Matthew," but now it was suddenly "the body."

"Yes," he answered as they climbed the steps to his room. "Matthew was dead between three and four hours before the judge found the body, according to the coroner's report."

"Right. I want you to tell me everything you know about the case; and then, if there's time this afternoon, I'd like to talk with the judge.

Then I want to read the coroner's report. Then we need to go up to the house. And I need a proper talk with that detective."

"Whoa, wait a minute. You're supposed to be relaxing, getting away from all this police stuff. And in any case the detective won't tell you anything. At least, nothing important. If he has any suspicions or sensitive information, he's not going to share them with a member of the public, even if that person is a detective sergeant. He's probably already told us more than he's supposed to."

He opened the door of his room and gestured for his sister to enter. A cloud covered the sun. He shivered at the sudden chill.

Joanna said, "Maybe, maybe not. In any case, it's a puzzle, and puzzles are what I'm trained to solve. I've been doing it for fifteen years and it's become a habit, I guess. So humor me for a day or two, Martin. Honestly, this is the best relaxation I know; it takes my mind off everything else."

Martin knew when to admit defeat.

"OK," he began, "Here's what I know."

Joanna sat at the table, pulled a clean sheet of paper from a drawer, and began to take notes.

He was interrupted after ten minutes, when Joanna, furiously scribbling in shorthand, ran out of paper.

They returned to the car and proceeded to tour Pinetree for some time, looking for a stationer's, a bookstore, or a drugstore where they might purchase a ream of paper and a binder. Eventually they parked the car near a small group of shops — *Skislope Mall* a garish sign proclaimed — at the foot of the gondola that ran up to the restaurant at the top of the mountain. They searched among the boutiques and souvenir shops, and found the store they needed: *Healy's Books and Cameras.* As they purchased paper and a pack of pens, Joanna asked if the proprietor of the store was whom she guessed it to be.

"Yes, the mayor owns the business, but he's out of the store this afternoon, " the young woman behind the counter said.

"We saw him at the funeral," said Joanna. "Matthew Chambers — did you know him?"

"Only by sight. He occasionally came in. But I can't say I really knew him. He was friends with Mr. Healy though, I think."

Martin and Joanna left. The coalescing clouds turned darker as they returned to the car with their purchases. The first drops of cold, heavy rain came, thudding against the metal of the car roof and splattering against the glass of the windshield as Martin and Joanna got inside.

For a moment all was silent except for the sound of the heavy drops hitting the vehicle. They looked at one another; Martin's face burst into a smile, reflected immediately in his sister's face. Nothing was said. Nothing needed to be said. They were together again.

Martin drove through the thickening downpour back to the motel, where Joanna began once more to dissect Martin's knowledge and commit it to paper.

It was nearly six by the time that she finally looked up from the table and Martin said, at last, "That's all I know about the life and death of Matthew Chambers."

Joanna flicked through the pages of shorthand. It would take her some time before she was sure that she had everything memorized. There would be no time today for interviews.

Martin said, "Come on. It's getting late, and I'm exhausted. Let's go out and find a good restaurant and put all this away for the evening. It'll still be here in the morning."

———

Dr. Felix Taylor was a worried man. He hoped that neither his nurse nor his receptionist would notice. The patients he was less concerned about: they had troubles enough of their own, they would not remark that the doctor was preoccupied.

He had thought that the first two or three days would be the worst, but now he was not so sure. It was the waiting that was so hard.

He opened a drawer in his desk and withdrew a photograph. It was a copy of the one that stood on his desk at home. He looked at it, and his eyes began to water.

———

The first few days had passed slowly. He expected the police at any moment. It was the weekend, and time hung heavily on his hands. He played his habitual round of golf with Bill Healy on Saturday morning, after carefully searching the morning paper for any reference to Matthew Chambers. There was none.

Bill had commented how tense he looked. Bill's game was off — he shot an 84, five strokes worse than on a typical Saturday — but still he had won the weekly match by an easy three strokes.

"Anything the matter? You're playing even worse than me this morning," Bill had said as they approached the final tee. "At least I have the excuse of a city council meeting that went on until one o'clock. What's your excuse?"

Felix did his best to raise a smile. "None. Just left my luck in bed this morning, I guess."

They had completed their round by ten thirty. The course was unusually empty for a summer Saturday; only half a dozen groups — all foursomes — were visible. Bill offered another game, a chance for Felix to get even, but the doctor declined.

"No. I've got a round booked at Cherry Hills with Jerry Kuykendall later in the day, and you can have too much of a good thing, even golf. Anyway, the way I've been playing, it would be easier just to hand you another $20 right now."

He opened his billfold and took out a single $20 bill, the stake for their Saturday-morning game. Bill accepted it with genuine pleasure. It was not often that he beat the doctor.

"Thanks. You'll just take it back again next week, anyway."

The two clambered into the golf cart. Bill depressed the throttle, and the cart slid off smoothly in the direction of the clubhouse.

Felix was unusually quiet. Bill filled the journey with talk about the harangue the council had received for failing to deny a mining permit to a company that wanted to blast some exploratory holes on a slope two miles south of town.

"It's not our fight," Bill said. "It's the county that issues the permits, not the city. The most we could do is to register our disapproval with the county commissioners. But you know what a bunch of bastards they are. If they knew we disapproved of something, they'd gleefully approve it." The bitter fight over the city's new sewage treatment plant was still fresh in Bill's mind.

He continued, "Of course, you can't say that sort of thing at a public meeting. I'd been careful to tell the council members beforehand, so even though all the citizens were screaming for us to stop the mining, we voted against any action. I heard mutterings of a recall petition as we were leaving. I guess I'll have to get on the phone to the most vocal citizens later and let them know why we did what we did." He looked at his golfing partner; "Never run for office. It isn't worth it."

Felix forced another smile. Bill Healy thoroughly enjoyed the rough and tumble of local politics. Politics left Felix cold. Indeed, listening to Bill's stories he sometimes felt almost sick at the gyrations and contortions needed to hold down even such a minor post as mayor of a small mountain town.

They arrived at the clubhouse.

"Time for a quick one?" Bill asked. It was unusual for them to drink so early in the day, but Bill quickly added, "Lucinda is out of town, you know. She's visiting her parents back east; she left early this morning and won't be back until next Sunday."

Felix had forgotten. Despite the early hour, he decided that perhaps a drink was what he needed.

"Just one, then, since you're slumming it this weekend."

The two men placed their golf bags in the trunks of their cars and re-entered the small clubhouse. They made directly for the bar.

Neither was surprised to see that, apart from the Hispanic bartender behind the counter, they were alone. The barroom was built on a corner of the building, and nearly two full sides of the room were devoted to windows, giving those within an unencumbered view of much of the course. The bar itself ran almost the entire length of a third wall; the fourth wall, which contained the doorway through which they entered, comprised dark paneling interrupted by a generous complement of aerial photographs of the course.

Bill ordered white wine (no ice) and Felix a Coors Light. Bill paid for the drinks and Felix dropped two quarters into the ashtray in front of the bartender.

"Good morning! Good morning!" came an unmistakable voice at the doorway.

Phillip ("Two ells, don't you know") Aitcheson entered, looking for all the world like a colonial Englishman from the early years of the century in his khaki shorts, beige short-sleeved shirt, white socks and brown sandals. The florid face that underlay a thin patch of white hair completed the picture of a more or less idle Englishman who dipped frequently into the port. The only anomaly was the accent: though he had been trying for years, the local anglophile had yet to imitate convincingly the English accent.

Phillip sidled up to them.

"I'm early for an eleven o'clock tee-off, and just thought I'd down a quick one to steady the nerves beforehand."

Felix almost expected him to complete the sentence with "what, what?" but the postscript never came.

"Do join us, Phillip," Healy offered. "We've just finished our round. The course is playing awfully hard today. Unless we're getting old, that is. We both played just about our worst rounds ever."

The pseudo-Englishman retrieved the glass of white wine that the bartender had poured without being asked. Felix saw the bartender make an entry in the tab list under the bar as Phillip walked with them to a table near the window.

"Cheerio!" The glass of wine was tilted and half-drained in a single movement.

"Cheers!" Felix and Bill replied, taking more decorous quantities of their respective tipples.

"I say! Did you people hear about Matthew Chambers, that lawyer chappie?"

For a moment, Felix thought his heart had stopped. He lifted his silver-colored can of beer and slowly drank two full mouthfuls, until he was sure that he could act normally.

Prompted by Bill, Phillip was already into the story.

"Judge Madison — you know, that black fellow; not that I mind that, of course — well, apparently he went around to see this Chambers fellow late last night for some reason or other" — his expression made it clear that he thought that this was highly suspicious — "and found him dead in his own living room. No signs of foul play or anything.

"I heard about it this morning when I did some early-morning shopping for the wife. It was the talk of the supermarket. It seems like he might have been murdered, although the police aren't saying anything, of course. But there was no suicide note — at least, none found as yet, or so Mrs. Dingle down at the market says."

Felix wondered what the source of Mrs. Dingle's information might be. But still, one always did wonder where Mrs. Dingle received her gossip. He remained silent, listening intently while Phillip Aitcheson finished his story.

"At least it will give our beloved police force something better to do than issue traffic citations, eh, Bill?"

He grinned at the mayor and jabbed him in the side. Bill, as unobtrusively as possible, rubbed where the blow had been struck and managed a feeble grin in reply.

Felix looked confused.

"Oh, don't you know about that one, old chap? It must have been before your time, I suppose. When was it, Bill? Four, five years ago?"

"Eight," came the instant reply, and Bill immediately realized that he had betrayed how the memory still rankled.

"It was before Bill's elevation," Aitcheson expounded. "He was a lowly council member in those days, but he'd had his name put up for mayor by the outgoing incumbent. It was just a few weeks before the election wasn't it?"

The jovial Aitcheson looked across at the glum Healy, still rubbing his side, who gave no indication of having heard the question.

"Anyway, it wasn't long before the election when Bill here managed to get himself a speeding ticket. What was it, Bill? Doing fifty in a twenty zone? Something like that, anyway."

"I didn't do it. You know that as well as I do, Phillip. Sure I was speeding, but nothing like that. The policeman just had it in for me, the bastard."

"Anyway, Bill decided to fight it in court, in front of this Judge Madison fellow. He was a municipal judge back then, before he was booted upstairs to his current eminence on the state bench. Anyway, the story goes — correct me if I'm wrong in any of this, won't you, Bill? — that Bill here vehemently denied the charge and the policeman stuck to his story that Bill had been driving recklessly and at over twice the posted speed limit. Basically, it came down to Bill's word against the policeman...."

"...and that damned judge accepted the cop's story. He had no evidence, none whatsoever. What the hell has become of 'innocent until proven guilty' in this country? That's what I want to know."

"And that, apparently, is pretty much what he said in court too, when Madison handed down his decision."

Phillip waited, to see if Bill would pick up the story. Reluctantly, after a few seconds' pause, he did.

"I guess I lost my head, because I started shouting about lack of justice in Madison's court. I was more angry at him than the stupid policeman, you see. I'd been found guilty without so much as a shred of hard evidence against me, that was what galled me so much. And I looked up to see that judge just sitting there, as if he was somehow better than me, knowing that he was above all this, and something just sort of snapped inside me. I guess I called him some names and things, I don't remember — anyway the long and short of it was that I spent a night in jail for contempt of court."

Phillip Aitcheson continued with the story. "Strange thing was that it didn't go down too badly with the voters in the end. Bill here won the election easily, and now it looks like we're stuck with him for mayor as long as wants the job. Strange, isn't it, how things turn out? Anyway, I must be going, otherwise I'll miss my tee-off."

Felix wanted to interrupt, to bring him back to the subject of Matthew Chambers, but he knew that that might be a mistake. Probably the man had shared with them all that he knew on the subject. Aitcheson stood, bade them good day, and was gone.

Bill was leaning back in his chair, morosely swilling the remnants of his drink around the bottom of his glass, as if he were reliving memories.

"So what did you call Madison?" Felix prompted.

"You don't want to know. It's water under the bridge. We get along just fine now, don't we? After all he's on the board of the Rotary Club with me; I have to get on with him, don't I?"

He gave the glass one final twirl, raised it to his lips and downed the remainder of the wine.

"Better be going. Even with Lucinda away, she left me a bunch of honey-dos. We had a small dinner party last night and I still need to clear up. Strange, you know, Matthew Chambers was the guest. He must have died not long after he left us. I wonder what killed him. I suppose there'll be an autopsy or something."

Felix shrugged, looking much calmer than he felt.

"I suppose so. I should imagine it was a heart attack; that's the most likely cause of sudden death for a middle-aged man. An aneurysm maybe. He came to me only a couple of days ago with a shoulder problem and I gave him some capsules for it. He should have taken one last night. Maybe I missed something. I thought it was just a racquetball injury, but maybe there was more to it than that.

"One thing," — he smiled faintly — "he had no close relatives, at least none around here that I know of, so I doubt I'll get sued for malpractice if I did miss something."

He raised the nearly empty can to his lips and drained it.

Felix Taylor spent the remainder of the weekend in Denver, playing golf, trying to relax. He returned to find a single message, from a youthful-sounding detective, on his answering machine.

He returned the call and had a surprisingly superficial conversation with the detective, whose sole purpose seemed to be to confirm that Chambers was a diabetic and that Taylor was his physician. There was no hint of suspicion in the detective's voice.

Taylor wanted to ask whether an autopsy had been performed and whether the results of blood tests were available yet. With difficulty, he bit his tongue and kept his questions to himself. He put the telephone down and gazed at the photograph on his desk in his home office.

So beautiful. He loved her so much. And she had been getting so much better.

Until Matthew Chambers had entered her life.

Chapter 11

It was a surprisingly effective procedure, one that had helped him numerous times in the past and which, Harry Jones hoped, would aid him once more in this most perplexing of cases.

It had taken him most of Thursday evening to complete the necessary paperwork and he had left the building only when he knew he was finished, shortly after one in the morning. His last act before leaving for the night had been to leave a Post-It on Chief Salter's door: "Request that you review Chambers case for me when you have time; write-up in my cubicle, in the folder marked with his name." He had signed it; then, as an afterthought, marked the date and time, so that the chief would have no cause to be angry when he showed up at work late in the morning.

He slept badly, going over the facts again and again. It was hardly surprising that they were on his mind; he had just spent an entire evening laboriously writing down every factual detail that might be relevant to the case. And, after the facts, he had committed to paper two pages of rambling, incoherent speculation about the circumstances surrounding Chambers' death.

From the facts alone, he could prove nothing — not even that Chambers had been murdered, although since the arrival of the toxicology report it was hard to see how it could be otherwise.

After the funeral, he had returned to his cubicle feeling defeated. Somewhere in all that he had unearthed, though, surely there was a

118

clue as to the who, the how, and the why of Chambers' death? Even in his speculations, all he had was the who, with no indication of either the motive or the *modus operandi*.

What possible reason could Felix Taylor have to kill Matthew Chambers? And, surely, if Chambers had known that Dr. Taylor posed a threat, he would hardly have visited him the day before his death for medical treatment? In some ways, the toxicology report served only to make the case even murkier, although it did seem to imply that at least there *was* a case.

But he could not prove even what little he suspected about Dr. Taylor. He tried to console himself with the thought as he tossed restlessly in bed that his boss might be able to put the pieces together more coherently.

It would not be the first time. In fact, the technique had been introduced by Chief Salter, imported, according to rumor, from Scotland Yard: when completely at a loss as to how to proceed with a case, sit down and in long hand write down every single fact of which you are sure. Facts, and only facts. After the facts of the case, list your hunches, deductions, suppositions and guesses, keeping them clearly separate from the facts. Then take the whole lot and give it to a colleague with enough time on his hands to digest and consider what you have written. Nine times out of ten, your colleague will find something you have missed.

The technique would never work in a big city police force like the one the chief had left: there was too much rivalry in city departments. Only a fool would admit defeat on a case and then promptly hand it over for a fresh pair of eyes to review and, quite possibly, solve for him. Besides which, it would be next to impossible to find a colleague with sufficient time to review the case in the first place.

But here in Pinetree things were different: Salter made it clear that he was always more interested in promoting what he called "team players" than rewarding "macho TV detectives." "Our job is to get the case solved, not to massage one another's egos," he would say. And so the system worked. Out of courtesy, Harry was giving his boss first crack at the case; if he was too busy to handle it, it would be passed on to someone else who knew little or nothing about the case. Maybe something would come of his evening's work, maybe not. But at least he had tried.

Unable to clear his mind, he continued to toss underneath the bedclothes.

Chapter 12

Joanna Salisbury was awake by seven o'clock, ready to begin work.

As a concession to Martin's sensitivities, she walked the few steps to his room rather than picking up the telephone, and saw that the curtains were still tightly drawn. No light escaped through the peephole in the door. She turned away with a discontented grunt and made her way to the lobby of the motel, where she indulged her impatience by drinking two cups of barely-acceptable coffee and gorging herself on a large sweet pastry smothered in cloying bright pink icing, which she immediately regretted.

Didn't Martin realize that there was work to be done?

She picked up a copy of the local newspaper, the *Pinetree Reporter*, and flicked through it. There was nothing of interest. In particular there was no mention of the discovery of the poisoned medication that had been in Matthew Chambers' possession at the time of his death. Frustrated, she refolded the paper and replaced it on the counter. She briefly considered risking a third cup of coffee, but decided that her brother had slept long enough. She climbed the steps to Martin's room.

Although the curtains were still closed, the round peephole shone with the yellow of incandescent light. She rapped on the door, then waited.

After a minute she knocked again, even harder. This time the light at the peephole flickered. Martin opened the door. He was dressed, but stubble adorned his chin.

Joanna cheerily breezed past him into the room.

"About time you got up, sleepy head," she chided. "I've been thinking, and there's lots that I want to know. I want to see this detective fellow, Harry Jones, and find out what he thinks is going on. How soon do you think we can see him?"

Martin, still bleary, shrugged.

"Dunno. Let me finish getting ready first, then we need to get some breakfast, and then we'll think about our plans for the day."

"Some of us have already had breakfast," teased Joanna while Martin made his way to the bathroom.

"Fine. In that case you can go away and leave those of us that are still asleep alone. I'll see you in the morning."

The sound of an electric shaver curtailed any reply that Joanna might have thought of making.

Detective Harry Jones was in no hurry. He wanted to be sure that Chief Salter had plenty of time to digest his work and mull over the facts of the case.

He awoke late and breakfasted leisurely in his pajamas. It was ten thirty before he arrived at the department. Signing in, he was given two telephone messages. Both, he saw with some surprise, were from Martin Salisbury. The first, timed at 8:10, was a telephone message, "Would like to meet," and gave the phone number of the motel. The second was a personal note, timed at ten o'clock. Written in a bold handwriting, the message said: "Would like to see you whenever possible to discuss Chambers case. Am going up to Chambers house."

He crumpled the messages and dropped them into the trash. Deep in thought, he walked slowly to his cubicle. There were no more messages and no urgent work waiting for him. Tearing off the top sheet from a yellow legal pad, he scrawled a note in case anyone tried to find him: "Gone to Matthew Chambers house. Telephone 494-2862."

Seven minutes after entering the building, he left it.

As Martin drove her up the mountain towards the house, Joanna breathed deeply of the cool air breezing in through the open window.

Looking at the trees that surrounded the vehicle, she contrasted her surroundings with her own neighborhood in Sutherland. It was a different world.

Somewhere along the way, people had become so engrossed in accumulating wealth and prestige, or merely in remaining employed, that they had forgotten that life should be about more than mere existence. Seventeen years of life in the suburbs had made her forget that places like Pinetree existed.

It took no deep thought to understand why Matthew had abandoned a lucrative job in Chicago in favor of a gamble in Pinetree. Once one placed it in such stark terms, the puzzle instead became: why doesn't everyone do the same? She answered her own question: because people are scared to step out into something new. She had a secure, well-paying job. It would be hard to give that up and move to somewhere like Pinetree without some security to back it up. But maybe the trade would be worth it.

Martin slowed and climbed an especially steep rise. Seemingly out of nowhere, a flat space appeared before them, and Matthew's house suddenly looked down on them.

Joanna's breath was nearly taken away. It was the kind of house in which she had never even dreamed of living. And now, as her brother quickly reminded her, half of it was hers.

When she followed Martin up the stone steps and then turned to look at the view, her breath *was* taken away.

"Wow!"

The vista of mountain slopes; peaceful Pinetree stretching along the valley below; the deep blue sky contrasting with the greenery — it was all postcard perfect. She stood imbibing the view while Martin unlocked the door.

Her attention was distracted by a sudden movement at the periphery of her vision. For a second she could not find the source of the movement. Then it happened again. She spotted a blue-green hummingbird hovering under the eaves, drinking from a large feeder one-quarter filled with bright red liquid. The buzzing of its wings complemented the low soughing of the trees.

She watched the bird intently for more than a minute until it darted away around a corner of the house, temporarily satiated. She turned and nearly bumped into her brother who was standing next to her, watching the bird as intently as she.

"Amazing," she said. "This has to be one of the most gorgeous places in the world to live."

"It's a bit different in winter," he cautioned, then ushered her into the house.

She felt oddly uncomfortable in the face of such understated opulence. There was not much furniture, but everything was of the highest quality. The contrast with her tract home could hardly have been more stark.

The living room, into which she descended down two wide steps, was easily as large as the apartment in which she and Kevin had lived the first five years of their life together. She crossed to the piano. A Grotrian. Stunning. She shook herself to try to break the spell.

Taking her notebook from her handbag, she said, "Right, let's get down to business. First off, can you show me around the house?"

Martin obliged, and Joanna said nothing for several minutes as he led her around the residence. She sketched a plan of the building in the notebook, along with descriptions of the contents of each room. They completed the tour in the living room, where it had begun. Martin pointed out the chess game, still untouched, and the location near the kitchen where the body had been found by the judge.

"Not quite, Martin," cautioned Joanna. "That's where the body was found by the police. There's no independent corroboration that Judge Madison found it there."

"Good God, Joanna, you *do* have a suspicious mind, don't you? You aren't telling me that you suspect the judge of foul play, are you?"

"I'm not telling you anything, other than an obvious fact. At the moment, we aren't even sure that a crime was committed, never mind who the perpetrator was, if in fact there was one. But it never does to jump to conclusions. That's the way a clever criminal gets away with his crime: he depends on a combination of his brains and police stupidity. Just one of those by itself is almost never enough for a crime to succeed; both have to be present. So, if we make sure that we aren't stupid, we'll get our man — or woman — in the end."

"So what you're saying is that no one is above suspicion?"

"You could put it like that. In fact, if I were handling this case, my list of suspects would include both you and me...."

Martin's right eyebrow shot up.

"But we were both thousands of miles away when it happened."

"Doesn't mean a thing. Both of us might have had a motive. Maybe we needed the money. This house must be worth a fortune."

"Less than you might think. Real estate seems surprisingly inexpensive around here. I know, I checked. Of course, I'm comparing it with prices around Oxford, which isn't really fair."

"Well, in any case, if one of us was strapped for cash — and I for one could certainly do with an infusion at the moment — this might be a ready source. Or maybe Matthew knew something about one of us and was blackmailing us, or... who knows? It could be anything. There are a hundred and one reasons why one of us might want him dead."

"But you could say the same about almost anyone. He could have been blackmailing anyone."

"Exactly. Even the judge. Anyway, the point is that no one is above suspicion. For myself, I know that I didn't do it, so that leaves one less suspect, but you've got to admit that that doesn't narrow the field much."

"So I'm still a suspect?"

"Well, not really. I was just trying to make a point. But still, you aren't off the hook entirely."

There was a smile on her face as she spoke, but Martin found it impossible to interpret.

"So, apart from your brother, is there anyone else you particularly think might have done it?"

"It's too early to say. Until I've had a real talk with our friend Harry Jones I can't form much of an opinion. I'm still trying to gather facts; I'm not yet trying to decide where they lead. Now, for example, you just said that property values are quite low around here. How much would this house be worth, would you say?"

"I asked Harry Jones and Judge Madison exactly that question. Independently, of course. They thought somewhere between $150,000 and $180,000. Apparently, even though the house looks beautiful in summer, real estate values are lower than you would think, partly because Pinetree is so far from Denver and partly because living here in the winter can be rough, especially some distance out of town like this.

"Don't forget that in a typical winter Pinetree sees between twelve and fifteen feet of snow. I was here the winter before last and can vouch for the fact that getting into town from here can be very tricky.

"There's a four-wheel-drive vehicle in the garage under the house; it's not for show. Matthew told me that most years there were several days when he was stuck here, unable to get into town. A lot of people come to Pinetree for the skiing, of course, but there are plenty of houses and condos much closer to the ski lifts, so this wouldn't bring in much income as a rental property. So you see it's not worth as much as you might expect."

"And Matthew owned it free and clear, did he?"

"Yes. He had lived pretty frugally in Chicago and made a couple of good investments in real estate there. When he bailed out of the law firm, he left with just over $100,000 in his pocket. He arrived in an autumn when the winter the year before had been particularly severe. The owners of this house had had it on the market all summer and were willing to sell at almost any price to get out before the snows started. He paid $95,500 for the house four years ago and immediately moved in and set up his business in town. He told me that he never regretted the move, even for one moment."

"And who was the source for this information? Matthew himself?"

"Yes."

"Then we'll need to check it. There should be records of all real estate transactions somewhere. I'll ask the detective what the system is over here."

"You really do have a suspicious mind, don't you?"

Joanna took this as a compliment. "Only when there's a possibility that someone is trying to pull wool over my eyes. Then you wouldn't believe how suspicious I can be."

Martin mulled this for several seconds.

"You know, I've been thinking these past few days that because I'm so good at programming computers, I'd make a pretty good detective, but now I'm beginning to realize I was mistaken. Programming is more like writing, it's basically a creative process, while detecting is deductive, which is quite a different talent."

Joanna opened her mouth to say something, but closed it again as a sound intruded from outside: an engine sounded nearby, suddenly followed by a squeal of brakes, then silence. A moment later, a car door slammed. She and Martin reached the front door in time to see Harry Jones mount the last few steps.

Martin and Joanna greeted the newcomer. As he followed them into the living room, he said offhandedly, "That's quite a padful of notes you have there, miss."

125

She turned and eyed him for a moment, as if appraising what she saw.

"Yes," she said. "I'm a detective sergeant with the New South Wales Police. It's habit, I suppose, to write everything down."

There was a distinct pause as Detective Jones assimilated this information.

"That would be New South Wales, Australia, miss?" He gave her no time to reply. "I don't think Pinetree would be in your jurisdiction, then."

He said it politely, but the meaning was clear enough: this is my case, not yours; I might accept help, but not interference.

Martin, watching, was astonished by the change that now took place in his sister. And he began to appreciate Joanna's professional abilities.

Before the young detective had joined them she had been alert, commanding, briskly in charge. Now she lowered her eyes submissively.

"Oh, I quite understand, Detective Jones. Please don't take offense; none was intended, I assure you. I was just trying to understand the circumstances of my cousin's death, that's all. Martin, you see" — she waved deprecatingly in her brother's direction — "is a businessman and when he was explaining things to me he must have got confused or left out a few things, because from what he told me there's quite a lot that I don't understand. And I'm afraid that my tidy mind makes me uncomfortable when I don't understand something. And you must call me Jo, Mr. Jones."

She looked up, her eyes unnaturally wide, looking directly at the detective. He held her gaze for only a fraction of a second, unaware that he was taking part in a contest. He looked away, towards Martin's expressionless visage.

"I'm sorry, miss... er, Jo. And you must call me Harry. I didn't mean to offend you. And I must defend your brother. I don't know exactly what he told you, but there's actually a lot about Mr. Chambers' death which isn't clear to me either. I'd be happy to tell you anything I know." He had so thoroughly fallen into Joanna's trap that he almost added, "Two heads are better than one," but he stopped himself just in time.

"Yes, I'd like that. You wouldn't mind if Martin joined us as well, would you? He does seem rather confused. Maybe we could all have lunch later and go over things then?"

"Yes, good idea. In the meantime, let me show you around the house."

Martin opened his mouth to explain that he had already done that very thing, but Joanna pre-empted him.

"That would be very kind of you, Harry. I don't know if Martin wants to join us or if he has already seen as much of the house as he wants to...." She looked at her brother.

Martin got the message. "No. You two go on without me. Tell you what, if it's OK for Harry to take you in his car, I'd like to go back into town for a while. Where would be a good place for us to meet for lunch?"

"Sure," Harry said. "No problem. Tell you what, why don't we meet at *La Patisserie* at noon. Would that be OK?"

Brother and sister agreed and Martin took his leave of the two professional detectives, keeping his thoughts firmly to himself.

Martin had to admire the way Jo had handled the local detective. And the way she had made sure that the two of them would be alone for an hour. Still, it rankled to be so firmly excluded. By lunchtime, though, Martin was feeling more charitable towards his sister. He had returned to his room and, in a fit of pique, aggressively set about two *Daily Telegraph* crossword puzzles and completed them both in less than an hour. He triumphantly filled in the final clue — *Dish of green peas as an exception (7)* — glanced at his watch, and saw with some surprise that it lacked only two minutes of noon.

He was several minutes late arriving at the restaurant. There was a line of people waiting to enter the popular eatery. Joanna and Harry had arrived a few minutes earlier, and the name "Salisbury" was called just as Martin entered the building.

A pert waitress led them to a white metal table with three chairs spaced around its circumference on the restaurant's patio. The patio commanded an unremarkable view of downtown Pinetree, but above it towered the ubiquitous grandeur of the mountains. The sun shone from high overhead, the first cumuli of the day beginning to dot the sky like slowly waxing flecks in a blue sea. An umbrella in the center of the table shadowed its surface but did nothing to provide shade to the diners.

For a few seconds, the sun dimmed as a thin cloud passed overhead. Harry glanced at his watch. "It's a bit early for clouds. Like as not we'll see a thunderstorm this afternoon."

"Now, you were telling me about the toxicology report on the capsules...," Joanna prompted.

Harry continued where, obviously, he had left off, leaving Martin to catch the thread as best he could.

"Just one capsule, that's all. Dr. Taylor claims that he gave Matthew a total of six capsules, with instructions to take two a day with food. He says that he told Matthew to take one at lunchtime on Thursday, and at breakfast and dinner after that. That would have been enough to see him through to the end of Saturday evening.

"Dr. Taylor says he gave Matthew a prescription, which we found in Matthew's medicine cabinet, for a further course of the same drug, and instructed Matthew to have the prescription filled if his shoulder was still sore when he finished the samples. Unfortunately, Dr. Taylor's information does not tally with what we found; there were three capsules remaining in the bottle that was found on the body, not two as there should have been.

"Mr. Healy could not confirm that your cousin took a capsule with what turned out to be his last meal. Mrs. Healy doesn't remember seeing him take a capsule either, but she spent most of the time before they ate preparing the meal in the kitchen, so it's hardly surprising she saw nothing. Her husband says that Mr. Chambers went to the restroom to check his blood sugar and give himself an insulin shot shortly after arriving. He had ample opportunity to take a capsule then without being seen."

"Or perhaps he was feeling better and decided against taking one."

"Yes. Or maybe he simply forgot. Or maybe he did take one and there was one more capsule in the bottle than Dr. Taylor has told us about."

"Sounds awfully speculative to me," contributed Martin.

"Exactly," said Joanna, looking pleased, as if her favorite pupil had just demonstrated that he had learned a lesson well. "So we'll just remember the fact for now: when he was found, Matthew Chambers had on him a pill bottle containing three capsules, two of which were indomethacin, and one that contained a lethal dose of cyanide."

"Exactly," said Harry. "As I told you yesterday, we sent the capsules in for testing simply as a precaution. We certainly never expected that one of the capsules would contain half a gram of cyanide."

"And the other two were completely untainted?"

"According to the toxicology report, yes."

"So... I'm sorry. I just want to be sure I've got this right. You're saying that when he died, Matthew Chambers was carrying on his person a pill bottle containing three capsules, one of which, had he or anyone else swallowed it, would have been fatal."

"Yes. That's it exactly."

Joanna's brow furrowed. Somehow, in some way that she did not understand, this must be the starting point from which she had to follow the thread that would lead to unraveling the how and why of Matthew Chambers' death.

Harry Jones reentered the Pinetree Police Department parking lot at half past two.

Driving back to the drab concrete building after lunch, it gradually dawned on him that he had told Joanna Salisbury everything he knew about the case. It occurred to him that maybe that was exactly what she had had in mind.

He shrugged off the uncomfortable thought, settling on the more pleasant rationalization that Jo was simply a lively, intelligent (and pretty) woman who was merely very inquisitive about her cousin's death. Of course, she *was* a detective.... He realized that she had spent almost no time at all talking about herself. He wondered exactly how good a detective she was, what types of cases she handled, what was her track record? The uncomfortable feeling that perhaps he had been used returned as he drove his car into a space and killed the engine.

There were no calls for him, but lying on top of his white plastic-coated desk was a handwritten scribble from his boss: "Come by when you are available to discuss matters."

There was nothing to keep him in his cubicle, and two minutes later he was knocking on Chief Salter's door.

"Enter!" barked the chief.

As Harry sat across the desk from his superior, another uncomfortable thought struck him: even though he had shared everything with Joanna, she had given no indication of how her own mind was working or what she thought of the case. Indecision struck him again; maybe she had no thoughts, maybe she wanted information merely for its own sake. But somehow he doubted it.

Chief Salter interrupted his thoughts.

"So, Harry. Any ideas or developments since you made these notes last night?"

Harry decided that he had to be honest with the chief about Joanna Salisbury.

"Only one thing; it slightly complicates things, maybe, but it's not really germane to the case itself."

His boss raised an interrogatory eyebrow.

"I spent most of the morning up at the Chambers house, where I ran into the Salisburys. You know, the two cousins, one from Australia and one from England."

Salter nodded.

"Actually, we ended up having lunch together at *La Patisserie*. As far as I can gather, there's been some kind of long-term estrangement between the two of them, but Chambers' death seems to have helped them reconcile. They certainly seem friendly enough now. Anyway, the slightly disconcerting news is that Joanna Salisbury is about thirty five, disarmingly pretty, very intelligent and... a detective sergeant in the New South Wales police."

John Salter hmmmed. Then there was silence for several seconds before he spoke.

"So; how does that affect you? How much have you told her?"

"Almost everything, chief. Sorry. She kept asking questions and it all sort of came out before I knew what I was saying."

He felt every bit as sheepish as he sounded.

"Is she interested in the case professionally?"

"I don't know. She didn't tell me what she was thinking. But she pumped me very expertly; I didn't even notice what she was doing until after it was over."

Salter shrugged.

"Oh well. Nothing we can do about it now. Probably no harm done. I'll check her credentials and see if I can get some background, just to be sure that she isn't leading you on with a pack of lies. But I don't think she's too much of a concern. It's not like she's a suspect or anything.

"Now, Harry, to work. I read the report thoroughly, of course. You did a good job writing it up, and it looks like you've been pretty thorough. Now, the question is, do you have any suspects besides Dr. Taylor? And do you have any means or motive for murder?

"Don't forget, there are always three puzzles to be solved in any murder: who did it? why did they do it? and how was it done? Without a solid case on all three, the defense will be able to sow a reasonable doubt in the mind of the jury and we won't be able to convict no matter how certain we are. And given the way things are today, if the defendant *did* do it, he'd probably go on to sell his story for half a million bucks to some publisher or other. So, what are your thoughts on the who, the why and the how?"

"You think it was murder, then?"

His boss shrugged.

"Your guess is at least as good as mine at this point. But it's safest to treat it that way. Until the toxicology report came in I wasn't prepared to waste much effort on what was simply an unexplained death. But now it's obvious that there's more to this case than I initially thought. So I think it warrants more effort until we are satisfied about what went on at the Chambers house last Friday evening. So, provisionally, yes, let's treat it as murder. Just don't tell the press, that's all."

Harry was grim. The memory of last year's fiasco returned to mind. "No fear of that, sir. If they get hold of it, it certainly won't be from me.

"Well, first of all, the question of who did it, assuming, as we are, that it *was* murder. Obviously, at this point, Felix Taylor has to be the prime suspect. Although even that simple supposition provides us with plenty of problems. By the time of Chambers' death on Friday evening, four of the six capsules that Dr. Taylor claims he gave to Chambers were supposed to have been used. So why were there three left in the pill bottle, not two? Maybe it was something as simple as that Chambers skipped a meal or forgot to take one of the capsules. Maybe there were more capsules in the bottle than Taylor claims. Maybe the poisoned capsule was introduced later and has nothing to do with the ones that Taylor gave him."

"But the poison was inside what was undoubtedly the gelatin covering of an indomethacin capsule, according to the lab report."

"True," admitted Harry. "So it does look likely that it was in the bottle when Dr. Taylor gave it to Chambers. It would have been hard for someone else to plant it. But not impossible. And there is a bigger question: if Chambers had died of cyanide poisoning, it would have been obvious at the autopsy. There's no way that the coroner and the blood tests would not have found cyanide in the blood; yet they found nothing. Obviously, ingestion of potassium cyanide was not the cause of Chambers' death. That, we have firmly established, was hypoglycemia."

"A puzzle, I agree. Carry on."

"So, we really have no case against Dr. Taylor. All we have against him is that he was the one who gave Chambers a bottle of capsules, one of which, we believe, was laced with sufficient poison to kill him. Not much of a case."

"Maybe. Maybe not. Go on; what other thoughts do you have?"

"Let's look first at the chemical facts as we know them. One:" — he raised his hands and tapped the index finger of his right hand with the corresponding finger on his left — "at the time of his death, Matthew Chambers was suffering from acutely low blood sugar; so low, in fact, that the coroner concludes that that was the cause of death.

"Matthew Chambers was a known diabetic, but he had been a diabetic for many years and was fully aware of how to test his blood sugar and how to administer insulin when necessary. In fact, we have two statements to the effect that shortly before his last meal he tested himself and gave himself a shot of insulin, although the latter was done out of sight. Mr. Chambers' stock of insulin has been tested, and it all seems untainted. The syringe that he used for that final injection has been recovered and tested, in case the insulin he injected had somehow been tampered with, but everything looks completely normal.

"Chemical fact number two:" — he ticked off the middle finger of his right hand — "there was a trace of a hypnotic in his bloodstream at the time of his death. The drug was triazolam, which is commonly used to treat insomnia. The amount of the drug in the blood sample corresponded to a typical dose taken between four and seven hours before death."

"Sometime in the afternoon, then."

"Yes. According to the coroner's reading of the report, it would have to have been between lunch and supper."

"Did Mr. Chambers suffer from insomnia?"

"There's no evidence of it in the medical records. Neither was there any triazolam in his medicine cabinet, nor could we find any among his personal belongings."

"Any indication of why he might have taken the drug?"

"None at all. In fact, according to the statements we received from people he saw during the afternoon, he gave no indication of drowsiness.

If he had in fact taken the triazolam shortly after lunch, it would most likely have knocked him out for several hours. Yet he attended two meetings that afternoon, and we have several witnesses prepared to attest that his behavior was perfectly normal all afternoon. In fact, the only abnormal behavior during the entire day was his brief loss of consciousness at the Healys', shortly after he had injected himself with insulin."

"Anything else?"

"Regarding the chemical facts? No, not really."

"And have you any suspects other than Dr. Taylor?"

There was a hint of something — impatience, perhaps — in Chief Salter's voice. His subordinate began to think that something, some important fact, had escaped him. He continued to talk, while worrying about what he might have missed.

"No one else comes even close. We don't have a motive for Felix Taylor, but at least we are partway to an M.O. With anyone else we have nothing at all. I suppose that a complete list of the most likely suspects would have to include his secretary, Kathleen Freeman, if only because she had the most contact with him and because, presumably, she was in the best position to know of anything strange or unsavory in his past. I've interviewed her, of course, and gone through the office reasonably thoroughly, and found nothing out of the ordinary, just as there was nothing suspicious at the house.

"Then there's Judge Madison, who found the body. I suppose that a degree of suspicion must always rest on the person who finds the body. The two of them, Chambers and the judge, were obviously close friends. They played chess together and as I understand it they were both members of the Rotary Club, where they usually sat together for lunch."

Salter interrupted. "There was a meeting of the Rotary last Friday, right? The day of Chambers' death?"

Harry nodded. "Yes, sir. And Chambers and Judge Madison both attended. As did Felix Taylor and Bill Healy, the mayor. According to statements by Healy and Judge Madison, the judge and Chambers sat together as usual. Felix Taylor arrived a few minutes late and also sat next to Chambers.

"Although he arrived late, the doctor left early. According to his appointment secretary, he was running late in the morning and had scheduled his first patient for one thirty in the afternoon, which meant he had to leave the meeting early. His secretary claimed that he usually schedules his first appointment on Friday afternoons for two o'clock, but he made an exception because the patient had to go to Denver that afternoon to meet a relative who was flying in from Illinois. I checked with the patient, a Mrs. Brenda Lyle, and she confirms that the doctor was originally hesitant to schedule an appointment so early in the afternoon."

"So we are not to read anything into the fact that the doctor arrived at this Rotary meeting late and then left early?"

"No, sir, I don't think so. The only other suspects I've really considered are Bill and Lucinda Healy, with whom Chambers dined on the evening of his death. As I said, Bill Healy is a member of the Rotary Club. In fact, he's the president this year, so naturally he was present at the meeting on Friday and he presided as usual. None of the members of the club that I spoke to could think of anything unusual at the meeting. In fact, they said that it was memorable only because it was a particularly interesting program."

"Oh?"

"Apparently, at these meetings there is half an hour of business, and then there is usually some sort of presentation for another half an hour or so. They all remembered the program last Friday: a dentist came up from Boulder to play ragtime music for them. It seems this dentist has hosted a weekly radio show on ragtime music for years in Boulder and is something of an expert on the subject. He writes his own pieces as well and has even recorded a compact disc. I didn't even know that ragtime was written any more. Anyway, this dentist came up from Boulder and played a selection of well-known rags interspersed with snippets of history and some of his own compositions. I guess it went down well; they all seemed to like it. But I can't see that it's relevant."

"OK. So the long and the short of it is that all our suspects knew one another pretty well; in fact they spent some time in each other's company on the day of Chambers' death. That right?"

"Yes, I think so. For what it's worth, Madison and Taylor had better access to Chambers than the others at lunchtime, but no one sitting nearby saw anything untoward going on between any of them."

"Any possibility that one of them could have lifted Chambers' glucose candy then?"

"Hmmm..., I hadn't thought of that. Sounds pretty difficult to me, to remove a roll of candy from somebody sitting next to you. Anyway, wouldn't Chambers have noticed when he got changed to go out to the Healys'?"

"Yes, I suppose he would. What about the meal with the Healys? Anything there?"

"Well, it's hard to ascertain facts there, of course, because of the lack of independent corroboration, although there are some things we can be sure of. Chambers was the only guest for an early dinner. Apparently he knew the Healys fairly well, and they would dine at one another's house once a month or so. It happened to be an early meal on Friday because of the council meeting that evening.

"If you remember, the meeting a couple of weeks earlier had been postponed because too many councilors were out of town. The dinner date had been set up some time in advance, but rather than cancel it when the council meeting was re-scheduled, they simply shifted the time earlier so that Mr. Healy would be able to join his wife and Chambers."

"The wife, what's her name... Lucinda, she doesn't attend the council meetings?"

"Apparently not. I interviewed Healy and his wife independently, and their stories match. Matthew Chambers arrived for supper at five, they had the meal, and he left at about seven, leaving Bill Healy just enough time to get to the council chambers in time for the seven-thirty start of the meeting."

"So the two Healys agree with one another, but there is no outside corroboration of the story?"

"Exactly, sir. One other thing which I don't think I put in the report is that Lucinda Healy left Pinetree very early the next morning, six a.m., to fly back east to see her parents. She cut the trip short so she could attend the funeral yesterday. I interviewed her yesterday afternoon after the funeral."

"And her story matches her husband's?"

"Substantially, yes, sir. Of course, there's never exact agreement, but basically, yes, they agree."

"So tell me a bit more about this incident at the meal that you mention in the report."

"It was rather strange; perhaps it was a precursor of some kind. It seems that while Mrs. Healy was in the kitchen preparing the dessert, Matthew Chambers had a fainting spell.

"He and her husband were together in the dining room, which is adjacent to the kitchen but can't be seen from it. She heard a clattering sound, but she was busy so she couldn't immediately go see what had happened. She thinks that there was a delay of perhaps twenty seconds — her husband puts it closer to ten — before she was able to go into the dining room to see what had caused the noise.

"She saw her husband bending over Chambers, who appeared to be unconscious on the floor next to his chair. Mr. Healy was slapping Chambers in the face, to try to bring him round. Chambers had spilt his drink, which was plain orange juice. Mr. Healy asked his wife to bring an ice pack and something for Chambers to drink. Mrs. Healy watched for about ten seconds and saw that Chambers was beginning to come around. Then she returned to the kitchen to get the ice and some more juice.

"By the time she returned to the dining room, Healy was helping Chambers to his feet. Within five minutes Chambers was pretty much back to normal, although still rather groggy."

"And Bill Healy; did he tell you any of this independently?"

"Yes, sir; neither spouse was present during the other's interview. I guess it was hardly the sort of thing you would forget. Mr. Healy said that he and Chambers were sitting, chatting about hummingbirds of all things, when Chambers suddenly looked pale and slipped off his chair, unconscious. He said it happened just like that, with no warning at all. He spilled his drink all over the hardwood floor.

"Mr. Healy brought him around by slapping him gently a few times; then he administered the ice pack. He thought that Chambers might have hit his head against the table leg when he went down. Mrs. Healy somewhat corroborates that by saying that he was rubbing the top of his head when she first saw him, as if it was sore."

"Water. Why did Healy have to go to the kitchen to get something for Chambers to drink? Surely there would have been a jug of water in the dining room?"

"Good point, sir. I wondered about that myself. Chambers was drinking orange juice; the others were drinking wine from a bottle Chambers had brought. Apparently, they had simply not gotten around to bringing in a jug of water."

"OK, I see. Anything else I should know?"

"No, sir; I don't think so. Chambers seemed slightly groggy through the meal. He left to go home at roughly the same time that Healy left for the council meeting. The Healys agree that he looked tired, but neither of them was particularly concerned that he wasn't safe to drive. And after that there's nothing until the judge found the body maybe five hours later. The long and the short of it is that if Matthew Chambers was killed, then we don't know who did it and we don't know why, and we don't know how. Up until the moment of his death, his day looked more or less like any other."

"Any theories about the candies; or, rather, the lack of them?"

Harry shrugged. "Four, sir: one, he lost them; two, unlike most diabetics he didn't carry glucose candy; three, he forgot to put them in the pocket of the clothes he was wearing; or four, Judge Madison removed them when he found the body."

"And which of those four do you most like?"

"None of them, sir."

Salter leaned back in his chair and steepled his fingers in thought. Harry remembered the edge that had entered his voice when they had been discussing Felix Taylor.

Here it comes, he thought.

"What about Chambers' life?" the chief asked. "Would you say that his life up until the moment of his death was fairly normal?"

"Depends what you think of as normal, really, doesn't it, sir? But I didn't uncover anything strange, if that's what you mean. It's all there in the summary at the beginning of my notes."

Salter leaned forward and began to read from the sheet in front of him. It was a biography of Matthew Chambers prepared by Detective Jones.

Matthew George Chambers

Birthdate: 18 August, 1950
Birthplace: Penshurst, Ohio
Citizenship: United States
Parents:

George Matthew Chambers (Professor of English, Penshurst College. Penshurst, Ohio)

Dawn Melissa Chambers *née* Barton (Homemaker)

Summary: The subject was an able student, and his father's income was sufficient to send him to private boarding school. He graduated from Market School at age eighteen, as class valedictorian. Although eligible for draft deferment, he instead volunteered for the Marine Corps and was sent on a thirteen-month tour of duty in Vietnam with the 3rd Marine Division.

He participated in major actions at Apbia Mountain and Lang Vei in 1969. He completed his tour of duty without injury and returned to Camp Pendleton in California with the rank of Lance Corporal.

In 1970, he was diagnosed with diabetes mellitus and shortly thereafter discharged from the armed services.

He applied for and was accepted at Harvard, where he took prelaw. During his sophomore year, both parents were killed in an automobile accident in which their vehicle was hit by a car driven by a drunk driver. The driver of the other vehicle survived, but is a paraplegic. Matthew Chambers attended none of the trial in which the survivor was found guilty of vehicular homicide and has, as far as can be determined, never attempted to make contact with him.

The subject graduated third in his class at Harvard and proceeded immediately to law school, from which he graduated in 1976, second in his class.

For two years he clerked for Justice Borges of the United States Court of Appeals for the Ninth Circuit, in Pasadena, California. In 1978 he accepted a job with the law firm of Herman, McCarthy and Soward in Chicago.

In the early 1980s, he began visiting Pinetree twice a year, once in the summer and once in the winter. He left Herman, McCarthy and Soward suddenly in 1990, shortly after winning an important case to which he had been assigned, in which he was defense counsel for a young negro male, Harold Williams, who was charged with vehicular homicide. Mr. Williams was found not guilty.

Immediately following the decision, the subject took a two-week vacation in England with his cousin, Martin Salisbury.

On his return from vacation, the subject tendered his resignation. He immediately moved to Pinetree and set up a small office specializing in domestic law. He continued to be sole proprietor of his own law firm from then until the time of his death.

It is apparently well known that the immediate cause of his resignation from Herman, McCarthy and Soward was disillusionment with the litigation system in the United States: the youth his talents exonerated was, in fact, guilty of the crime as charged and the subject felt that he could no longer work under a system wherein truth was so easily perverted.

The subject had few friends, apparently by choice. In his spare time, he enjoyed tinkering with electronic gadgets, reading and playing games of all kinds (in particular chess, at which he was generally recognized as one of the best players in the state, although he refused to play competitively, except locally). Judge Henry Clarence Madison was the subject's closest acquaintance; it was he who found the body. The judge is also a first-rate chess player and the two frequently played one another, and maintained an ongoing game which progressed at the rate of one move per day.

The subject was never married. His sexual orientation is unknown. As far as is known he had no intimate relationships with either sex.

All the subject's close relatives are deceased. The only remaining living relatives are a pair of sibling cousins: Mr. Martin Salisbury of England and Ms. Joanna Baker (*née* Salisbury) of Australia, to whom the bulk of the subject's estate passes in equal portions.

The chief finished reading and looked up. "OK, Harry, here's a couple of thoughts I had. The first one concerns our friend Felix Taylor.

"I've done a bit of digging about him. I haven't found a motive yet, but I thought you might be interested in this little coincidence that I discovered by looking up Dr. Taylor in the *Directory of Medical Specialists.*"

He pushed across a single photocopied sheet on which a paragraph was circled in yellow highlighter. He continued to speak as his subordinate read the paragraph.

"You see what this means, of course. Dr. Taylor arrived in Pinetree six months after Matthew Chambers. So much we should have known. What we didn't know was where Dr. Taylor practiced before he came here. As you can see, he came to us from Oak Park, Illinois. I looked it up on a map; it's essentially a suburb of Chicago."

He waited for Harry's response. He did not have to wait long.

"Could be just a coincidence, sir."

"Yes, it certainly could. And we still don't have an explanation of why, if Chambers took a fatally doped capsule, no trace of the poison was found in his bloodstream. That seems an insurmountable obstacle to any theory that casts Felix Taylor in the rôle of murderer. Still, it makes Dr. Taylor more interesting than ever. We need to find out why he moved when he did and why he chose to settle in Pinetree. I checked with the PD in Oak Park, and Taylor has no hint of a criminal record, but you may want to dig a bit deeper.

"One thing," he cautioned, "don't forget that Taylor is a doctor. That means that he's intelligent, and if he is somehow involved, he's going to do his best to confuse us. In other words, he's unlikely simply to break down and confess if he realizes that we suspect him. On the other hand, if you drop hints that we think he's involved, he may not be able to leave well enough alone and he might begin actively trying to misdirect our thinking. That might be just the break we're looking for. Do you understand what I'm saying?"

"I think so, sir. You think I should talk some more with Taylor and leave him with the impression that we suspect him and have more evidence than we really do. And then watch him carefully to see what he does."

"Exactly. And while you're at it, try to do some digging in Oak Park. I know it's all a bit desperate, and it's probably all a dead end, but at the moment it's the best we've got."

"And the second thing, sir? You said you had two thoughts."

"Yes. One thing about Chambers really troubles me: his lack of sexual activity. Here's a fit, healthy, extremely eligible bachelor in his mid forties. He went to church, but he doesn't seem to have been any kind of religious fanatic. I have a hard time believing that he wasn't sexually involved somewhere with someone. Either it's someone in

Pinetree and he was extremely discrete or there's something in his past that we haven't discovered yet.

"Maybe something damaged him psychologically and that's what he was really running from when he moved to Pinetree. My guess, and it's only a guess, is that he was homosexual and he kept it quiet because of some sort of scandal in his past. I may be wrong about details, but there's *something* there. There has to be. Dig into that, Harry, and you may be surprised at what you turn up."

"Yes, sir. I'm sorry I didn't think of that; I should have."

"No, don't blame yourself. It's just a fresh pair of eyes looking over the facts, that's all. It's how the system is supposed to work, remember?"

"Yes sir, and thank you."

"You're welcome. Keep me informed of anything you find."

Dismissed with several new leads, Harry Jones left his superior's office with renewed optimism.

"How's your chess?"

Joanna asked her brother the question with no warning. They were wearing swimsuits, seated by the side of the motel pool, she with her notes and the day's copy of the *Pinetree Reporter* open on the table before her, he with a furrowed brow as he tackled a particularly fiendish crossword.

"Huh? What was that?"

He hadn't been paying attention, wrestling instead with: *Lover of wisdom returns without a taxi*; five letters.

"Oh! Of course!" he exclaimed and filled in the answer.

"Chess. How's your chess? You used to be pretty good at school, I remember."

"Yes, I wasn't bad. Not in Matthew's class. We played a few games over the years, but it was never much of a challenge for him to beat me. I played for college a bit when I was there. I won some and lost some, about fifty-fifty, I guess."

"Think you could hold your own in a town chess club?"

"What, a town like this?"

He lifted his eyes to look around the town, but from the poolside the view was limited to little more than the motel and the surrounding mountains.

"I should think I'd be better than average somewhere like this. Although except for a couple of games against Matthew eighteen months ago I haven't played in years. I gave up playing when one of our software guys at work who didn't even know the game spent a month programming one of our computers to play. The stupid program beat me three times running. I haven't played seriously since then."

"OK, well you only need to play people here, not machines. And you don't even need to beat the people, I just want you to ask a few questions and keep your eyes and ears open."

She handed him her copy of the *Pinetree Reporter*, folded to show a column headed *Things To Do*.

She continued, "There's a meeting of the Pinetree chess club tonight. With Matthew's interest in the game, he was probably a member; and even if he wasn't, some of the people who are members must have played him and might have known him fairly well. I'd like you to go to the meeting and see if there's anything new that you can dig up about him."

"What sort of thing? What exactly do you have in mind?"

Joanna shrugged. "I don't know. We seem to be at rather an impasse, and I'd like more information about Matthew, that's all. I'm not looking for anything in particular."

"So what kinds of questions do you want me to ask?"

"If he was a member, find out how good he was, who he usually played, if anyone noticed any changes in his play recently, that sort of thing. If he was aware that he was in some sort of danger, he might have been able to hide it from the rest of the world, but he probably couldn't hide it from his chess-playing friends. His game would almost certainly suffer if his mind was preoccupied with other matters, and they'd notice that, you see."

Martin nodded. "Yes, I get it. Now I know why you're the detective and I'm simply a software manager."

"Who earns ten times as much as I do...." She said it without rancor, a statement of fact, softened by the smile on her face. "Anyway, aren't you going to ask what I'm going to be doing while you're enjoying yourself playing games?"

"No. But I'm sure you'll tell me anyway."

"Just for that, I won't. So there!"

Martin deliberately closed his book about his pen and placed them carefully on the table. Then he unceremoniously stood to his feet, pulled his sister from her chair, dragged her to the poolside, and together they fell laughing into the water.

———————————

Martin Salisbury was nervous.

The announcement in the *Things To Do* column in the newspaper had said simply: "Pinetree Chess Club meets tonight at the Pinetree Lodge and Center at 7:30. All levels of play catered to. Players and non-players welcome." He wanted to be neither too early nor too late, and had carefully timed his arrival at the parking lot of the imposing log lodge on the edge of town for twenty five minutes to eight. There were a dozen or so cars already parked, and another vehicle drove up as he locked his car door.

He took a few deep breaths of the cool, thin mountain air. There were butterflies in his stomach. *Chess is only a game*, he reminded himself as he recalled the real reason why he had given up playing: the crushing feeling of inferiority, of stupidity, of worthlessness that he felt whenever he lost.

Fifteen years ago he had made a promise to himself that he would never again voluntarily put himself in a position where he could receive such blows to his self-esteem. He argued with himself that tonight was different, that his principal reason for being here was not to play chess, but to seek out information from the other players. He did not convince himself.

"Good evening. You here for the chess club?" an amiable voice intruded on his thoughts.

"Yes, and you?" His voice sounded dry.

"Yes. Harold Winterson."

The overweight man wearing a tee shirt and khaki trousers that bulged at his paunch stuck out a hand. Martin grasped a large, squishy hand and limply shook it.

"Glad to have you with us," the man continued. "You must be a visitor." He nodded towards Martin's car, the license plate and the plate holder both proclaiming that this was a rented vehicle.

"Yes. Martin Salisbury, visiting from England."

They began to walk towards the large glass double doors at the entrance of the lodge.

"England, eh? Well, hope you like it here. Most people come in the winter for skiing, of course, but for my money it's better to visit in summer. So," his obese partner suddenly changed the subject, "do you play much chess?"

He held the door open for Martin.

"Thank you. No, not much. I just sort of dabble these days. It got to the point where machines started beating me routinely and I sort of lost interest really. I just thought that it might be a congenial way to spend an evening."

"Right you are, Martin. Nothing as sociable as a chess club. Here we are, then. The bar's in the room next door if you want a drink. Don't worry about it affecting your game, none of the rest of us will notice. It's more of a social evening than anything else."

"How often do you meet? And how many members are there?"

"Every Friday. Except when there's a town council meeting, when we postpone the club because a couple of our members are on the council and most of the rest of us go to the meetings. We have twenty five regular members and most of us show up if we're in town."

They had arrived in a medium-sized hall. Fluorescent lights were already switched on, augmenting the early-evening sunlight filtering in through the west-facing louvered windows. Ten tables were set up, boards and pieces ready for play, clocks wound, pads and pencils laid out for the players to record the moves. Half a dozen members were standing around, chatting, all but one with a drink in his hand. All the players were male.

Play started at 7:45, by which time there were fourteen club members in the hall, with Martin the odd fifteenth. Martin had scrutinized the membership ladder, and recognized only one name: Henry Clarence Madison, at the top. Matthew Chambers' name was absent from the list. A sixteenth person entered the hall, the judge himself. He vaguely waved an affable greeting to his friends and, not seeing Martin, made for the bar in the adjoining room.

"The ladder's informal." The voice at Martin's elbow was Winterson's. "Ah, I see that the judge is at the top now."

"Isn't he usually?"

"No." Winterson injected the monosyllable with a hint of polite grief. "Our best player died last Friday evening. Very sudden and completely unexpected. He'll be missed. He and the judge were in a class of their own. It'll be tough to find anyone to beat the judge now. Unless you're willing to take on the challenge?"

Martin laughed as best he could. "Me? No thanks. I'm too rusty; and besides, I never was much good even when I was in my prime. Which was a long time ago."

"Well, I've got a game already, otherwise I'd offer to play you. Come on, let me introduce you to some of the others and we'll find you an opponent."

He grasped Martin's arm with one pudgy hand, the other holding a glass which was already empty save for several blocks of ice and the remnants of a golden liquid sloshing around at the bottom.

Martin was introduced to several members of the club who greeted him with polite enthusiasm. He could not remember their names, which were shot at him in quick succession. One of the men, an insecure-looking, thin, youngish, bespectacled man going prematurely bald, offered him a game.

"I just started learning to play a few weeks ago, so I'm not very good; but I'm trying to learn." He encouraged and apologized in the same sentence.

As he and Martin located an empty table, Winterson whispered a little too loudly in Martin's ear, "You want to be careful of young Flinders, my friend. He looks like a brain, and in his case looks don't deceive. It's true that he's only just started playing and he's at the bottom of the ladder, but that's only because he hasn't yet played any official games. Rumor has it that he's deadly. Just a friendly warning."

Martin thanked Winterson and took a seat opposite "young Flinders." Judge Madison re-entered the room and without so much as a glance at his surroundings went immediately to a table where an elderly man in a florid yellow Hawaiian shirt sat waiting to start play, already absorbed in the placement of the chess pieces even though they had yet to be moved.

"Martin Salisbury, from England." He offered his hand to be shaken across the board.

"John Flinders."

The young man shook Martin's hand weakly and took a pawn of each color from the board. Martin guessed incorrectly and the board was turned so that he was black. Before he could start the clocks, Flinders made the first move, pawn to queen's pawn four.

Martin tried to dredge his memory. Was "young Flinders" merely a poor player, or was he attempting a standard queen's pawn opening? He moved a pawn to block.

Within ten minutes, all thought of his real task for the evening had been forgotten. It was no longer important. The room was deathly silent, apart from a quiet background of chairs moving, occasional coughs or exclamations, the unsynchronized ticking of eight clocks interrupted sporadically by the louder sound of a button being hit to stop one clock and start another. There would have been no opportunity for conversation even if Martin had remembered his objective.

But Martin was fighting for the game. He had already made two mistakes whose only consolation was that they had revealed the strength of his opponent. The first error had cost Martin a pawn and the second a weakening of his position in the central part of the board. The opening had been a white queen's pawn gambit refused, and as soon as the standard opening moves were over, Martin had found himself against a very able opponent.

For twenty minutes the game could have gone either way. The first of the other games was completed, and the two players from that game silently wandered around the games still in progress, pausing only briefly at Martin's board before finally settling on Winterson's board as the most interesting. But now, well in the middle game, although he was still down a pawn, Martin had regained control of the center of the board and he was quietly setting a trap which should leave white's queen's bishop in his hands in five moves.

The first check went to Flinders, but it was meaningless and accomplished nothing. Two moves later Martin captured the bishop as planned and looking over the board he realized that he now had a commanding position.

Flinders' play began to go downhill. He made two unforced errors on consecutive turns and Martin found himself ahead by two pawns and a rook. The board was beginning to clear and Flinders obviously realized that he was doomed to lose. Wordlessly, he calmly knocked his king horizontal.

"No point in prolonging the agony. Well done."

Martin accepted his opponent's hand, perspiration and all. The five onlookers who had gathered around drifted away, talking quietly amongst themselves, dividing between the two remaining tables where games were being fought to conclusion.

Both games were finished within ten minutes, and by common consent there was a general exodus to the bar.

Winterson explained to Martin: "We usually have a drink or two and then those of us who want to go back in for a second game. I must say that you rather made mincemeat of Flinders from what I saw. You should try someone higher up the ladder for your second game. Now, can I buy you a drink?"

Martin requested a beer, not that he wouldn't have been grateful for something stronger, but because he realized that this was his best, and perhaps his only, opportunity of the evening to extract information and gossip from people who were now taking seats around tables near the bar. While he waited for Winterson to get his drink, he sidled up to a group of players. One of the players turned, separated from the remainder of the group, and started to chat with Martin.

After the initial exchange of names — the other's was Harvey Brewster — and initial smalltalk about the weather and Martin's status as a visitor, Martin tried to guide the conversation to more substantive topics.

"I hear that you lost one of your members last week. He died unexpectedly?"

"Yes. Awful shock. Normally it would have been a club night, but it was canceled because of a city council meeting. He would have been here, otherwise. As it was, I guess he just collapsed at home.

"Chambers, his name was, Matthew Chambers. He was our best player. In fact, it was one of our other members who found him late in the evening. That black man over there" — he nodded in the direction of Judge Madison, who was standing with a group near the bar. The movement must have caught the judge's eye, for he looked up and his eyes met Martin's for a moment. There was a brief flare of recognition and Henry Clarence nodded at Martin. Martin realized that the judge would extricate himself from his conversation as soon as he could. He interrupted Brewster just as Winterson returned with the beer.

"Oh, Judge Madison. Yes, I've met him already. Seems like a nice enough fellow."

"Oh, sure enough," the other continued. "Likes his booze a bit too much for my taste, but they say he's a hell of a good judge, and he's certainly the only one of us who ever stood much of a chance against Matthew."

"Yes," interjected Winterson, "it's a pity he doesn't get to many meetings. He often goes away for the weekend. Quite a turn up for the books, really, him showing up here tonight. After all, he was in town last weekend as well. That was when he found Chambers' body, you know."

Martin nodded.

"He and Chambers had an ongoing chess game. They met here at the club, oh, it must be three or four years ago now, and it was immediately obvious that at last we'd found someone who could go up against the judge. Anyway, the two of them really hit it off and they set up a one-move-per-day game. That's what the judge was doing when he went up to Chambers' place and found the body, you know: he was going to get Chambers' latest move."

None of this was new, but at least they were talking about something related to Matthew's death. Martin tried to guide the conversation.

"So where does the judge go on his weekends out of town?"

Winterson shrugged. Brewster said, "Beats me. You can ask him if you like, he's coming over."

Martin greeted the judge quickly, to try to pre-empt him from saying the wrong thing.

"Good evening, Judge. I didn't realize you were a member here. Do you come every week?"

"Hello, Martin."

The speech was clear and the eyes shone, despite the fact that to Martin's knowledge the small, rather rotund man had consumed at least five drinks in the past two hours.

He continued, "I get here whenever I can. I hear that you dismantled our newest member."

The conversation was going to return to chess, which was fine with Martin. If the topic was chess, then the judge was unlikely to intimate to the others that Martin knew a lot more about Matthew Chambers than he had let on. And he had found out something which might be useful, which should keep Joanna happy.

"Luck, really, I think. It's so long since I played," Martin said.

"Well, I'm not so sure of that. Why don't you give me a game? Only the first game of the evening counts for the ladder, so those of us who want to stay on and play a second game can choose our opponents. I'd like to give you a game."

"You'll thrash me, no doubt. But yes, all right, if you like."

"OK. Let me just get a top up. You all right with your beer? Right, I'll meet you in the playing room in a minute."

Martin took his leave of Winterson and Brewster, and made his way back to the hall where two other matches were already in progress. He seated himself at a table and waited for Judge Madison to return from the bar.

Chapter 13

Felix Taylor was tired (which showed) and nervous (which did not). He was tired because he had spent the night unable to sleep. A successful, intelligent man, he found it hard simply to switch off his brain just because he needed rest, and so the scenarios had played themselves over and over as the night dragged on. It was the scenarios, not the insomnia, that made him nervous. They all ended badly.

It was not that he regretted his actions. No, never that. Rather, it was that whereas beforehand he had carefully rationalized that it was worth spending the remainder of his life in jail, more than a week had now passed and there was as yet little sign that the expected price would be demanded of him.

He had expected his actions to bear fruit quickly, as indeed they had. But then the inexplicable had happened. He was fully prepared to be taken into custody and charged within hours, or at most a few days. From then on things should have been simple: he would have explained himself to a lawyer — he could afford someone like Trenton Byers; after all, he had plenty saved and little use for money now — and put himself entirely in the hands of a professional who was being paid to get him off with as short a sentence as possible.

There was always the possibility, given the fickleness of juries, that he would get away with it entirely. But that was merely a hope which he had been careful to ensure never rose to the level of expectation.

But instead of all that there was... nothing.

Well, almost nothing.

The young detective had talked to him on Sunday on the telephone — on the *telephone*: he wasn't even worth a personal visit — about Chambers' state of health at the time he had died. The questions had been almost perfunctory and the entire conversation had lasted no more than five minutes. Taylor had rationalized away the lax nature of the investigation when he realized that the lab reports on the blood samples were probably not yet in the hands of the police. Things would change soon enough when those reports arrived.

They must have arrived on Thursday. That was the day the detective had called again. This time he made an appointment to meet the doctor in person, an appointment that unnerved Dr. Taylor because instead of a direct accusation the detective's threats were indirect and insubstantial.

Then another day passed without contact from the police.

What were they playing at? Could it really be possible that he might get away with it?

No; that was simply unbelievable. That would require too much incompetence. But why hadn't they confronted him directly yet?

Then the telephone call came, just as he was leaving the office yesterday. Detective Jones would like another half hour of Dr. Taylor's time as soon as convenient. Would first thing tomorrow be possible? Say at eight thirty in the morning? It shouldn't take more than half an hour, if that. Sorry for the inconvenience. Would it be all right to meet at Dr. Taylor's office?

And so he had passed the night fitfully. Now he was exhausted and, frankly, frightened. He glanced up at his office clock. Five minutes to go. Hell! Where was that detective? Why didn't he just come in and get it over with? Why should he have to suffer while a pipsqueak of a youngster, twenty years his junior, played cat-and-mouse games?

He probably learned all he knows about murder cases from watching television. He's going to act stupid and wait for me to make a mistake. Well, I'm not going to do his job for him. Maybe I'm guilty, but I'll be damned if I'm going to convict myself for him. If he wants to arrest me, he's going to have to find just cause for himself; I'm not going to give it to him.

Taylor, in a detached way, noticed that his anxiety was being replaced with anger with Detective Jones. *Good*, he thought, *it will keep me on my toes.*

Harry Jones was parked in an unmarked car out of sight of Dr. Taylor's office window. He still had not decided how to handle the interview and was becoming more nervous by the minute. The only decision he had made was that he was going to arrive at Dr. Taylor's office ten minutes late. With any luck, that would unnerve his quarry enough to make him careless; but he had no plans for what would happen after that. He looked at his watch for the third time in the space of a minute. 8:29. Seven more minutes, then he would leave the car and walk slowly to Taylor's office.

"So how'd it go last night?" Joanna asked.

She and Martin were walking side by side from the motel to the unpretentious old-style diner that had replaced *La Patisserie* as their customary breakfast venue. They had refrained from talking shop most of the way, but now that they were in sight of the squat wooden structure with the faded poster in the window advertising "Breakfast — all you can eat: $2.99 — real home cooking — free fill-ups" she thought it was time to ascertain how well her brother had done.

"Not before coffee," Martin replied.

They walked the final fifty yards in silence. Martin opened the door, which produced a flat jingling sound. As usual, there were half a dozen patrons scattered around the diner, regulars sipping their first (or second, or third) coffee of the day. The door closed itself behind them as he and Joanna steered themselves towards "their" table, next to the window, basking in the early morning sun.

They ordered without glancing at the menu: blueberry pancakes and maple syrup for him, "Pinetree Special Omelet" for her, and cups of coffee for them both.

Joanna tried again.

"Now will you tell me? How'd it go at the chess club?"

"Nothing doing. You first. Spill the beans. What were you up to last night?"

"OK. If you insist. Are you getting fed up of living in the motel?"

"Huh? Why? Where else is there? Do you have somewhere better in mind?"

"Let me put it this way: I lay claim to the master bedroom."

"What? Would you like to say something that makes sense?"

"I'm telling you what I did last night. I talked with Harry Jones, and he agrees with me that there's no reason why we shouldn't live in Matthew's house for the duration of our stay. I didn't tell Harry, of course, but I'd like to go through that place carefully myself. And it seemed stupid to be paying daily room charges at the motel when between us we own a very nice mountainside house just outside of town.

"Harry says that as far as he's concerned we can move in immediately. That way we'll kill two birds with one stone: no more motel rates and I get to take as long as I like to go through Matthew's things. But, as I said, I'm taking Matthew's room. You get the spare room."

Martin laughed.

He said, "That's a great idea. Let's move in later today. And now for what I learned last night...."

He was interrupted by the arrival of their food and coffee, and for perhaps a minute both of them were too preoccupied to speak.

"First thing," Martin eventually began. "For what it's worth, Matthew was the star of the chess club. The only person who ever beat him was Judge Madison, and that happened only rarely. Matthew really was pretty good; the judge thrashed me last night even after he was thoroughly intoxicated. Anyway, that's the first point. The second is that the chess club meets weekly, on Friday evenings, except on nights when there's a council meeting like there was last week. And third, perhaps the most interesting snippet of information was something about the judge himself.

"Apparently, he misses quite a few meetings because he often goes out of town at weekends. No one seemed to know where he goes. I asked several people as surreptitiously as I could without seeming suspicious. I even asked Henry Clarence himself, but the question slid past him as if I hadn't asked it. I did check and everyone was most definite that Matthew usually attended the meetings, even when Madison was absent, so wherever the judge went, it wasn't with Matthew. Still, it does raise a question doesn't it?"

Joanna nodded enthusiastically. "It does indeed."

She fell silent as she wolfed her omelet, lost in thought.

153

The office door was barely ajar, and Felix Taylor could not see out into the corridor beyond. He heard the sound of footsteps, followed by a brisk knock on the door. The clock over the door read nineteen minutes to the hour.

"Come in," he said.

He sounded hoarse. He hoped that the detective would notice neither the frog in his throat nor the sweat that had erupted on his forehead.

Detective Jones walked into the room. With khaki slacks and a short-sleeved green Aertex shirt he could have been mistaken for a tourist, except for the presence of a dark notebook held firmly in his right hand.

As the detective was closing the door, Dr. Taylor rubbed his palms against the legs of his trousers. The perspiration left a dark smudge. He rose; they shook hands and sat. *Will he get straight to the point this time, or will he continue to play cat-and-mouse?* wondered the doctor.

Harry appraised the man across the desk. He looked tired and nervous. Still, one had to be fair. Even the most innocent of people get nervous when being interviewed by a policeman. *Should I get it over with or beat about the bush and see what comes out?* the detective wondered.

He said, "Thank you for your time, Dr. Taylor. I'm sorry to intrude again, especially on a Saturday morning. It's good of you to meet me like this. As I said on the phone last night, it concerns the Matthew Chambers case. I want to thank you for being so forthright in our previous conversations and for letting me have a copy of Mr. Chambers' medical file."

"You're very welcome, Detective Jones. It's always unfortunate when someone is suddenly struck down in the prime of life. Is something amiss? I must say that it seems a bit... what shall I say?... out of the ordinary that you're still asking questions."

"I'm afraid I'm not at liberty to say anything about that, sir. I'm sure you understand. Anyway, I was wondering if there was anything you might like to add to your previous statement?"

As he was talking, Harry opened his notebook and extracted a pen from his shirt pocket. He clicked the pen, ready to write. His manner was one of someone expecting a reply.

Dr. Taylor became even more nervous. Obviously, the detective expected that he *did* have something to add. Desperately, the doctor wondered what reply he could give. His mind, racing, was blank; he could think of nothing that was not incriminating.

He shook his head. "No, nothing I can think of, I don't think."

So much for that, thought Harry. Still, it had been worth a try; the doctor was suffering an attack of anxiety about *something*.

"I'd like to clear up a couple of points to make sure I've got them straight. According to the medical file, and I think you said this before, Mr. Chambers became a patient of yours about eighteen months ago. Is that correct?"

Dr. Taylor looked vague and uncertain at the new line of questioning. What on earth was the detective playing at?

"Yes. His doctor had been Dr. Henry, who was also in this practice. Dr. Henry died of a heart attack, so Matthew needed a new doctor. I knew Matthew slightly from the Rotary Club so I guess that's why he chose me to be his new doctor. Diabetics need frequent checkups, so they don't generally like to be without a physician for any length of time. As to the exact date, I don't rightly remember. But wasn't all that information in the file?"

The detective ignored the question.

"So you and he knew one another before he became your patient?"

"Yes, slightly. As I said, we were both members of the Pinetree Rotary Club. We didn't really know one another very well, though, just nodding acquaintances really. He seemed nice enough." He shrugged.

"And so, when Mr. Chambers needed to change doctors because of Dr. Henry's death, he chose you because he already knew you from the Rotary?"

"Yes, I imagine so. It happens quite frequently."

"Now, let's see, according to the medical record, that was in February last year. How long had you been practicing in Pinetree at that time, Dr. Taylor?"

"I arrived in November, 1990, so that means I'd been here a little more than two years."

"And where were you before that?"

"I was in practice for twenty years in Oak Park, Illinois. My wife died, you see, and I decided that a move would be best for me. I heard about Pinetree from someone so I came and looked it over. I fell in love with the place and decided to sell up and move out here."

"I see. Sorry to hear about your wife. Oak Park; let's see, that's near Chicago, isn't it?"

"Yes. It's a suburb, really."

"Were you aware that Mr. Chambers resided in Chicago before moving to Pinetree?"

"Did he? He never mentioned it to me."

The fact that the doctor had not directly answered the question was not lost on the detective. He paused for several seconds, then decided on a simple, frontal attack.

"Dr. Taylor" — he kept his voice level, his eyes fixed on the doctor's face — "had you ever seen Mr. Chambers before you moved to Pinetree?"

This time the evasion was more obvious.

"What is this? Some kind of interrogation?"

The doctor's eyes were locked on the detective's. They contained no hint of any emotion other than righteous hurt. If anything, the doctor seemed more relaxed than at the beginning of the interview.

"I'm just trying to establish facts, that's all...."

"I'm sorry. I just don't see the point of all this." Dr. Taylor continued, "Anyway, in answer to your question, Mr. Chambers and I had never met before I joined the Rotary Club here."

Harry Jones considered this response carefully. It answered a question, but not exactly the one he had asked. There was a difference between seeing and meeting. *You aren't going to lie to me because that might set you up for trouble later*, he thought. *You're hiding something all right, but I'm not going to get it out of you here unless I push harder than I'm willing to do right now.*

"OK, Dr. Taylor. Thanks for everything. I think that'll be all for now. Sorry to take up your time like this."

He decided, on the spur of the moment, to drop one last bombshell.

"Murder investigations are always rather stressful on everyone involved."

There was a silence of fully five seconds before the doctor responded.

"Murder? What? Mr. Chambers was murdered? You're joking. Aren't you? How?"

"Sorry, Dr. Taylor, I'm not at liberty to say anything more just at the moment. Anyway, thanks again."

His revelation had produced nothing more than normal surprise from the doctor. Another trick tried, another trick failed. The detective stood and extended his hand across the desk. The two men shook hands and the detective left the room.

Dr. Taylor leaned back in his chair while the sounds of footsteps faded down the corridor and let out a sigh of nervous relief. He opened his desk drawer and removed a photograph. He looked at her face.

"We can do this," he said.

"Nice house. Now that we're here, what are we going to do?"

Martin was leaning back on the sofa, a glass of iced water in his hand, looking across the expanse of what had been Matthew Chambers' living room.

Joanna was sitting cross-legged on the hardwood floor, pawing her way through the day's edition of the *Pinetree Reporter*. She turned the final page, glanced at the full-page advertisement for a local supermarket, and looked up at her brother.

"Nothing there. Well, Martin, I suggest, as it's nearly lunch time, that we find ourselves somewhere to eat before we get to work this afternoon and rip this place apart looking for something that our detective friend overlooked."

"Good idea. How about the *Top of the Mountain*? I've never been there and it's supposed to be a wonderful place to eat."

"Great. Let's go."

They hurried out the house and made their way carefully down the narrow driveway in Martin's rented Camry. They arrived at the road just as a large white car was pulling away from the mailbox at the end of the drive. A handwritten sign on which the words "U.S. Mail" were scrawled stood on the car's back shelf. A yellow flashing light was between the sign and the window, partially obscuring the words.

"The mail. I hadn't thought of that. Hang on a minute."

Joanna jumped out the car, hurried over to the battered box and extracted the contents. There were about two inches of mail, most of it, it was obvious at a glance, of that peculiarly American genre known as "junk mail" — colorful flyers sent out *en masse* in the hopes of persuading the recipient to part with money.

She began to sort through the remaining mail as Martin pulled away from the mailbox. By the time they reached the small parking area in front of the Skislope shopping mall, the mail had been sorted into two piles on Joanna's lap: the larger pile was colorful, glossy and utterly uninteresting; the smaller contained three letters addressed to Matthew by name and a single picture postcard addressed to Martin.

"Yours, I think," she offered the postcard as Martin killed the engine.

He took it and immediately recognized the handwriting. A wave of guilt swept over him. In the happiness of being reunited with his sister and the excitement of puzzling over his cousin's death, he had barely thought about Davina.

He examined the photograph. "Kenya — Home of Wild Africa" the card announced over a color photograph showing zebras, giraffe and elephants apparently living peaceably within a few hundred feet of one another at a watering hole.

He turned the card over once more and had to smile when he saw that the card was "Printed by Henry Solbourne and Sons, Liverpool."

"Who's it from?" Joanna asked.

"Davina. Here, you read it."

He handed the card to his sister. The message was dated six days earlier.

> Dearest Martin
>
> Hope you've been enjoying camping in the wilds with Matthew. I've been enjoying ditto with Roger. Photos going v. well. Will be finished early at this rate.
>
> Love,
> A secret admirer.

Joanna handed the card back to Martin.

"You miss her?"

"I hadn't, up till now. But yes, now that you mention it, I do. Very much."

"Who's Roger?"

"Roger? A raving poofter, or so she claims. She just put that in to make me jealous."

"You hope."

"I hope."

They got out the car and began to walk towards the ski lift.

"You going to marry her?"

Martin would have forgiven his sister if there had been a note of warning or even of condemnation in her question, given her sorry experience of marriage. But it was just a simple enquiry.

"If she'll let me," he said. "I ask her with a regularity bordering on the monotonous. So far she's always refused, but she urges me to keep trying."

They arrived at the ski lift. The operator took $4 from them and within seconds they were ensconced in the gondola.

The town fell quickly away. Ahead, the mountain looked as tall as ever, but within seconds they could see the entire town spread out behind them.

The dull, low, background sounds that accompany the business of life in the late twentieth century faded away.

There was a rattle as the gondola passed a cable support, then peace fell. There was no birdsong, only the quiet susurration of a slight wind. The trees beneath them moved silently. No words were necessary; brother and sister looked around and marveled in silence, absorbing the beauty.

The journey came to an end fifteen minutes later with a rattling bustle. They found themselves standing outside the gondola, looking across a short rise to a building painted smartly in white and electric blue, a wall of glass looking out across the valley, *The Top of The Mountain* emblazoned boldly across a signboard on the roof of the building in letters three feet high.

The air here was cooler and noticeably thinner than down in town. Nearly eleven thousand feet above sea level there was conspicuously less oxygen. They walked slowly up the gradient towards the restaurant. They were winded by the time they reached it.

A young greeter smiled and took them to a table overlooking the valley.

The town was obscured by the rise up which they had walked. But the sight of the Rockies that formed the backdrop took what remained of their breath away. Even now, in the middle of summer, snow glistened dirty-white on the peaks of the taller mountains. The sky was a deep blue, the kind that seems to be ubiquitous on postcards but is rarely seen in real life. A few puffy clouds were scattered across the sky, their whiteness serving to emphasize the blueness in which they were embedded.

They ordered. Joanna removed the rest of Matthew's personal mail from her handbag and slit it open. It was a disappointing collection of the commonplace: a newsletter from the Rotary Club announcing the program for yesterday's meeting; notification of the annual Ice

Cream Social at St. Peter's Church; and an innocent letter from an ex-colleague in Chicago, Fred Gilbert by name, obviously created on company time on a day when he was bored.

"Nothing there," Martin said.

"No. We should call this Fred Gilbert in Chicago just to make sure he's on the up-and-up, but no, I think you're right. Nothing there."

"So then, Detective Sergeant Salisbury, where exactly are we in this case? If there is a case."

"Oh yes, Mr. Vice President Salisbury, there's a case all right. We just don't know for sure what the crime is. Personally, I'm betting on murder. And where are we? Well, I know that I didn't do it, and I'm reasonably sure that you didn't, but it could have been anyone else."

"You aren't still playing that game, are you? Come on, you must have some theories."

"I do. But first things first. Here's the food."

It looked delicious and tasted even better. It would have been hard to believe that the word "spectacular" could justifiably be applied to a club sandwich, but that was the adjective Martin used. Joanna had to agree: her Caesar's salad was equally superlative.

"You're not getting away with changing the subject so easily," nagged Martin after a while. "What's going on in that mind of yours, Jo?"

"Look, you must have seen plenty of cops and robbers shows. Why don't you tell me?"

"Actually, no, I rarely watch television," Martin said. "But let's see now. One needs to find motive, opportunity and method, isn't that the way it works?"

"Yes, that's fair enough. Why don't you take a stab at them, in any order you like?"

Martin thought for nearly a minute before continuing.

"OK. To my mind it's the opportunity that narrows it down the most."

"Precisely."

"The motive could be almost anything, and in any case we probably haven't yet found it. And the method, well, that hardly stands out as being obvious, does it?"

"Go on."

"So that just leaves us with the question of who had the opportunity of doing in poor old Matthew."

"And the answer is?"

"Well, I suppose the judge could have done it. In fact, when one thinks about it, anyone who wasn't at the council meeting could have done it."

"Nope. I don't agree."

"Why not?"

"You first. What else can you deduce, Mr. Holmes?"

"I give up. Your turn."

"Pretty feeble, I have to say. Suppose we limit ourselves to those who knew Matthew well or who stood to gain from his death. Even though it could, theoretically, have been almost anyone, it actually takes an awful lot of guts to go through with a premeditated murder. This wasn't a crime of the moment; there was no sign of a struggle, at least according to the judge's testimony. Certainly there was no blood at the scene and the police found nothing to cause them to question the judge's story.

"So, if Matthew died at someone's hand, it was premeditated. Murder, not manslaughter. And the mere fact that we are relatively clueless about everything to do with his death actually gives us a pretty big clue: whoever did this was nobody's fool. This took brains. Which is not to say that the exact timing of Matthew's death was premeditated. It could have been that someone was merely waiting for a particular set of circumstances to occur before putting a plan into action."

"Like a Friday night with a council meeting?"

"For example." Joanna shrugged.

"You said 'his plan.' Do you have reason to believe that whoever did it was male?"

"No. Sorry. I was just being generic. I have no idea if the killer — if there was one — is male or female. Now, think about the scene of his death. What can you tell from that?"

"I don't know.... I suppose it's important that there was no struggle, and that his death wasn't caused by something external — there was no gun, no heavy object, nothing of that kind. Even if he was murdered by a friend, it's hard to imagine there wouldn't be evidence of some violence."

"Which leads us to what conclusion?"

"Er...."

"Think. You were always supposed to be the clever one."

"Er... oh!" Martin's face lit up. "The murder was performed somewhere else entirely."

"Explain."

"Something was given to Matthew, some kind of a drug, at some other time and place. Its effect just happened to manifest itself on that Friday evening."

"Good boy; you'll make a detective yet."

"I hadn't thought about that before."

"That's all right. I wasn't sure about it until I had another chance to look over the living room this morning. If there had been any kind of a struggle, something would have been knocked over. Or there would have been marks on the body. But you've ignored the biggest clue of all."

"I give up. Just tell me."

"The candy. My mind keeps coming back to that. I'm more and more convinced that Matthew's murder was committed somewhere other than in the living room. He might have died there — probably did, in fact — but I don't think he was murdered there."

"So you don't think it was the judge?"

"I didn't quite say that. All I said was that the real murder, if it *was* murder, occurred somewhere other than the place where the body was found. Anyway, who do you think did it?"

Martin shrugged. "Don't know. Who do *you* think it?"

"You really want to know?"

"Yes."

"Well, you won't be happy with this. I'm still worried about the judge. He got $10,000 out of it, after all. I'd love to know *why* Matthew left him that money. That's an awfully big thank you for a few games of chess. And where does he go on weekends? I won't be happy until we've resolved those questions."

"Well, maybe we'll find the answer this afternoon, going through the house once more."

"Maybe." Joanna did not sound optimistic.

Chapter 14

Harry Jones was exhausted. As far as he could tell, his afternoon had been thoroughly unproductive, which only increased his fatigue.

Ten telephone calls had been made to Matthew Chambers' closest acquaintances, and not one of them had recollected ever seeing Matthew with a woman in any but the most proper of circumstances. To each person in turn he had put the difficult question: "To the best of your recollection, did Mr. Chambers ever give you cause to think that he might be homosexual?" The answers had been uniformly brusque and negative.

No one had answered the Healys' home phone, but he had reached the mayor at his store. Bill Healy's replies were no different from the others'. On his list, he placed a checkmark next to the Healys. There was only one person left to ask. He dialed, and the phone was answered on the fifth ring. For reasons not wholly connected to the case he preferred to conduct this interview in person.

"Good afternoon, Miss Freeman. This is Detective Jones, from the police."

"Good afternoon, Detective Jones."

"I was wondering if it would be possible for me to see you? I have a couple of questions regarding Mr. Chambers that I thought you might be able to help me with. They won't take long."

"Well, I'm not planning on going out. You can come to my house."

"Thank you. In twenty minutes or so, if that's all right?"

"Certainly. I'll expect you then. You know where I live?"

"Yes. I have your address. So I'll see you in a few minutes. Thank you."

"You're welcome. Goodbye."

In deference to neighborhood gossip, Harry drove his personal car. The sight of a police car standing outside Kathleen's house would doubtless raise suspicions in neighbors' minds. And if there was one person he did not suspect of killing Matthew Chambers, it was Kathleen Freeman.

A gray Porsche was parked in front of Kathleen's house, distinctly out of place in the rundown neighborhood. With a twinge of disappointment, the detective guessed that it must belong to the boyfriend.

The boyfriend — six feet tall, a shock of dark hair, cropped mustache and commanding air — opened the door.

"Come in, come in. Kathleen's expecting you. I'm Jim Billings."

The detective followed him into the diminutive living room, where music was playing. Kathleen arrived from the kitchen and reduced the volume.

"Anything to drink, Detective Jones?" she offered as he took a seat.

"A glass of iced water would be fine, Miss Freeman. And you can call me Harry."

"I'll be right back. And you must call me Kathleen."

He settled down and whiled away two minutes in silence as Billings took a seat near him and the two men proceeded to ignore each other.

Kathleen returned with a glass and handed it to the detective. She sat opposite him. She crossed her legs, and her skirt climbed well above the knees of her tanned legs. A sexual thought flitted momentarily through the detective's mind before he could suppress it. He began with a polite question to set her at ease.

"Miss Freeman... Kathleen, have you found a job yet? I wouldn't think there are many jobs for legal secretaries in Pinetree."

"No, there aren't. But I've been lucky. Jim here is a lawyer in Steamboat and his firm has agreed to take me on. I start next week. So all in all it hasn't been as bad as it might have been. At least, for me," she added, recognizing that it could hardly have been worse for her erstwhile employer.

"I'm glad you've been able to arrange something so quickly. It doesn't always work out that way. Anyway, I'm sorry to intrude like

164

this, I just wanted to ask you a couple of questions. But before I start, I must ask you both to keep this conversation in strict confidence."

There were two murmurs of assent.

The detective continued, "I must tell you that we are now treating this as a case of murder."

Kathleen's mouth dropped open and, underneath the Colorado tan she turned pale.

She was incredulous. "But who... and why?"

"Those are the questions, aren't they? We were hoping you might be able to shed some light on the answers for us."

"Me? I don't think so."

"You knew Mr. Chambers as well as anyone. Possibly better. As far as you know, can you think of anyone who held a grudge against him?"

"Enough to kill him? No. No one would do a thing like that."

"There we believe you are wrong. Now, it is only natural that you are upset. But I must ask you to think carefully. Did Mr. Chambers ever give offense to anyone? He was a lawyer, and he practiced in town for four years. In that time there must have been *someone*."

Kathleen considered carefully before answering. The music stopped at the end of a track; another track began.

She shook her head. "No, I really don't think there was. His business was confined to wills, real estate closings, occasional tax advice, that sort of thing. Not the kind of things one might kill for. And anyway, I never heard anyone say they were displeased with his services."

"Never? In the entire four years?"

"No, never. He was a good lawyer and a friendly person. He liked to get on well with everyone. I never ever heard him say a bad word about anyone. Who would want to kill him?"

Suddenly, she seemed on the verge of tears. Her fiancé rose and knelt uncomfortably next to her chair. His hand lay gently on her arm and remained there for the rest of the interview.

"I'm sorry, Miss Freeman. I'm sorry about Mr. Chambers' death, and I'm sorry to have to distress you by asking you these questions. But it is important. I must ask you these questions, distasteful though they are. We want to catch whoever did this."

Kathleen nodded wordlessly. She sniffed back her tears and said, "Yes, yes, I see. Of course. Anything I can do help. I'll be all right now."

"So you are quite sure that Mr. Chambers had no enemies?"

She nodded again. "Yes. Quite sure."

"How well did you know Mr. Chambers?"

"What do you mean?"

"Well, you worked in his office for four years, but even so you might not know much about his private life."

"I see.... Well, he didn't strike me as secretive; but you're right, our paths rarely crossed socially. He was a Rotarian. I'm just a secretary, and Jim lives in Steamboat, so I spend a lot of time there. So we didn't run into each other very often outside of work. He was fond of chess and somewhat less fond of bridge; that's about all I know."

"Thank you. Now, I'm sorry to have to ask you this, but was there ever anything between you and Mr. Chambers?"

"You mean... sexually?"

"Yes, er... was your relationship strictly business, or did you and he ever have, shall we say, any romantic engagements? You are, after all, a very attractive young woman and it would be hard to blame Mr. Chambers for making a pass at you."

"No, there was never anything like that between us. He knew about Jim, of course, but even before Jim, Matthew was always the perfect gentleman."

Harry wondered if she were telling the truth. Her fiancé's presence might have affected her answer; he had to trust Kathleen that even if she lied now, she would call him later to give him the truth as soon as she was able. He kicked himself for not asking Jim to leave the room. Oh well, too late now.

"Was there ever any indication during the years you worked for Mr. Chambers that he was involved with any other women? You must have screened most of his calls."

"Yes, all his incoming calls went through me. And no, as far as I know, there was never any particular woman. There would be times, of course, when a woman would call several times a day for a week or two, but as far as I could tell it was always strictly business. The same happened with men as well. The only woman who was a fairly frequent social caller was Mrs. Healy, the mayor's wife. Matthew was a frequent guest at the Healys', so she called him quite often, setting up the next meal I suppose."

"And when was the last time she called him? Do you recall?"

"Let's see... that would be the day Matthew died. He told me he was eating an early supper with the Healys that evening, and she called to leave a message for me to remind him when he got back from Rotary. I don't remember whether or not he ever returned the call, but I imagine he did; he was usually punctilious about returning phone calls. Most lawyers are."

"Thank you. And one more question, if you don't mind. Was there ever any indication that Mr. Chambers might have been homosexual? I'm sorry for asking, but we need to know."

Kathleen opened her mouth, ready to answer in the negative. But she closed her mouth again and gave the question more thought. It was not something she had ever thought about before. And it *would* explain Matthew's lack of involvement with women. After all, he had been a rather attractive man. But even after ransacking her memory, she decided that there was no evidence to support the conclusion.

"No. I'm sorry. If he was gay I never saw any indication of it."

"But you can't say that he definitely wasn't?"

"No. I'm sorry. He seemed to treat everyone pretty much the same. I guess that's what they call 'politically correct' these days isn't it? But with him it was just his nature. Didn't he have any close friends you could ask? Surely someone must know. What about the judge?"

"Yes. Of course. I'll ask him." Harry rose from his chair. "Anyway, I mustn't take up any more of your time. Thank you for your cooperation."

"You're welcome. Anything I can do, don't hesitate to let me know."

"Thank you. And you'll let us know your telephone number when you move to Steamboat, won't you? Just in case we need to reach you."

"Oh, I can give that to you now. I'll be with Jim."

Harry jotted down the number. Closing his notebook, he thanked her again and let her lead him out of the house while her fiancé hovered possessively in the background.

On his way home, Harry stopped at a public telephone outside a supermarket. It was nearly half past five. There was one more task remaining for the day, one simple act whose sole purpose was to rattle his prime suspect.

The telephones rang throughout Dr. Taylor's house. The physician was seated at the desk in his home office, barely a foot from the closest phone. His head was in his hands.

Felix Taylor was becoming more and more depressed at the situation in which he found himself. He raised his head and looked at the telephone. It continued to ring mercilessly. Eventually, he reached out and wearily picked up the instrument.

"Dr. Taylor." The physician's flat intonation gave no indication of the jumbled state of his thoughts.

"Ah, good evening, Dr. Taylor. I'm glad I caught you."

A tight knot formed in the pit of the doctor's stomach. He recognized the voice.

"This is Detective Jones. I was wondering if you had any plans to go out of town over the next few days?"

Plans? No, Felix Taylor had no plans. He had no plans even for supper tonight, never mind where he might go in the course of the next week. Why couldn't the detective just get it over with?

"No." He cleared his throat and tried again, "No, Detective Jones, I don't expect to be traveling at all."

"OK. Thank you, Doctor Taylor. If you change your mind and do decide to leave town, for whatever reason, please inform me first. You may leave a message for me at any time at the department. Thank you."

The detective hung up without giving the doctor time to respond.

After helloing a couple of times into the disconnected instrument, Felix Taylor re-seated the receiver in the cradle and replaced his head in his hands. An even deeper despair overwhelmed him.

Chapter 15

"Any idea what we're looking for?" Martin asked his sister.

"None whatsoever. We probably won't even know we've found it when we see it. Just go through the house looking at everything. Turn things upside down; look inside everything. The chances are that it won't be obvious. As like as not, it'll be something that neither of us suspects, something completely ordinary; it'll only become important when one of us fits it with something else, something apparently unrelated. It's like those cryptic crosswords you like so much. Or one of those Rubik's Cubes: chaos will suddenly turn to order."

She paused a moment, then added, "Of course, that's if we're lucky. If we're unlucky, we won't find anything at all."

"Well, that'll certainly be true if we don't get on with it."

The two heaved themselves out of their chairs. "Music while we work?" offered Martin.

"Sure. Some kind of rock, if you don't mind. It was one of my ways of escaping Kevin."

For a moment, a cloud descended.

"Want to talk about it?"

She shook her head.

Martin nodded, only partially understanding, and crossed to the stereo. He cast his eyes over the collection. It was limited to compact discs: no cassettes and, surprisingly, no vinyl records. It was hard to find them in stores now, of course, but still most people, especially of his generation, had a substantial investment in the old black plastic.

He commented to Joanna who was standing at a window, watching a hummingbird hover under the eaves.

She said, "That's exactly the sort of thing that I mean. It probably means nothing more than that when he moved here from Chicago, he got rid of all his old records. But maybe there's more to it than that, although I doubt it. And while you're there, you should open up all the CD cases to make sure there's nothing inside. Maybe it was suicide and he'd been depressed for the past few months and he used to write down his thoughts when he listened to music. Or maybe he was blackmailing someone with photographs and he hid the negatives in a CD case. Who knows? It could be anything."

She seemed undaunted by the possibilities, which seemed to Martin to multiply without end. He looked over the collection.

"Must have thousands of dollars invested in CDs."

This time he evoked no response from his sister, who was absorbed at the window, watching the hummingbird's dartings, her thoughts obviously far away.

His eyes found the CD almost of their own accord. There was no decision to be made. It was not what she had asked for, but even so he knew it was the *right* one.

He turned the stereo on and popped the disc into the caddy. Seconds later the first quiet notes floated through the room.

Joanna turned to him and without any warning she burst into tears. He hurried to her and they held one another tightly, crying unashamedly. The sound of Vaughan Williams' *Fantasia on a Theme by Thomas Tallis* continued. It evoked much the same memory in both the siblings, made all the more painful and poignant for Joanna by the barrenness of the intervening years and her own, failed marriage.

It was their parents' favorite music. The siblings remembered arguments between their parents when they were young. Nothing out of the ordinary: the common, minor flare-ups that occur in every family when nerves are frayed or tired. And always the same ending: one parent or the other, deciding that enough was enough, would go to the record player and put on an old recording of this piece of music.

It was, for both, oddly disconcerting to hear the piece without the intrusion of surface hiss, the sharp thud which occurred just as the theme was stated for the first time, the clicks 1.8 seconds apart two minutes into the piece. It was as if the CD were oddly defective.

The last time that Joanna had heard the record was only hours before she had eloped with Kevin. The argument between her parents had started late, after she had gone to bed, and it had continued longer than usual. She did not know the exact reason for the argument, but she had little doubt that it was something to do with her and Kevin. The music signaling the end of the argument had not started until half past midnight. Three and a half hours later she was standing outside the house, watching for the glare of headlights that would take her half a world away to a new life with the man she loved.

———————

Martin was dispirited. For nearly five hours, he and his sister had worked on tearing Matthew Chambers' house to pieces. Every room had been searched as thoroughly as a detective sergeant knew how. Any object that might conceal a piece of paper had been moved, opened, searched. From every book in Matthew's meager library to every jar of herbs in the kitchen — everything had been looked at, shaken, opened, returned to its place.

Now, exhausted, they reclined in the living room. The buzzing sound of amplified hummingbird wings filled the room, courtesy of microphones installed by Matthew near the feeders under the eaves. The sky was beginning to darken as the evening drew in. On side tables next to their chairs were drinks, the ice nearly melted.

"Any ideas?" Martin asked.

"No. But it's here somewhere. There's got to be something."

"Maybe it was a natural death after all."

Joanna shook her head.

"No. Every time I begin to think that, his empty pockets and that poisoned capsule force me to reconsider. No. It's here and we've missed it, that's all." She leaned back and gazed up at the cathedral ceiling. "You know, it must cost a fortune to heat this place in winter."

"Yeah, I guess so. Although he usually keeps a fire in the fireplace; at least, he did when I was here the winter before last. Actually, it's not as bad as it looks. Most of the rest of the house has ceilings and...."

They said it together: "The attic!"

Joanna jumped to her feet.

"Where's the entrance?"

Martin pondered. "I don't know; but there's got to be one."

171

It took them two minutes to find it: a square hole cut into the ceiling in the closet of the master bedroom .

"We'll need a ladder to get up there; I think there's one in the garage."

The phone rang. Joanna left Martin staring up at the etched square and picked up the telephone by the side of the bed.

"Hello?"

"Hello, Jo? It's Harry Jones."

"Good evening, Harry."

Martin's head swiveled and he looked questioningly at his sister.

Joanna continued, "What can I do for you?"

"I was sort of at a loose end this evening and I was wondering if you and your brother would like to go out somewhere to dinner. We could talk over the case, or just be sociable, whichever you prefer."

"We'd be glad to. Martin and I ate at the *Top of the Mountain* at lunchtime, so I don't think either of us is up for a big meal, but sure, we'd be happy to join you."

"OK. How about..." — there was a pause while Harry's mind raced through the possibilities — "...*Dino's*? It's on Princeton Avenue, just past the Skislope Mall."

Joanna lifted her mouth away from the mouthpiece and spoke to her brother: "*Dino's*, near the Skislope Mall; do you know where it is?"

"Sure. I've seen it."

To Harry she said, "OK. We know it. What time?"

"About twenty minutes?"

"OK. We'll leave right away. See you there."

She put down the phone. "Harry Jones wants to have supper with us. Maybe we can all pick one another's brains."

"What about the attic?"

"It'll keep until tomorrow. Besides which, we should really wait until daylight before exploring up there. And if we haven't found anything, we don't need to feel guilty about not telling our detective friend about it, do we?"

Martin shrugged. "I suppose not. But if he's going to share his thoughts with us, the least we should do is tell him."

"You're too honest, Martin. What kind of a businessman are you? Anyway, we'll see how it goes. Now, come on. I promised him we'd be there in twenty minutes."

Harry was embarrassed. A thirty-five-year-old bachelor, he was not used to having visitors to his apartment, and it was especially embarrassing that one his guests on this occasion was a beautiful woman who probably outranked him.

He fumbled with the key, partly through embarrassment, partly because his motor functions had been palpably affected by the three large glasses of dark beer he had consumed with dinner. At last the key slid into the lock. He turned it and pushed the door open.

He walked into the apartment ahead of the others, casting his eye around nervously. It was not as bad as it might have been. What could be seen of the kitchen was fairly clean, and he had vacuumed the floor only two days ago, so there were fewer crumbs and dirty marks on the carpet than there might have been. He stood to one side to let the others in.

"Come in and take a seat." He gestured towards the small living area.

His guests walked into the apartment. They kept their thoughts to themselves. Martin swept his eyes once around the apartment and thought, *There, but for the grace of Davina, go I*, and Joanna merely decided that Harry needed a woman's touch around the place. They settled themselves, Joanna on the cheap, hard sofa, Martin in a chair whose green upholstery clashed with everything else in the room.

Outside, lights were scattered in the crepuscule of the midsummer evening. The black shape of the mountain south of town obscured much of the gray sky.

"Drink?" Harry offered. "I only have beer as far as alcohol goes. But there's coffee, and I think I have some orange juice."

Joanna accepted the coffee, Martin declined the offer entirely. They were left to their own devices while Harry disappeared into the kitchen to prepare Joanna's coffee.

The room was barren of interest. There was nothing that reflected the interests (whatever they were) of its occupant. No paintings hung on the walls, only a light beige paint. There were no bookcases, no stereo, not even any photographs. A room belonging to a lonely man who was rarely home. Joanna empathized.

Thinking their quite different thoughts, Martin and Joanna were silent until their host returned with Joanna's coffee.

He sat on a hard chair, completing an uncomfortable triangle.

"So, you've been listening to me all evening. What about you? What are your thoughts?"

He looked at Joanna.

Joanna noticed Harry's glance move from her face to her legs. She uncrossed them while she considered what to say.

Over dinner, Harry had done most of the talking. He had brought them up to date anent his suspicions but lack of hard evidence against Felix Taylor. He had also shared his plan for trying to unnerve the doctor.

Joanna had listened, interrupting only occasionally when she required elucidation on some point, but she had offered no thoughts of her own until the end of the meal when she had rather clumsily asked about the thoroughness of Harry's search of Matthew's house and discovered that the attic had not been examined because, like her and Martin, Harry had simply never thought of it. Initially, Harry had wanted to be present when they searched, but they had finally agreed simply to let him see anything that she and Martin found up there. There was no point in all three of them wasting the morning.

Harry had made it clear at dinner that the doctor, Felix Taylor, was his principal suspect. Joanna was less sure.

"So your money's on the doctor, then?" she asked.

"I think so, don't you?"

"I don't know. I'd been wondering about the judge, but I'm not at all sure."

"The judge? Henry Clarence Madison? Why do you think he was involved?"

Harry was clearly interested in the notion that such a respected member of the community might have been involved in something as unsavory as a murder.

"Two things, really. Firstly, there's the matter of the $10,000 that Matthew left him. It would be interesting to know what the judge's financial situation is and why Matthew left him such a large sum of money. It may just have been friendship, I suppose" — Joanna obviously thought this unlikely — "but still it's a lot of money to leave a chess partner. And then there's the question of what he does with himself on Friday evenings when he's not at the chess club. I know it's probably got nothing to do with anything, but still I'd like to know. Mmmm, good coffee," she complimented its maker.

In his somewhat inebriated state, the friendly smile she threw at Harry pleased him more than her interest in the Chambers case. But he forced himself to concentrate.

"I'll call on the judge tomorrow," he said, "and ask him those very questions. It shouldn't take long to check out his answers. But what do you think I should do about Felix Taylor?"

"Well, if American TV is anything to go by, the answer's simple, isn't it? You just haul him into custody and beat a confession out of him."

Harry wasn't sure whether she was joking.

Martin asked, "How long can you detain someone without charging him?"

"A sticky point, that," Harry said. "It's been the subject of quite a few Supreme Court cases. The most recent ruling basically says that a person may not be held against his will for an unreasonable period of time. Of course, the Court, as usual, doesn't bother to tell us how it defines 'unreasonable', except that the forty eight hours in the case before it was regarded as being too long. Our rule of thumb is that one day is probably OK, two days probably isn't."

Joanna asked, "Are you permitted to tell him lies about the evidence you have against him?"

"No, that's out; also, I don't know what the law is like in either of your countries, but here he has the right to remain silent, and if he chooses to exercise that right the fact can't be held against him in court. And, of course, he has a right to his lawyer."

Martin said, "In other words, your hands are fairly well tied. You really need to have quite a case against someone before you bring them in?"

"Yes. And when you're dealing with someone as intelligent as Felix Taylor, it's going to be very difficult to get even that far. Right now, we'd be laughed out of court even on something as simple as attempted manslaughter."

There was silence for nearly a minute. It was Joanna who broke it, in an oddly brittle voice.

"Harry, how sure are you that Felix Taylor killed Matthew?"

Harry looked uncomfortably out the window.

"I don't know. He was involved somehow, I *am* sure of that. But how he did it and why, I haven't got the faintest idea. He's nervous for one thing, too nervous to be completely innocent. He knows what he did, and he's afraid that we're on his track. But I haven't discovered yet what he's hiding. Maybe when I do the case will break."

"But until then you're reduced to scare tactics, hoping he'll make a mistake?"

"Yes. And I don't think he's quite that scared yet."

Joanna nodded, her lips drawn into a tight line. "Maybe we can do something to change that."

Chapter 16

Sunday, August 21

They were both out of bed early. Even Martin, never one to start his day unnecessarily early, was ready by half past seven.

The morning was still cool. Neither of them was yet accustomed to the wide daily temperature swings at this altitude.

The predawn temperatures were in the mid or low forties, yet only eight hours later the shade temperature would reach the mid eighties, and the unshaded temperature would be well over a hundred. Then the air would cool again as clouds gathered in the early afternoon, threatening rain. Yesterday, lightning had been clearly visible in the distance, dancing around the peaks to the east that marked the continental divide.

Today dawned the same as every day: chilly, with a bright sun in a pellucid sky.

While Joanna prepared breakfast for the two of them, Martin worked on a crossword puzzle in the living room. He was two thirds of the way through the book. He laughed out loud at: *Athenian space?* (5).

Joanna called him to the kitchen table, and over breakfast they discussed the evening's conversation with Harry Jones.

"It'll be interesting to see what comes of his meeting with the judge," Martin ventured.

Joanna nodded and paused, a spoonful of Special K in front of her face. "By the way, if it's OK with you, I'd like to attend the service at St. Peter's church this morning."

Martin was surprised. His sister had never been religious. His puzzlement must have been evident, because she quickly added: "Matthew obviously had an attachment to the church, because he left it a bequest. And you never know when you might learn something important."

Martin nodded. "Good idea. When is the service?"

"Nine thirty. At least, that's what it said in yesterday's paper. We'll have time to take a quick look up in the attic first."

They finished breakfast and then, without bothering to clear away the breakfast dishes, Martin went in search of a ladder. He found a six-foot wooden step ladder in the garage. He maneuvered it awkwardly into position.

"You should wear gloves, just in case you find something. And you might need a torch," said Joanna.

Martin returned to the garage and reappeared two minutes later carrying a flashlight in gloved hands.

"Satisfied?"

"Yep. Go ahead."

Joanna stood at the foot of the ladder while Martin climbed it. Moving the loose square in the ceiling, he released a cloud of insulation material that showered down on them. For nearly a minute he was helpless, coughing and spluttering as the dust caught at the back of his throat.

Eventually, eyes still watering, he recovered.

"Are you all right?" his sister asked.

"Yes. I'll be fine. I wasn't expecting it, that's all."

Standing on the flat top of the ladder, he peered into the darkness. He could see nothing. The only illumination came from the small square in which his body was inserted. The dark insulating material seemed to absorb light as readily as it absorbed heat. The air in the attic felt comfortably warm.

Switching on the flashlight, he saw boxes not far away. There were perhaps half a dozen of them, about eighteen inches on a side.

He called down, "There're boxes up here. About six of them. Let me just take a look."

He lifted himself into the attic and worked his way on to a dusty wooden board adjacent to the hole in the floor.

"Yes. Six of them. Let me take a look."

He opened each of them. They were ordinary cardboard boxes, with no writing on the outside.

"Looks like we found his vinyl records, anyway. And there's old correspondence and clothes and some books. Nothing very interesting."

Joanna's voice reached him, muffled and distant.

"Can you haul them down? We'd better take a look at them anyway."

Martin tried to lift one, found it difficult, and then tried sliding it across the floor to the hole. It slid easily, propagating a wave of gray dust before it. He heard the sound of coughing.

"Watch out! You could have warned me!" Joanna shouted through her fit of spluttering.

"Sorry, I didn't think."

Joanna's head and shoulders appeared through the hole in the floor. Between the two of them they maneuvered the box on to the floor of the bedroom below. It took fifteen minutes to move all six boxes.

"You're filthy. Go get a shower or something," Joanna suggested as Martin descended the stepladder.

"Take a look at yourself in a mirror," he said with a grin.

She looked across to the bedroom mirror and laughed. It was a laugh of silly pleasure. Martin realized that the scars left by her relationship with Kevin were healing.

"Come on, showers for the two of us and then we'll go to church. We'll look at these things when we get back."

He idly kicked one of the boxes, releasing another small cloud of gray dust.

Martin looked at the church. He had never suffered from the virus of religion and indeed, insofar as he thought of religion at all, it was with a kind of superior air, believing that the crutch of faith was only for those who needed to rationalize the vagaries and unfairnesses of life.

To Martin, churches were old, quaint structures that one sometimes visited while on vacation and wherein could be found ominous, threatening, cold silences that merely grew deeper through the centuries. In his mind, church buildings should be cavernous and sepulchral, needing a tax break simply to pay the heating bills.

But St. Peter's was utterly unlike the church in the village a mile down the road from Birchwood Cottage. This building, if it weren't for the enormous cross atop the roof overlooking the town, could have been mistaken for a large house.

The parking lot was nearly full. There must have been at least thirty five vehicles already parked when he drove up. As he was locking the car, he caught sight of a white Mazda.

"Look," he said to his sister.

She followed his gaze.

"Harry," she said.

He nodded. Together, they crossed the tarmac and went inside. Inside, the church was bustling with activity. Someone wearing a plastic name badge that identified its wearer as "Mal Bartlett" stepped forward and pumped Martin's hand.

"Good morning. Glad to have you with us."

His hand was released. The scene was replayed with his sister.

"Good morning. Glad to have you with us."

Mr. Bartlett took a step backward, his duty performed, and hovered in wait for the next congregant.

The doors to the sanctuary stood open immediately before them. To one side another man stood, his badge askew and unreadable without more effort than Martin was prepared to expend. Martin and Joanna moved towards the sanctuary and the man thrust a pair of bright yellow folded sheets at them. Martin accepted them with insincere thanks. Passing one to his sister he glanced down. "St. Peter's Episcopal Church. Order of Service," he read.

They entered the sanctuary and Martin halted momentarily to get his bearings. The sanctuary was a large room, capable of seating maybe a hundred and fifty on the comfortable-looking, padded pews. It was perhaps half full. There was a murmur of quiet conversation which competed with a prelude from an electronic organ that was not immediately visible.

People were entering the sanctuary behind them. He could not immediately see Harry Jones and he began leading Joanna towards a pew near the rear of the church on the right hand side. He finally spotted Harry, seated by himself nearer the front on the opposite side of the church. He was about to move to join Harry when a young man leaned forward from the pew behind, held out a hand and said, "Good morning. You're new here, aren't you? Are you visiting?"

Trapped, he greeted the young man, who exclaimed delightedly, "You're English, aren't you? I love your accent. We were in England just last year, weren't we, Martha?" And before he quite knew how it had happened, he was seated in front of the young man and his wife

— neither of whom were wearing a name tag — uncomfortably trying to twist in the pew to converse with the man about England.

The prelude ended, the young man said, "It's starting," and Martin turned thankfully to face the front of the church. Joanna, next to him, shot him a reassuring smile. A man walked up to a microphone at the front of the room, tapped it, and said, "Good morning, and welcome to St. Peter's Episcopal Church. Let us pray," and with that the service began.

Martin squirmed throughout the entire performance. It began with fifteen minutes of singing, accompanied not by the electric organ, which he discovered was not far away at the rear of the room, but by guitars and piano. The singing was interspersed with people seemingly at random saying "Praise the Lord" and "Hallelujah" in loud voices, as if somehow declaiming that they were so pure that they felt a special kinship with the Maker. Martin found it all rather nauseating.

Confessions and prayer followed the singing, to be followed in turn by a tedious message from the Reverend Steven Allbright, the thrust of which seemed to be: "Thank God that He loves us even though life is easy for us." Martin had the uncomfortable feeling that somehow he was missing the whole point of the sermon.

Halfway through the preaching — and partly to keep himself from nodding off — Martin surreptitiously audited the congregation. There were eighty five adults in the room. Every one was white.

After the sermon there was one more song, an offering (feeling no guilt whatsoever, he passed the plate without adding to it; Joanna dropped a folded dollar bill into it) and the benediction. The organ began a postlude as the pastor walked to the rear of the church. People began to move. The sound of the organ was once more relegated to the background as people began to converse.

"Glad you could join us," said the young man who had visited England. "Come again."

He looked like he was going to say more, but Martin pointed apologetically at Joanna as she left the pew.

"Got to go," he said, and followed her out into the sunshine.

They were joined by Harry Jones perhaps half a minute later.

"Good morning," he smiled. "Interesting service." There was a note of caution in his voice.

"Yes," Joanna agreed with a similar edge. "Are you a member here?"

"Me? Oh, no. I just came out of interest. This was where Matthew came to church."

"Great minds think alike." And with that everyone relaxed, now that they had established that none of them had taken the service seriously.

"Notice anything useful?" Harry asked.

"No. Waste of time, really."

"Yes. Had chance to look in the attic yet?"

"Yes. We found some boxes and we've got them down. Haven't had chance to look at them yet, though. Want to join us for lunch? Then we can go back to the house afterwards and look at the boxes."

"Sure, thanks. I'll follow you."

An hour later the three were gathered in the living room with the unopened boxes before them. While Joanna made coffee in the kitchen, Matthew and Harry began to empty the boxes and place the contents in piles on the living room floor.

By late afternoon, the boxes' contents were strewn haphazardly around them: books, papers, vinyl records and old letters. Every envelope and every dust sleeve had been carefully and systematically opened in a search for anything out of the ordinary. The only remaining task was to read through the six-inch stack of old letters, a final desperate attempt to find a clue.

Harry yawned for the tenth time in as many minutes.

"Sorry," he apologized. "I didn't sleep well. This case is keeping me awake nights."

He did not like to admit that the excess of yesterday evening had culminated in a headache that had blossomed in the small hours of the morning and had not yet run its course.

"Look, if it's all right with you," he continued, "I'll leave the letters to you. I'm going to go home, have a nap, do some shopping, and then see if I can find out from Judge Madison where he spends his weekends and why Matthew left him $10,000."

Martin said, "We'll let you know if there's anything in the letters. Although I doubt it; they all look pretty old to me."

Harry left, and Martin and Joanna turned their attention to the correspondence. All the letters were old, none more recent than five years. Most were personal: private correspondence that could easily be sorted into piles depending on the handwriting on the envelope. A few were obviously business related. When they had finished sorting them, Joanna attacked the business letters while Martin picked up the oldest pile of personal correspondence.

"This looks like the oldest one," he said, fingering a letter addressed to Matthew at an FPO number and postmarked Newington, Connecticut. He lifted an old, blurred snapshot from the envelope. It showed a young couple in a garden. The male was Matthew, the female unknown. It was hard to be sure from the photograph, but she looked acceptably pretty. He replaced the photograph in the envelope.

Joanna grunted distractedly, concentrating on the business correspondence; Martin set about reading.

It took two hours to read all the letters. Neither of them found anything worthy of interest.

Martin fixed them sandwiches: bread, ham, cheese, tomato, lettuce and English cucumber. When he returned to the living room, he saw Joanna immersed in a letter that he recognized as the very first one he had read. She looked up as he entered the room. "This one is much older than all the others; but you can see why he kept it."

Martin rolled his eyes heavenwards. "Yes, Jo. I told you that about two hours ago. Obviously, you weren't listening."

"Sorry. One thing though, we should call and tell Harry that this kills the homosexual blackmail theory."

"Yes. It must have hit poor Matthew pretty badly."

Joanna scanned the letter she had been reading. It was addressed to Private Matthew Chambers and dated 1969, at the height of the Vietnam War.

> Dearest Matthew
>
> This is the hardest letter I have ever had to write. You can't imagine how hard it is for me to know that you are half a world away fighting for our country, trusting me to protect our love while you are away, and now I find that I must betray that trust. Oh Matthew, if only you were here, things would be so much easier. Engagements are broken all the time, but with you so far away it seems so callous of me.
>
> You *must* understand that it has nothing to do with your not being here and someone else being available. That's not it at all. I have tried and tried to analyze my feelings

carefully, to be sure that I am doing the right thing. And I am certain that even if you were here, my decision would be the same. I have to break the engagement.

I love you Matthew, I really do; but now I realize that it is not a love that will last. I have met someone else, and now I know what true love is. I am sorry, Matthew, but you must accept that I could never love you in the way that I love him.

And so, my dear, dear Matthew, I have told him that I am willing to marry him. We are due to be married in a couple of months. Please don't be angry. Instead, be happy (if that is possible) that I have found the true love of my life, and that we will not be making the mistake of confusing a very physical mutual attraction with a true lifelong love. I thank you for everything you have been to me. No one can take those memories away.

All my love

The letter was signed with a single letter, "L," in a curved, flowery style.

Joanna looked at the postmark. "Matthew was from Ohio, wasn't he? How far is that from Connecticut?"

Martin shrugged. "I don't know. Look it up. Quite a way, I think."

Joanna went to the bookcase, where she found an atlas. She flicked through the pages.

"Here it is. You're right, it's not exactly next door. I wonder how he came to know someone in Connecticut? It sounds like it had been going on for some time."

"Who knows? Maybe she moved there after he was assigned overseas. Did Martin volunteer or was he drafted, do you know?"

"I asked Harry. He volunteered. That must have made this letter even harder on him."

"Yes, well, at least we found out about his sexual leanings, so the afternoon wasn't quite a total waste. Come on, let me make some coffee and then we can think about where we go from here."

It was the kind of question that had to be asked in person if one was to be certain of the veracity of the reply. He had decided against calling ahead, gambling that the judge would be home.

Harry Jones looked at the cars parked neatly in the underground garage. There was no way to identify the judge's car. One car's license tag was out of date. Idly, he crossed to that car and felt the hood. It was warm. He'd warn Patrolman Stevens that he should keep his eye out for a yellow Corolla.

He crossed the half-filled lot to the elevator. Inside was a directory of the building; H. C. Madison (no honorific) lived in apartment 312. He rode the elevator to the third floor. Outside apartment 312 he pressed the doorbell and heard an electronic chime.

It was several seconds before he heard the sound of movement. After a brief delay, the door opened. Judge Madison stood before him, five feet two in his moccasins, a smile on his face and an almost-empty glass — a third of an inch of tawny liquid lost amongst the ice — in his hand. There was no hint of recognition in the judge's face.

"Detective Harry Jones with the Pinetree Police Department," offered Harry.

"Ah yes, yes. I thought I recognized you, Detective Jones. You've testified in my courtroom, haven't you?"

"Yes, sir."

"Well, I'd invite you in, but I must remind you about the rules regarding *ex parte* contact. We aren't allowed to discuss anything that might have any bearing on any case in which you and I are both involved, you know."

"It's all right, your Honor; it's nothing like that. Although I assume that it's permitted for me to compliment you on your handling of the Josephson case last year."

The smile strengthened into a grin. "Yes, well, thank you. Let's say no more about it, shall we?" He stood aside for the detective to enter. "Do come in, won't you? Can I make you a drink, or is this an official visit?"

"If you're asking whether I drink on duty, the answer is: sometimes, your Honor. And in this case, I don't mind if I do. One of what you're having looks like it would go down well."

"Certainly, certainly."

The judge busied himself for a minute out of sight in the kitchen, while Harry looked around the living room. It was spacious, especially for a single man. Bookcases lined the walls, occupying nearly every spare foot of wallspace. The titles were an eclectic mix, and there seemed little or no order in the way in which the books were arranged. *Pudd'nhead Wilson* was adjacent to *On a Clear Day You Can See General Motors* and three shelves away from *The Adventures of Huckleberry Finn*. There were no law books.

A single birthday card stood at eye level on one of the bookshelves. It bore a cartoon of a haggard face looking into a bathroom mirror. In large print were the words "You know you're getting old when...." The detective peered inside, not so much to read the punch line ("...you look like this on one of your good days") but to look at the signature, which turned out to be that of Judge Felicity Clayburn, a colleague of Judge Madison's who was known to disagree with him on almost any issue that mattered.

His host returned carrying two glasses of amber liquid.

"Ah, caught out, I see. It's my sixty fifth birthday."

"Today?"

"Today."

Harry accepted the glass and toasted the judge.

"Happy birthday, your Honor."

"Thank you. She can afford to be kind, you know, sending me cards. She'll still be on the bench a quarter of a century after I'm safely underground. Then there'll be no one to keep her in check."

The judge looked serious; it was impossible to know whether he was jesting. Harry guessed not.

"And yes, for your information, I've read just about all of the books."

Harry realized that something had been niggling him since he had walked into the room, and now he realized what it was.

"No television?"

"No. I see no need for it. Rots the mind; kills the brain cells." With no trace of irony, he drank deeply from his glass.

"Take a seat," he offered a chair and took one himself.

Harry sat next to a table on which a chess game was in progress, and realized that it was adjacent to one part of the bookshelves where order did dominate: all the books were concerned with chess.

The judge continued, "So, if this is not an illegal attempt at *ex parte* contact, and it's not a social visit — which seems unlikely in view of the fact that I've lived in Pinetree nigh on twenty years and never in all that time borne a social visit from a member of the local constabulary — then I can only conclude that it somehow involves the late Matthew Chambers."

Harry laughed. "You'd have made a good detective, your Honor." He raised his glass. "*Salut.*"

"Good health," the judge responded. "But you are quite incorrect. I'm the wrong color for a detective."

"But not for a judge?"

A chuckle. "Oh, no. A colored judge demonstrates to the world how open-minded and liberal a community is. A colored police officer is quite another matter.

"Judges are expected to be impartial; few people would openly accuse a judge of bias, although, of course, we are human and therefore it is only poor judges who don't admit, if only in the privacy of their minds, how strong their biases sometimes are. But a policeman is something else entirely.

"A colored policeman in a Caucasian town like this — of course, I discount the invisible Hispanics, without whom the town could not function — a colored policeman would be accused of bigotry or racism every time he annoyed a white person. And do you honestly think that the populace of Pinetree would divulge to me things that they tell you? I hope you're not that naïf. Anyway, I'm not tall enough or sufficiently imposing to be a policeman. So, Detective Jones, are you here to impart information or to extract it?"

"Extract it, your Honor."

Harry paused to sip his drink while he gathered his thoughts.

He continued, "You were probably the person who knew Mr. Chambers the best?" He made it a question.

"I suppose so. Although I imagine that his secretary was probably privy to far more details about his business life than was I. But regarding his social activities, yes, I would imagine that I knew him better than anyone else."

"So I must ask you a hard question, your Honor, and I can assure you that I shall keep the source of your answer to myself."

"That's a rash promise, Mr. Jones. You should never make promises that you might not be able to keep."

Harry accepted the reprimand. "You're quite right, your Honor. But still, I would not pass on the source of the information unless it proved to be absolutely necessary to the prosecution of the case."

"That's better. So... your question?"

The judge emptied the dregs from his glass. Harry had taken but a couple of sips from his.

"Have you any knowledge, or even suspicions, of Mr. Chambers' sexual proclivities?"

The judge's laugh was as immediate as it was unexpected. It continued for several seconds before dying down to a mirthful chuckle and, finally, dissolved into speech.

"Quite well done, Detective Jones. Yes, quite well done indeed. You see a middle-aged man, fit, healthy and undoubtedly attractive, die unexpectedly under puzzling circumstances. You investigate and discover that the man had no obvious sexual liaisons, even though he has been a resident of a small town for four years. His closest friend, apart from being an esteemed judge, is also, although more than twenty years older than the deceased, known never to have married. And immediately the mind begins to work."

Harry Jones had never put the facts together in such a convenient way before; but now, stated so baldly, they did indeed look suspicious.

"But I can put your mind at rest, Detective Jones. Although you have only my word for it, of course, and you can decide for yourself what that's worth in the circumstances. Nevertheless, you have my word that there was nothing of that sort.

"Should it interest you — and I would quite understand it if it did not, because there are few things so boring as when a man starts to spout personal facts about himself — I was once engaged to a beautiful young law student, some forty years ago now. It was a perfect match, so we thought, except for the one tiny incidental fact that she was white.

"Her family disapproved. Hardly unusual in those days. Quite the contrary, really. They even tried to buy me off, which was one of the less-agreeable events in my life. In the end we arranged to elope, but her parents must have discovered our plan because before we could set a day she was whisked away to Europe. She stayed four years. When she returned, she did so as the wife of a Texas oilman. Her family made no secret of their pleasure.

"As to Emily's feelings, I could never bring myself to try to discover them for myself."

He fell silent, looking at the empty glass, rotating it slowly in his hands. At length he continued, his eyes still on the glass.

"Anyway, the point is that I have no discernible tendencies to homosexual behavior, and as far as I know the same was true of Matthew." He looked up. "Maybe something similar happened in his past; I don't know, but I wouldn't be surprised. It's not as uncommon as you might think. Many men have the capacity to love but one woman. Or perhaps it's simply that we can withstand only a certain amount of pain...."

"Thank you, your Honor, for being so frank. I'm sorry. I didn't mean to pry."

The judge's lined face broke into a smile. "Of course you did. You're a detective: it's your job. Excuse me a moment while I get a refill. How about one for you?" It was said out of politeness. The detective's glass was still more than half full.

"No thanks, I'm driving."

The judge disappeared into the kitchen. There were several clinks, and he returned.

"I just want to be clear on this," said the detective, taking another sip. "You never saw any indication that Mr. Chambers was homosexual?"

"Right."

"But you also never saw any indication that he was heterosexual?"

"True. A mine of useful information, aren't I? Sorry." He raised his glass. "Good health."

There was a sharp knock on the door. The judge put his glass down and looked at his watch.

"Nine o'clock on a Sunday evening? Now who could that possibly be? I can't remember the last time I had two unexpected visitors in one evening."

He rose to answer the door.

He opened it and someone shouted, "Surprise."

In the corridor stood three of his erstwhile colleagues on the local municipal bench, apparently led by his nemesis and current colleague on the state bench, the Honorable Felicity Clayburn. She hefted a bottle.

"We came to celebrate with you, you old reprobate."

She breezed past Judge Madison and stopped when she realized that there was another person in the room. For a moment she looked nonplussed.

"Oh! Sorry. If you're busy...."

The detective stood and drained his glass. "No, it's all right. I'm just leaving."

"Don't leave on account of us."

"No, really, I'll be going now."

Harry shook hands with Judge Madison. "Thanks very much. Perhaps we can continue some other time?"

"Yes, yes. That would be fine. Whenever convenient."

The detective left, nodding greetings to the local judiciary, and made his way thoughtfully to the elevator.

Chapter 17

Monday, August 22

Harry waited all morning in the courtroom.

Judge Madison never once directly looked at him, although he must have realized that the detective was present. There were no other members of the public in the seats at the rear of the courtroom, just lawyers sitting waiting for their cases to be heard.

The cases were a depressing litany of failure: a string of divorces, the only variations the names of the parties, the faces of the lawyers representing them, and the degree of acrimony between the estranged spouses. Harry found himself feeling embarrassed at the airing of so much dirty laundry in public, even though the public, fortunately, had singularly failed to avail itself of the opportunity to survey the filthy clothing. He wished that he had bought a book in which he could immerse himself as an escape from the dreary recitation of mistrust and greed.

Eventually, it was over. Judge Madison banged his gavel.

"All rise," the clerk commanded, and the judge strode out of the room with as much dignity as his overweight five-foot-two-inch frame would permit.

The last two lawyers left the courtroom. Moments before they had been at loggerheads over the assets of a wealthy middle-aged couple; now they were chatting amicably about golf on Saturday.

191

Harry ambled through the low swing gate that separated the public gallery from the front half of the courtroom. The clerk was tidying his table. Harry approached and, out of habit, flashed his badge at him.

"Excuse me. Detective Harry Jones, Pinetree Police Department."

The clerk glanced at the card and nodded.

"I'd like to meet with the judge in his chambers. Would that be possible?"

"If you'll follow me, I'll let him know you're here."

The clerk gathered up the remaining papers and led Harry through a side door, down a corridor, and into his office, which acted as an anteroom between the judge's chambers and the hallway. Dropping the papers on his desk, he knocked on the inner door and poked his head inside.

Harry heard the judge instruct the clerk to let him in.

The judge greeted him with a friendly smile.

"Ah, good morning, Detective Jones. And how did you find another dull day in court?"

"It's a bit different from what I usually see," admitted the detective, seating himself on a plush leather chair.

"Yes. Most people somehow have the idea that being a judge entails making lofty decisions or instructing juries on how to proceed in murder trials. In fact, of course, most of the time it's mundane matters: watching marriages torn apart and trying to dispose of the combined assets in a legal and preferably fair manner. I tell you, Detective Jones, being a judge can ruin whatever faith one has in human nature faster than any other job I know."

"Except, perhaps, being a cop?" Harry ventured.

"*Touché*; you have a valid point. Well, it's nearly lunch time. Assuming that this isn't an *ex parte* meeting, would you care to join me?"

Harry was surprised by the offer. In all his years in the department, he had never been offered lunch by a judge. He hesitated, concerned about the propriety of accepting.

"Don't worry. I've already had to explain your presence in my apartment yesterday evening. I told them the truth, of course: that you're investigating Matthew's death and were pumping me for information. And be assured that I'll be just as hard on you as always next time you're in my court. If it makes you feel guilty, don't accept. But I don't see that any harm can come of a simple lunch in the cafeteria."

"Well, your Honor, as I think you've guessed, I didn't finish asking my questions last night, but I think you might prefer to answer my questions in the privacy of your own chambers rather than in a place where someone might overhear."

"And what else do you want to know? Not more about Matthew's sexual proclivities, surely?"

"Not quite, your Honor. I'm afraid there's a couple of things about yourself that we need to clear up."

He took his pad and pen out of his pocket, and turned the top sheet to expose a virgin page.

"Questions about me? OK. Well, perhaps you're right and it would be best to answer them here."

"Your Honor, my first question concerns Matthew Chambers' will. As you are probably aware, he bequeathed his estate to five parties. There were sums of money to his secretary, Miss Freeman, and to St. Peter's church. Nearly all of the remainder of his assets are to be split equally between his only living relatives, Mr. Martin Salisbury and Mrs. Joanna Baker, now Joanna Salisbury."

The judge nodded.

"All of those bequests are understandable. However, the fifth major bequest, the sum of ten thousand dollars, was to you, your Honor. Would you be able to speculate why Mr. Chambers might have left you such a large sum?"

The judge mmmmed in thought or, possibly, agreement. He asked, "And the second question?"

With anyone else, Harry would have demanded an answer to his first question before continuing; but here, on the home territory of an influential member of the community, he was willing to table the question temporarily.

"Well, your Honor, there's a matter of your attendance at the Friday night meetings of the chess club. As we understand it, you are an experienced and rather capable chess player."

Again the judge inclined his head.

"It is our information that you attended the meetings of the Pinetree Chess Club, but your attendance was somewhat irregular, due to engagements that would frequently take you out of town for the weekend. If you don't mind my asking, your Honor, where exactly did you go on those occasions?"

"Do these questions have some bearing on the case, Detective Jones?"

The detective shrugged. "I don't know, your Honor. Quite probably not, but they are pieces of the puzzle that need to be fitted in place. We know that Mr. Chambers was a keen chess player and that you were the only other member of the chess club who was able to give him a good game. We also know that Mr. Chambers died on a Friday evening, the day of the week when there was usually a chess club meeting. We know that on that particular week, the chess club was canceled because of the meeting of the town council. We know that you were in town that Friday evening, whereas often you went away to some unknown destination for the entire weekend...."

"As I say, it may be nothing; but it may not. Would you answer the questions please, sir? Both of them."

The lines on the judge's aging face deepened in a wide smile. "And, of course, there's always the fact that I happened to be the one who found the body...." He let his voice trail away.

"As you say, sir, there's always the fact that you were the one who found the body."

The detective waited.

"Yes, well, I suppose it was too much to hope that I'd be able to keep it secret for ever. I don't know what answers you are expecting, young man, but your suspicion that I might not want to discuss these matters in public was well founded."

Harry did not react; he wondered what was coming next.

"I shall have to make a clean breast of it, I suppose. You understand that I am putting myself in your power. I shall trust to your discretion, Detective Jones, and your commitment that this will be kept between the two of us."

He paused. The silence lengthened; he obviously wanted an assurance from the detective before continuing.

"Yes, sir. Insofar as anything you tell me has nothing to do with the case, you can be assured that I will respect the confidentiality of the information."

The judge continued. "Well, your questions, whether or not you suspected it, are not unrelated."

Harry had not been able to formulate a connection, but he was hardly surprised that there was one.

"I should go back to the beginning, which was about ten years ago now. One lunchtime I chanced to overhear a conversation between the county attorney and his assistant in the courtroom cafeteria. I could barely believe what I heard; after all, such people are supposed to have a modicum of intelligence and training in logic, although I confess that long experience has, sadly, shown me little evidence to support that proposition. Sometimes, you know, I despair of our system of education."

He brought himself up short, realizing that he was beginning to ramble.

"Anyway, the gist of this conversation was that the deputy county attorney was telling his superior that he spent every vacation at Las Vegas, playing roulette. That someone would willingly spend their precious vacation time in such a way was perhaps not so much of a surprise as the statement that followed, which was to the effect that this attorney always bet on his lucky numbers and on his last trip to Las Vegas had shown a substantial profit.

"For a while I was contemptuous, thinking to myself in my superior way that anyone who believed in lucky numbers was a fool. And so, I hasten to assure you, I still feel."

Harry wondered where this was leading, but he maintained a look of interest.

"But one thought led to another and somehow I found myself thinking that by never having visited Las Vegas myself, I had denied myself an experience that all intellectually curious Americans should experience at least once in their lives. My very next vacation, I went to Las Vegas."

The judge took a deep breath, as if preparing himself for an ordeal.

"Well, Detective Jones, I know of no easy way to say this: I was hooked. Gambling, you see, I did not know then, is like a drug to some people. It has nothing to do with education, nothing to do with social standing, nothing to do with intelligence. It simply acts on the brains of some people differently than it does on most. Unfortunately, I discovered this for myself in the worst and most direct way possible. I lost $5,000 in my first one-week trip to Las Vegas."

A "phew" of wonderment escaped the detective's lips.

"When I returned home, I was full of remorse and self-recrimination. I was far too embarrassed to tell anyone what I had done. Once away from the damned place, though, I was sure that the madness was gone.

For three years I thought that. I was certain of it. But the only way to prove it was to go back. So I did. I lost $7,500.

"Then something even more unforeseen happened: limited-stakes gambling became legal here in Colorado. Of course, we'd had scratch-off games and electronic Lotto for some time, but those aren't the same thing. Not at all the same thing. I buy a ticket or pick numbers occasionally, maybe every month or two, but I can take or leave those games at will. But real gambling, even with a limit of only $5 per bet, is something else entirely.

"I began to visit Central City, on the other side of the mountains, on weekends. Mr. Jones, do you have any idea how much money one can lose in an unlucky weekend of hard gambling, even with a limit of five dollars a bet?"

Harry shook his head.

"Well, all I'll say is that it's an awful lot of money. More than I can afford. Anyway, the long and the short of it is that I kept this addiction secret for a while, until Matthew Chambers came to town and we began to meet regularly over a chess board.

"Mr. Jones, do you play chess yourself?"

The abrupt change of subject caught the detective momentarily by surprise.

"No, sir. I used to, in grade school, but not now. I doubt that I could even remember the rules of the game."

"Well, chess is unique. I had always been the best player wherever I went, until relatively recently. Oh, I was beaten occasionally of course, but never with any consistency by any one player. I was at the top of the chess club ladder here for years. Then Matthew arrived.

"He appeared at the chess club one evening; it couldn't have been more than a couple of weeks after he arrived in town. It so happened that that evening we had changed our usual format slightly; all the people in attendance had their names thrown into a hat and the pairings were drawn at random. If it weren't for that, it would have been some time before Matthew and I played, since he, as a newcomer, would have entered the ladder at the bottom and I, as usual, was at the top. Even in elective games I don't often play against people more than half a dozen places below me.

"Anyway, as luck would have it, my name was drawn with Matthew's. I thought nothing of it. Even though he was a completely unknown quantity, I was beaten rarely enough that I gave little thought to the first few moves.

"Mr. Jones, I was thrashed — absolutely and totally crushed in a way I have never been before or, I'm glad to say, since. Never again did I refrain from thinking carefully about each and every move when playing against Matthew.

"In that first game, I think I woke up somewhere about the eighth move. I took my first real look at the board and pondered my next move for at least ten minutes. Five moves later and I knew that there was no way in hell I could recover the game. Two moves later, I conceded. We were the first game to be completed and, of course, no one realized that I had lost. We hastily set up the board again and played a second game. This time, naturally, I concentrated hard. The game went to twenty five moves before I conceded.

"Now, Detective Jones, let me tell you what is unique about chess. Since it is a game that has no element of luck, I discovered something for myself that evening that I had heard about, but which I had never experienced: I discovered that a man who consistently loses to another at chess feels himself intellectually inferior to the winner.

"That had never happened to me before, but once Matthew appeared on the scene, I discovered that it was a truth I had to face. We began to play often, away from the chess club — I found that I won perhaps twenty percent of the time — and I began to share confidences with Matthew that I had never shared with anyone before. Matthew, for quite different reasons — mainly stemming from insecurity and, to a degree I think, loneliness — shared equally with me.

"Well, you can guess what happened. It wasn't long before I told Matthew about my gambling weakness.

"At first, he had difficulty comprehending it. So I gave him a graphic demonstration; I took him with me for a weekend in Central City.

"Actually, it was a much better weekend than usual; I ended up only $50 down, as I remember. Anyway, once we returned to Pinetree, he conceded that I did indeed have a problem. He wanted me to enroll in Gamblers Anonymous, but there is no local chapter; the nearest is in, of all places, Central City, and I certainly wasn't going to go there. After three months of pressure, I finally joined a chapter in Denver.

"They meet on Saturday evenings. I can't get away every weekend — I'm sure you can appreciate how tiring that drive can be after a long week in court — but I manage the trip about half the time.

Generally, I drive down on Friday evening and catch a show of some kind. Saturday I relax, wander the bookstores, that sort of thing. Then there's the meeting on Saturday evening, another night at the motel, and then I drive back on Sunday morning."

The detective interrupted. "What about relapses? It would be easy enough to end up in Central City instead of Denver."

"Yes, it would. And if I was doing it on my own, just for me, then I dare say that I would have given in to temptation and done exactly that long before now. But I don't just do it for me. I made a promise to Matthew, you see, and if nothing else I am a man of integrity."

There was silence for several seconds, a silence filled by the shadow of Matthew Chambers.

Harry said, "Thank you for your openness, your Honor. You can be sure that your secret is safe with me. But that doesn't explain about the sum of money Mr. Chambers left you in his will."

"Oh, but it does. You see, when Matthew met me, I was teetering on the verge of personal bankruptcy. He gave me $10,000, just like that. 'A gift to a friend,' he called it. After that, of course, I could never disabuse the trust he had placed in me.

"The money, I hasten to add, was only a small portion of the gambling debts I had built up, but it was enough to tide me over until I got on my own two feet again. He never said anything directly about there being the possibility of more, but on a couple of occasions, I got the distinct impression that if I remained free of gambling" — the judge made it sound like a disease — "for five years, there would be more money as a kind of reward. I expect that the sum in his will was merely his way of ensuring that I got the money even if he died in the meantime."

"I understand." Harry paused, then added, "And I must say, sir, that considering how close the two of you were, you have been taking his death very calmly."

The judge's response was instantaneous and sharp.

"That, Mr. Jones, is because you have not been able to see me in the privacy of my own home this past week. If you had, I can assure you that you would not have felt me lacking in grief for the one true friend I have ever known." The judge's eyes bored into Harry. "Mr. Jones, you should know that just as Matthew relied on me to kick my gambling habit, I am relying on you to bring Matthew's killer to justice.

"Yes, I've seen the toxicology report and I've talked with John Salter. I know Matthew was murdered."

The judge leaned forward as he spoke, his words full of controlled anger. "And I'll also tell you that I will recuse myself from the case if it falls to me to try it, and by God! you police had better not screw this up. I want the man that killed Matthew behind bars, and I want him never to walk the streets again."

The old judge's eyes were watering; he seemed to have aged ten years in the past thirty seconds. He took several deep breaths, and his face softened.

Gruffly, he continued, "Now, come on, young man. Are you going to take me up on my offer of lunch?"

"Yes, sir." The detective rose, putting away his notebook. "And thank you, your Honor, for being so forthcoming. You have my assurance that it will go no further than necessary."

"Thank you, young man. I appreciate your rectitude. Now let us say no more about this."

Joanna had been playing mum all morning. It had started when Matthew surprised her in the living room in the act of replacing the telephone on its hook just after eight thirty, a guilty look pasted on her face.

"I'll be going out after lunch. Can I borrow the car, or should I use Matthew's?"

"You can have mine. But where are you going?"

"I'll tell you later."

She refused to be drawn further.

They spent the morning going through Matthew's boxes yet again. By lunchtime they were thoroughly fed up with going over the same ground repeatedly. They tidied the material into piles on one side of the living room and made lunch. Afterwards, and still giving him no clue as to where she was bound, Joanna left her brother to his book of crossword puzzles.

Joanna had already examined the map of Pinetree in the telephone directory, so she knew exactly where she was going.

She drove down the mountainside. She was happy. Her window was all the way down, her elbow exposed to the breeze. The cool, fresh mountain air was magnificent and invigorating. As she drove, she wondered at the transformation she had undergone since her arrival. For a second, she thought back to Sutherland: her real job, her real life. Her stomach tightened involuntarily. She forced herself to think of the here and now, driving down a narrow, winding road on a mountainside on a beautiful Colorado summer's day. The tension in her stomach eased.

She found herself thinking of Harry Jones' apartment. It was almost eerie how much it reminded her of her own home, even though there was little that the two places had physically in common. From his apartment, her thoughts drifted to Harry himself. He seemed a little old to be unmarried. Perhaps he, unlike she, had never found someone with whom he wanted to share his life. If so, he was lucky.

She joined the highway, and then, almost immediately, left it once more. She found the parking lot easily enough and parked in one of the many empty spaces. As she walked away from the car she rehearsed her lines in the act to come.

In the waiting room, Joanna gave her name to the receptionist.

"Have you ever seen Dr. Taylor before?"

But the receptionist already knew the answer to her own question, and she pushed a clipboard with a multi-page form across the counter towards the new patient even as she asked the question.

"No. I'm from Australia; I've just been visiting Pinetree these past few days and then this problem started with my leg and I wanted someone to look at it. Someone recommended Dr. Taylor so, well, here I am."

"Please fill this out and the doctor will be with you shortly."

Joanna took the clipboard and sat in one of the numerous empty seats. She cast her eyes around the waiting room. Two other patients were waiting: an old man, part Indian — Native American, she corrected herself — whose face was sun browned and lined almost to the point of disfigurement; and a young woman with an almost unnaturally pale skin whose eyes darted around the room, never alighting on any object for more than a second, looking as if she were unable to focus on anything.

An old, dark-skinned woman appeared, shrunken and shriveled but whose eyes were the very opposite of those of the young pale-faced woman; the eyes of the old woman sparkled with life. They, too, darted around the room, but they seemed to take a delight in what they saw.

They landed on the old man. The woman's face lit up and the man pushed himself slowly to his feet. They held hands for a moment.

"Come on, old man. I'll tell you what the doctor said."

They left.

A nurse appeared.

"Sunshine?" she said, apropos of nothing.

The young paleface looked up and a smile flitted across her face. She nodded and rose. Joanna felt suddenly sorry for the young woman.

Sunshine walked unsteadily towards the nurse, exhibiting more difficulty than the old woman who must have been three times her age. The nurse held out her hand to steady the young woman and together they disappeared down a corridor and out of Joanna's sight.

Joanna looked down at the sheets before her.

"Don't worry too much about the form," the receptionist offered. "Since you're an alien most of it doesn't apply. Just do your best."

Joanna bent to her task.

She returned the form to the receptionist, who smiled as she glanced at the extensive white space.

"That's fine," she said, encouragingly. "As long as we have your name and address and a method of payment, they're the only really important things. Oh, I see you put your address in Australia. Could you give me an address where you can be reached in Pinetree?"

Joanna thought for a moment and then gave the address of the motel. If Felix Taylor *had* been involved in her cousin's death, it might be better if he didn't know where she could be found.

She returned to her seat and flicked through a magazine called *Colorado Lifestyle* whose contents comprised photographs of sun, snow and forest, with young and remarkably pretty women wrapped in smiles (and often little more) having the time of their lives. *And aging their skin, and inviting malignant melanoma*, thought Joanna.

"Joanna?"

The nurse had returned; Sunshine was at the counter arranging payment.

"If you'd come this way please."

Joanna put down the glossy magazine and followed the nurse into a consulting room.

The nurse took her blood pressure: "120 over 70, pretty good"; her temperature: "99.7, slightly elevated"; and her pulse: "72, normal." Then the nurse asked her briefly about her symptoms.

"A pain in my leg. It comes and goes. Sometimes it's hard to walk properly. Right now it's not too bad, just a sort of dull throb." Joanna exhibited her calf so that the nurse could see the seat of the nonexistent pain.

"OK, well, the doctor will be in in a moment," the nurse said. She left.

A minute later, Doctor Felix Taylor entered the room. He was older than Joanna had expected, although it was obvious that he kept himself in good shape. He was tall and his face was etched with shallow lines; his hair was thick and gray, but not at all unbecoming. All in all, he appeared decidedly distinguished. He must have been quite a handsome devil in his youth.

He flashed her a smile, glanced at the chart the nurse had left, and said, "Now, Joanna, what exactly is the trouble?"

Joanna took a deep breath.

"Dr. Taylor, I'm here because Detective Harry Jones of the Pinetree police could not come."

A flicker of surprise crossed Dr. Taylor's features.

She continued, "I'll tell you right now that if necessary I shall deny in court that this conversation ever took place. Back home in Australia I'm a detective sergeant. I came to tell you something that Harry, because of legalities, cannot tell you himself.

"The game's up, Dr. Taylor. I've seen the evidence. It's not yet enough to be sure of convicting you in front of a jury, but he's nailed you and he's going to keep after you until he *can* convict you before a jury. If this were Australia, I would pull you in and hold you until you told us the truth, but Harry is softer than I am.

"But let me tell you something, Dr. Taylor: Matthew Chambers was my cousin, almost the only kin I had in the world, and I'm setting my own timetable on this. If you aren't in custody within two days, I'm coming after you and, believe me, you'll tell me what happened before I finish with you. Now, if you'll excuse me...."

Joanna pushed him aside — hard — and swept from the room. Her pulse racing, she walked rapidly back the way she had come, through the waiting room where she heard a surprised "Good day..." before the sound of the receptionist's voice was blocked by the door.

She forced herself to maintain her pace all the way to the car and then, without looking up at the building she had just vacated, she started the car and drove out the parking lot.

Felix Taylor stood, motionless and horrified. Rendered speechless by Joanna's assault, by the time he recovered she was gone.

He went to the window and watched her walk to her car, start the engine and drive away without so much as a glance in his direction.

The receptionist burst into the room. "Dr. Taylor? That Australian woman just walked out of here without paying...."

"No charge, Ginny, all right?"

"All right, Dr. Taylor, whatever you say. Are you all right?"

"Yes, Ginny. I just need a minute to myself, that's all."

The receptionist backed out of the room and left him staring vacantly out the window.

Joanna breathed deeply, calming herself as she drove up the mountain to Matthew's home.

The sunshine flickering through the trees and the breeze coming in at the window were not enough to calm her. She forced herself to slow down, but her heart was still beating rapidly and her breath remained staccato as she stopped the car in front of the house. She cut the engine.

For more than a minute she sat listening to the silence of the forest. Gradually, she recovered.

The meeting had gone better than she had expected. Dr. Taylor had been, quite literally, dumbfounded — rendered speechless by her unexpected vehemence. For a moment she wondered if she had gone too far. What if it was all a mistake? What if Dr. Taylor had nothing to do with Matthew's death? But he had to. The cyanide-laced capsule could only have come from Felix Taylor. No; whether or not he was the immediate cause of Matthew's death, Felix Taylor was hiding something. The question now was whether she had scared him enough to cause him to break cover?

She got out the car and climbed the steps to the house.

Martin was inside, seated on the sofa, book and pen in hand.

"Hello, Jo. You're back sooner than I expected."

She ignored him and made straight for a telephone. She dialed a number from memory. The phone at the other end rang for several seconds.

"Hello. You have reached Detective Harry Jones. If you'd like to leave a message for me, please press 1 now. If you need to talk to a dispatcher, please press 2. If this is an emergency, please hang up and dial 911 or, if that is not possible, press zero now."

Joanna pressed 2. The telephone rang twice more and then a bored female came on the line.

"Good morning. Sorry. Good afternoon. Pinetree Police. How may I direct your call?"

"I have an important message for Detective Harry Jones. I must talk to him immediately."

"I think he's out. Let me try his desk for you."

"No, I've already tried that. I got his voice mail. Can you please patch me through to him?"

"I'm sorry, I can't do that."

Joanna added steel to her voice. "I'm a detective sergeant and I need to talk to him *now* — it's about the Matthew Chambers murder."

She hoped that she was not laying it on too strong. Still, it was nothing like the liberties she had taken with the truth when talking to Felix Taylor.

"Can I have your name?"

"Detective Sergeant Salisbury; S-A-L-I-S-B-U-R-Y."

"Thank you. Please stay on the line."

She waited for three minutes. Martin mouthed the word "Coffee?" from across the room and she nodded. Martin disappeared into the kitchen. Eventually, a new voice, gravelly, male, came on the line.

"Detective Sergeant Salisbury?" He pronounced her name as it was written: Sal-is-bury.

"Yes." She didn't bother to correct him.

"My name is Salter. I'm chief of detectives with the Pinetree PD. I'm Harry Jones' boss. I've been following the Matthew Chambers case carefully. You are Mr. Chambers' cousin?"

"Yes." She nearly added "sir," but stopped herself just in time.

"OK. Now, what do you need to talk to Harry about? Anything you want to tell him, you can tell me."

Joanna did not want to argue with the man, but she knew that it was one thing to tell Harry that she had just put the fear of God into his prime suspect, and quite another to tell his superior.

"No, sir. With all due respect, I know Harry and I don't know you; you're just a voice on a telephone. I'll speak to Harry, no one else."

There was silence as Chief Salter digested this.

He said, "OK. Wait a minute, please."

He stabbed the hold button and rang back to the dispatcher.

"Put this through to Harry if you can find him. And this will be on tape, won't it?"

"Yes, sir, it will."

Salter stabbed a button on his phone, reconnecting him with Joanna. He said, "If you'll hold, they're trying to find him."

"Thank you."

Joanna heard a click as the chief of detectives disconnected.

Another four minutes went by. At last, Harry came on the line, competing with the whine of a car's engine.

"Harry, this is Jo."

"Jo? How on earth did you get through to me? That's against the rules..."

Joanna interrupted. "Get to a phone and call me as soon as you can. I'm at 494-6088."

"Got it. Give me two minutes."

Smart cookie, thought Joanna. Her opinion of the detective rose several notches.

Joanna put the phone down as Martin entered the living room with two steaming mugs. He handed one to his sister. Joanna had barely taken a sip of her coffee before the telephone rang.

"Jo? It's Harry. What's up?"

"This conversation isn't being recorded, is it?"

"If it is, then it's being done illegally. I'm at a public phone at the Safeway."

"Good. You remember on Saturday night how you were bemoaning the fact that you couldn't scare the bejesus out of Felix Taylor?"

"Uh-huh."

"Well, I've just returned from his office. If he wasn't scared before, he is now. If I were you, I'd watch him like a hawk. If he's going to crack, it's going to be soon."

"Jo! What the hell have you done?"

"I told him that you have enough evidence to be sure of his guilt, but not enough to convict him in front of a jury."

"Jesus!"

Joanna ignored the interruption. "And then I told him that if he isn't in custody within forty eight hours, I personally would force a confession out of him by whatever means necessary."

"Shit! Jo! You can't *do* that. You've ruined the case. Any halfway competent defense attorney will use what you've done to tear us apart."

"Use what? If Taylor did it, I'd swear on a stack of Bibles that I just went to see him in his office about a sore leg. And if you have any brains, you'd back me up."

"But I can't do that. Don't you see? You shouldn't've told me, Jo. I..."

"Listen. While we're sitting here arguing the niceties of the law, Taylor may be leaving the state. If I were you, I'd go stake him out and get a telephone tap as well, if this bloody country lets you do that."

"Sorry. 'This bloody country,' as you call it, has laws about tapping phones. That's out. We don't have enough evidence yet to convince a judge to issue a warrant." There was an hiatus while his mind raced. "OK, here's what I'll do. I'll go and see Dr. Taylor right now and ask him a few ambiguous questions. If I leave him with the impression that we are on to him, then it won't be my fault if he misinterprets the strength of our hand. Jo?"

"Yes?"

"I'm sorry. I didn't mean to get angry. It's just that we have rules that we have to play by. You'd've made one hell of a good cowboy, though."

"Just go get something useful from it. Keep in touch."

She put the phone down.

"Now what was that all about?" asked Martin.

Chapter 18

Felix Taylor, for all his education and the wisdom of his years, was feeling trapped. He had never expected to feel this way. Before, he had thought that he would feel nothing but relief and satisfaction that the deed was done. But he didn't feel like that at all. Maybe it meant that he was weaker than he'd thought he was. But whatever the reason, he now found himself looking for a way out. But there wasn't one. Not as far as he could see, anyway.

Several times his hand went out to the telephone only to be withdrawn.

The hands on the clock turned slowly. His receptionist interrupted him to tell him that a patient had arrived.

He said, "I'm feeling ill, Ginny. Please cancel all appointments for the rest of the day. Apologize for me. Send them to Dr. Murphy or Dr. Williamson if it's urgent. Otherwise try to fit them in as soon as possible."

His nurse interrupted him next. He assured her that he wasn't sick; it was just that something had come up that needed his undivided attention. He'd be all right by tomorrow.

She left him in peace.

The hands of the clock continued to turn.

Then there was another interruption. His receptionist pushed open the door.

"I'm sorry, Dr. Taylor. It's that police detective. He's in the waiting room. I told him you were feeling ill and not seeing any patients, but he insisted that I tell you. He says he has no warrant and you can refuse to see him if you wish."

She sounded puzzled and indignant.

He looked at her, considered the waiting policeman, and made a decision.

"Tell him I'll be with him in a few minutes. I just have to make a phone call first."

Detective Harry Jones paced to and fro in the doctor's waiting room, wondering what the doctor was doing that was taking so long. He had already been waiting for twenty minutes, much longer than the promised "few minutes," and there was still no sign of the doctor.

Frustrated, he mentally reviewed the case.

On the one hand, he was more convinced than ever of Dr. Taylor's guilt; but on the other there was still the one fact that vitiated every theory he could concoct — the absence of any poison in Matthew Chambers' bloodstream. There was no getting around the fact that if Matthew had taken a poisoned capsule, it would have left unmistakable signs. Something — something important — was still missing.

His mind wandered to Joanna Salisbury.

At first he had been less than impressed with her. He had felt used, the way she had pumped him for information the first time they had met, as if she was trying to show him up by solving the case for him. But over the past few days she had seemed to relax and become more forthcoming and cooperative — and with each passing day she had seemed both younger and prettier. His first guess when they met had been that she was in her early forties. He had now revised that estimate downward about ten years.

One thing about her was obvious: she knew her stuff. The *sub-rosa* message that he had sent her on Saturday evening, for example. He knew that to incite her directly to commit a crime was itself criminal. But there had been no direct incitement, just a few words of suspicion and frustration. Without even acknowledging that she had understood, she had followed through in the most emphatic way possible. In fact, a bit more emphatic than he had wanted.

Whatever she had said to Dr. Taylor, though, had clearly rattled the man, otherwise he himself would not now be cooling his heels in the waiting room.

He already knew what he was going to say to the doctor. His threats would be much less direct than Jo's: "we have our eyes on you," "are you sure there is nothing you want to tell us?" — that sort of thing.

There was a noise and he looked up. Dr. Taylor stood in the corridor at the entrance to the reception area. He looked tired. "Haggard" was the word that sprang to mind.

The doctor said, "Would you come to my office?" Neither offered a handshake.

A minute later, the two men were seated in the doctor's office, avoiding one another's eyes. Harry waited.

Eventually, Dr. Taylor broke the silence.

"I suppose it's about Matthew Chambers?"

"Yes."

Harry pulled out his notebook and flipped it to an empty page. Ostentatiously, he clicked a ball-point pen, ready to write.

"What exactly did you want to know?"

"Well, sir. I was wondering if there was anything you wanted to tell me."

"About what? You know, there was a woman in here earlier who did everything except accuse me of murdering him. I'm sure you know who I mean. Do you think I murdered him?"

The question was fair and deserved an answer. But not necessarily one as direct as the question.

"My opinion, Dr. Taylor, does not matter. What matters is what a jury of twelve of your peers will decide after weighing the evidence before them."

"In that case, Detective Jones, I think I must refrain from saying anything further without my lawyer present. I assume you are placing me under arrest?"

Harry was caught off guard. He had not come here to make an arrest.

"No, sir. I don't have enough evidence... yet. But I think it will come; it's just a matter of digging deeper, isn't it?"

Dr. Taylor stared at the young officer. Harry would have given a year's salary to know what was going on behind the mask that faced him across the desk.

"Is it?" the doctor said. "I think that this interview is over, Mr. Jones. And in future I want my lawyer present whenever we talk. He tells me I don't have to tell you anything."

So the doctor had already spoken to his lawyer. That, at least, was something. That must have been why Harry had been kept waiting: Dr. Taylor was talking to his attorney.

The pager on Harry's belt vibrated silently, interrupting his thoughts. He glanced down and saw Chief Salter's telephone number on the display. He stood to leave.

"Is there a telephone I could use before I leave? I'm being paged."

"Certainly." Dr. Taylor made a gracious gesture. "Use the one in the reception area. It's connected directly to an outside line."

Harry made his way to the desk in the waiting room and dialed his supervisor.

John Salter was seated at his desk, drumming his fingers against the brown plastic veneer. A fax curled on the desk in front of him. For the tenth time he tried to flatten the thermal paper. He had no more success than the first nine times.

His telephone rang and he grabbed the instrument.

"Salter," he growled.

"Sir. It's Harry Jones."

"Harry, bring Taylor in. We've got a motive."

"Sir?"

"A fax came in for you and because you were out it was brought to me. It's from that law firm that Matthew Chambers used to work for before he came to Pinetree. The one in Chicago. Let me read you the gist of it."

He held the telephone between his head and his shoulder, using his hands to hold the facsimile flat. His eyes scanned the text.

"It's from Mr. Donald McCarthy, senior partner with Herman, McCarthy and Soward. He says, and I quote:

> "In regard to your request for information regarding Mr. Matthew Chambers, I am pleased to oblige you with the following.
>
> "Mr. Chambers was employed by Herman, McCarthy and Soward for the period from 1978 to 1990 as an attorney in our litigation department. According to our records, he participated in a total of 119 cases in this period.
>
> "It is our practice always to have a senior partner responsible for, and to work with, each of our practicing attorneys.

Mr. Chambers worked closely with Mr. Jeremy Bullard, a senior partner in our firm who has only the highest praise for the quality of Mr. Chambers's work while he was with us. Mr. Bullard and I have reviewed the cases with which Mr. Chambers was involved and believe that we have located the one which interested you. I can provide more information if necessary but briefly the facts are these:

"On December 20, 1989, a young negro male was arrested on suspicion of vehicular manslaughter in a hit and run incident in the community of Oak Park. The young man's father was (and still is) a prominent local businessman. He engaged our services to defend his son against the charge. Mr. Bullard was assigned the case and he delegated much of the work to Mr. Chambers.

"The case went to trial and the young man was found not guilty of the charge against him in a decision rendered on July 2, 1990.

"The name of the person who was killed in the incident was Harold Taylor, an eighteen-year-old white male, the son of a physician in Oak Park, Dr. Felix Taylor. Shortly after the decision was handed down in this case, Mr. Chambers resigned from our firm to relocate to Pinetree, Colorado where he is believed to have set himself up in practice. I have made inquiries and as far as I have been able to ascertain Dr. Taylor is no longer resident in the Chicago area. His wife died shortly after the incident to which I refer above. Soon after her death he moved away.

"I have no further information regarding Dr. Taylor. I trust that this will be of use to you.

"So, Harry, bring him in. We have enough to hold him for a while now."

"Yes, sir." Harry made no attempt to hide the elation in his voice.

He replaced the telephone and made his way back to the doctor's office. He knocked on the door and then stepped into the room without waiting for an invitation.

The doctor was seated, looking out the window. He swiveled his chair to face the detective.

"Dr. Felix Taylor, I am arresting you on suspicion of the murder of Mr. Matthew Chambers. Anything you say will be taken down and can be used in evidence against you. You have the right to remain silent and should you choose to exercise that right it will not be held against you. You have the right to have an attorney present. If you are unable to provide an attorney, one will be provided for you." Harry paused. "Come on, Dr. Taylor. We have you now."

Chapter 19

Davina Dawson woke. She was uncomfortable and stiff, and cramp was gnawing at her left leg. She tried to stretch to relieve the cramp, but the bag stuffed underneath the seat in front of her prevented her from stretching properly. Not for the first time she envied Martin, who always flew first class.

She looked towards the aisle. She would have stretched her legs there if she could, but between her and the narrow walkway slept two old ladies who, she was sure, would be unbearably polite if she woke them. It was not worth the guilt.

She looked out the window. Far below the Airbus, the flat farmland of the northern central states was gliding by. A large town was falling away behind the plane.

She looked at her watch, and was surprised to see how long she had slept. She tried to calculate where she had been this time yesterday, but her brain was not up to the task. Sometime in the past day or so she had caught a terrifyingly ancient 707 in Nairobi, Kenya. From there she had flown to Cape Town and thence in a 747 to London. After making her way from Heathrow to Gatwick and kicking her heels for several hours at the latter, she had boarded the Airbus. Within the hour, she should be on the ground in Denver.

It would be a relief when the journey was finally over. From the moment her plane had touched down in Nairobi to the moment she left

East Africa, she had barely had time to catch her breath. Eighteen-hour days had stretched first to nineteen hours, then to twenty, as she and Roger became crazed at capturing the multitudinous wildlife of the East African plains on tape and film at all hours of the day and night, at all angles, in all lights.

It was not until they declared their mission a success several days early — with only the *real* work to come: the tedious editing, cutting, selecting, annoyance at having everything but the one *right* shot — and decamped in the direction of Nairobi and civilization that her exhaustion had overcome her.

Now, after nearly twenty four hours on airplanes and at airports, thirteen of them spent asleep, her body was succumbing to a completely different kind of tiredness: one that required solid ground under her feet, with regular hours and edible food.

Her leg spasmed, and she tried once more to stretch.

She wondered if her postcard had arrived. She had tried to phone Matthew's house several times since mailing the postcard, giving precise details of when she was going to arrive in Denver, but no one had ever picked up the telephone. *Lucky things*, she thought, *enjoying themselves camping in the wilderness of the Rockies.*

Dully, she looked out at the world through the layers of plastic, thinking hopeful and vaguely happy thoughts.

Martin rang the doorbell for the second time, then turned idly to look at the view. The Healys' house was on the opposite side, and also at the opposite end, of the valley from Matthew's. Here the sun shone brightly, surrounding the house with a light, airy forest rather than the slightly gloomy always-shadowed pine trees around the north-facing house of which he was now part owner.

Joanna stood at his side. She breathed deeply of the thin, cool air.

"I could get used to this, you know," she said.

Martin had no time to respond. Sounds came from the interior of the house and, seconds later, the door was opened by a well-preserved woman in her early forties. Blonde, with no sign yet of incipient aging, her hair fell about her shoulders and glistened in the bright sunlight. She tipped her head and smiled at her visitors.

"Yes?"

"Excuse me," said Martin. "Mrs. Healy?"

"Yes. Do I know you?" The woman looked like she was trying to place them. "Oh, yes. You were at the funeral."

"Yes, ma'am. My name is Martin Salisbury, and this is my sister, Joanna."

"Oh, yes," the woman's smile intensified. "Of course. You're relatives of Matthew's aren't you? Please come in."

"Thank you. Just for a moment, if you don't mind."

She ushered them inside. All along the south-facing walls were windows through which sunlight streamed. Dust motes danced in the beams of light.

"I was just about to make some coffee. Would you like some?"

Martin declined, Joanna accepted, and both followed Mrs. Healy into the kitchen.

The house was very open, much more so than either Martin or Joanna were used to seeing in England or Australia. The living room, which was on their left as they entered the house, segued into the dining room, from which it was separated by a low wall. Martin nodded appreciatively as he followed Mrs. Healy through to the kitchen. It was a refined house, very American, very chaste, declaring "middle class affluence" to anyone who entered.

They passed a telephone on a small table, above which was a cork board with scribbled notes pinned to it.

"Would you like some orange juice, Mr. Salisbury?"

"Oh, call me Martin. And yes, please, I'd like that very much."

"And you must call me Lucinda."

Mrs. Healy dived into the enormous refrigerator and emerged with a large carton of orange juice. She filled a glass and handed it to Martin, and then began to prepare the coffee.

"Please, sit down in the living room, both of you. I'll join you shortly."

Martin and Joanna took seats that looked out at the panoramic view.

The Healys' house was closer to the valley floor than Matthew's, and the conurbation of Pinetree was hidden by a knoll between the house and the town. The soil here was thinner than on the other side of the valley, and there were fewer trees. In the middle distance, across the valley, they could see the peaks of the mountains: to the right the permanent white cap of Mount Devonshire; somewhat closer and lower was green-topped Pinetree Mountain, up which climbed gondola cabins.

They sat gazing at the view without speaking until Mrs. Healy appeared with a tray carrying two cups of coffee and a plate of what she no doubt would call cookies, but were still biscuits to Martin and Joanna. Joanna took her coffee and she and her brother began to nibble on the cookies.

"Since you were close to Matthew, we wanted to tell you in person," Martin started. "The police believe that Matthew was murdered and that the person responsible for his death is now in custody."

For a second, there was no visible reaction. Mrs. Healy was sitting in a comfortable chair, a cup of coffee in one hand and a sugar-coated cookie in the other. She was in the act of bringing the cookie to her mouth as Martin spoke. The cookie never reached its destination.

She sat immobile, her mouth slack. Then, in a way that perversely enthralled Martin, the color drained from her face. She sat stock still; then she blinked several times, took two breaths, and her body dipped sideways. The cookie and the coffee fell to the floor.

Mrs. Healy had lost consciousness.

Joanna scrambled to her side and held her head firmly between her knees as Martin scurried around trying to mop up the mess of the spilled coffee on the beige carpet. By the time the liquid was sopped up, Mrs. Healy was sitting in her chair once more, breathing deeply and making twittering noises. She shook her head several times.

"I'm sorry," she finally said. "I'm sorry about that. I really don't know what came over me."

Joanna and Martin comforted her: "That's all right"; "No need to apologize"; "It was my fault for shocking you like that"; "Are you sure you're all right?"

Things became calmer. Mrs. Healy apologized again.

"I'm sorry. It came as such a surprise. Matthew was killed? On purpose? Murder?"

Shock filled her voice.

"It certainly looks that way," said Joanna. "But the police think they have the man who did it, and he's going to spend the rest of his life behind bars if they have anything to do with it."

"Who was it? And why? What possible reason could someone have for killing Matthew? He was so sweet... I'm sorry. I'm still having trouble taking it in...."

"Do you know a man by the name of Felix Taylor? He's a doctor in town."

"Felix? Yes, of course I know him. He's in the Rotary Club with my husband. He seems a perfectly nice man."

"Sometimes appearances can be deceptive, Mrs. Healy. There is substantial evidence that he killed Matthew."

"But why? What had Matthew ever done to him?"

Martin said, "That's what we didn't know for a long time. Do you know where Matthew lived before moving to Pinetree?"

"Yes, Illinois. He practiced with a large firm in Chicago."

"Exactly. And do you know where Felix Taylor lived before *he* moved here?"

"No... Chicago?" she hazarded.

"Near enough. He lived in Oak Park, which is a suburb of Chicago."

"So you're saying that they knew one another when they lived near Chicago?"

"Not exactly. They didn't know one another, at least as far as we know at the moment. But it seems that about four years ago Matthew defended a young hit-and-run driver. The driver, everyone seems to agree, was guilty of vehicular homicide, but the jury found him not guilty, mostly because of the job Matthew did defending him.

"The person whom the young man killed was Harold Taylor, Felix Taylor's son, his only child.

"Felix's wife suffered from depression, and when she heard the news that the alleged killer of her son had walked free, she took an overdose. She was dead when Dr. Taylor found her.

"Matthew knew what he had done. He didn't know about Mrs. Taylor, I don't suppose, but he did know that because of him a guilty man had walked free. He decided that he no longer wanted to work in litigation, so he resigned and moved to Pinetree. A few months later, Dr. Taylor discreetly followed."

"So you're saying he followed Matthew here in order to kill him?"

Martin shrugged. "I don't know. Perhaps the tranquility and change of pace that Pinetree offered was part of what brought him as well. But it certainly looks possible that he came here with murder on his mind. He didn't seem to be in any hurry, though. Perhaps he thought that the longer he waited, the less likely he was to get caught. Anyway, what looked like a good opportunity came his way a couple of weeks ago.

"Matthew needed some medication for a sore shoulder, and Dr. Taylor provided him with capsules containing an anti-inflammatory. But what he also provided was a potent poison. Some of the capsules were left after Matthew died, you see, and one of them was tainted with a fatal dose of poison. So there doesn't seem much doubt."

Mrs. Healy had been alternately nodding and shaking her head throughout Martin's narrative. Now she sat motionless in her chair. Joanna hovered nearby in case she suffered a relapse.

Mrs. Healy waved her away. "I'll be all right. It's just such a shock, that's all. That anyone would want to kill Matthew. And Felix Taylor, of all people...."

Joanna spoke, her voice clipped and professional.

"Mrs. Healy, I'm a detective myself" — Mrs. Healy was past registering surprise at this — "and you wouldn't believe what people are capable of when they think they have sufficient cause. I've seen people killed for a lot less than this. That's one thing about being a policewoman: you lose your illusions about human nature very quickly. There isn't very much people won't do given sufficient motivation."

"I suppose so. But to follow Matthew here, to wait all those years and then cold-bloodedly kill him — it seems so inhuman."

"To the contrary, it's very human. To have lashed out and killed in a rage would have been animalistic. It's the careful planning and execution, you see, that makes it so human."

"Yes, I suppose so."

Martin broke in. "Anyway, we're sorry to have been the bearers of the news. But we thought you ought to be told. We'll leave you in peace now."

He rose to leave, and Joanna moved to his side.

"If there's anything you want us for, we're staying at Matthew's house and you can call us there."

Mrs. Healy nodded. "Yes, yes. Thank you."

She tried to lift herself out of her chair. For a moment she looked old and frail, and it required little imagination to guess how she would look in thirty years' time.

"You stay here; we'll let ourselves out," Martin said.

Mrs. Healy raised no objection, and Martin and Joanna crossed to the door and quietly let themselves out of the house, leaving Lucinda Healy alone with her grief.

They stood outside and filled their lungs with the thin mountain air.

"I'm glad that's over," Martin said, barely above a whisper, so that the sound would not carry through the open windows into the room they had just left.

"Yes, it's tough, isn't it? It's not a job I like doing. Come to think of it, there's not much to like about being a detective except when you finally nail the bastard that's committed a crime like this. It's not the glamorous job that's portrayed on television, you know."

"No, I suppose not," conceded Martin. Then, brightening, "Come on, Jo. It's over now. Let's get something to eat."

Chapter 20

Davina stopped at the gas station. Finding Pinetree had not been hard — it had been signposted as far back as I-70 — but she remembered Martin telling her that Matthew lived in a mountain home outside the town, well hidden by trees.

She filled the car with gasoline — the price less than a third what she was used to paying in England — then pulled to one side of the forecourt to enter the station to pay. As she signed the credit card voucher, she saw that her hand was shaking. She suddenly felt a wave of weakness.

She looked at her watch and wrestled with the time change. How long was it since she had eaten? When had she last tested her blood? Five hours, she realized. Too long.

"May I use the loo?" she asked.

The man behind the counter looked at her blankly.

"Toilet? Restroom?"

"Oh!" The man handed her the key. "It's round back."

Recovering her kit from the trunk, she went to the cramped room, where she tested her blood with the portable glucose meter. She found, as she had guessed, that her blood sugar was much too high. She prepared her insulin shot and administered it, then sat on the plastic rim of the toilet seat for three minutes while the injection took effect.

Feeling much better, she returned the key to the station attendant. "By the way, I'm trying to get to 11750 Mountainside Drive; do you know how to get there?"

"Mountainside Drive? Let me think."

The attendant rubbed his chin. "Is that out on the other side of town?"

"I don't know. A Mr. Matthew Chambers lives there."

The name seemed familiar to the attendant, but he couldn't place it. Vaguely, he was sure that he'd seen it printed somewhere in the past couple of weeks. In the newspaper, maybe.

"Well, if it's the road that I'm thinking of, you want to get back on the highway and head through town. Take the exit marked 'West Pinetree'; it's the third exit from here. I think Mountainside is the road that goes right past the Safeway store on the west side; you just follow it to the south up Mount Devonshire and you should pass the address you're looking for before you go too far." He sounded uncertain.

"Thanks. I'll try that." Davina resolved to stop at the supermarket to ask again.

But there was no need to ask for further directions. As soon as she pulled off the highway at the third exit, a sign indicated Mountainside Drive. She turned left, passed underneath the highway, and almost immediately began to climb out of the valley.

The road was much easier to find than the house. She twice passed the mailbox with the chipped numbers before she decided to try the single-lane track which left the road at that point. The houses in the neighborhood were set back so far from the road that they were completely invisible behind the wall of trees. She climbed the long driveway and stopped herself in front of a spectacular house. The garage door was closed. There were no obvious signs of life.

She was not surprised. Matthew and Martin were probably miles away, camping deep in the backcountry. She intended merely to leave a note on the front door and then return to a motel in town and wait for a call when they returned. She found a sheet of paper and a pen, and made her way up the winding steps to the front door of the house.

After leaving her note, she decided that she ought to try to confirm that this was indeed Matthew's house. So, suppressing a guilty feeling, she walked around the outside of the house on the redwood deck, peering inside.

She found what she was looking for in the living room, where a chess game was in progress on a small table next to the window. Matthew was a chess nut, so this was probably the right house. She began to make her way down the steps back to the car when suddenly there was the noise of an engine, followed almost immediately by a harsh squeal of brakes. Another car had come within inches of rear-ending hers.

Martin jumped out of the car, a torrent of abuse at the ready for the fool who had left his car where it was asking to be hit.

He saw her standing on the steps, and all thoughts of anger fled. He had forgotten how beautiful she was. How his heart beat faster merely at the sight of her. He called her name and ran to her.

They embraced and kissed. Several times.

Joanna got out of the car and waited.

Davina's eyes moved to Joanna, and Martin saw both their movement and the suspicious narrowing that followed an instant later.

He hurried to explain.

"Darling, this is my cousin Joanna, from Australia."

"Cousin? You never...."

"Long story. I'll explain later."

"And you must be Davina," said Joanna, extending her hand. "Martin has told me a lot about you."

They climbed to the front door and let themselves in. It was almost two minutes before Davina realized that something didn't make sense.

"Where's Matthew? I expected you two still to be camping."

Joanna said, "I'll go make some coffee. Or tea if you prefer? Although that doesn't work well at this altitude."

"Oh, yes; I'd love some coffee."

Joanna departed for the kitchen, leaving Martin to explain.

When Joanna returned, it was to silence.

"Martin told me about Matthew," Davina said unnecessarily. She took the mug of coffee. "I'm sorry. What can I say? It's just terrible."

Martin said, "Yes, well at least they caught the guy that did it."

Silence descended once more.

Joanna decisively changed the subject. "Come on, I'll show you around the house. You'll stay with us, of course. Martin's in the spare room; it has a double bed."

Joanna nearly bit her tongue at the *faux pas*. Martin had never spelled out his sleeping arrangements with Davina.

She quickly grabbed Davina by the hand to hide her embarrassment, made it clear that Martin was not welcome, and began to lead Davina around the house.

"Pleased to meet you, Joanna."

Chief of Detectives Salter held out his hand to Detective Sergeant Salisbury. They shook firmly.

"Harry told me a bit about how you've been helping on this Chambers case. I'd like to thank you personally for your assistance. I understand you've been a great help."

"My pleasure," replied Joanna, wondering to herself how much Harry had really told his boss. Not too much, she hoped. "We have to stick together, don't we?"

"My thoughts exactly," Salter rejoined. "Now, let's go find a table."

Harry, Joanna and John Salter moved forward to catch the attention of the *maître d'hôtel*.

"Just the three of you? Smoking or nonsmoking?"

The three exchanged querying looks.

"Non is fine for me," offered Joanna.

"Fine. Nonsmoking, please," Salter said.

"If you'll follow me." The *maître d'hôtel* gathered three menus and led them to a booth on the far side of the restaurant.

They took their seats, the two Americans seated together on one side, Joanna on the other.

"Sorry your brother couldn't make it," said Salter.

"Well, to tell the truth, I have a confession to make. I didn't invite him. His girlfriend arrived unexpectedly today, you see, and I thought he'd appreciate the time alone with her. I told him that you'd invited me out, wished him well and then left the two of them alone. They have some catching up to do."

She became absorbed in the menu, desperately trying to suppress her blush.

"Well, anyway, thanks again for all your help. And pass that on to your brother as well, won't you?"

"I will. Now, what do you recommend?"

It was quarter of an hour before the subject turned to the death of Matthew Chambers.

Joanna asked, "Now, tell me, how sure are you that you're going to nail Felix Taylor?"

There was a long moment's silence before Salter replied.

"That's a good question, Jo. He did it; I don't think that any of *us* have any doubt about that. But convincing a jury beyond a reasonable doubt is going to be hard. I'm certainly not going to the DA until we have a lot more than we've got so far. I'd really like to have a signed confession, but Taylor is a canny bastard. He's not talking to us without his lawyer present, and the lawyer basically has told him to shut up and not answer any questions. Even the harmless ones. It took us an age to find out about his wife, even though he must have known we'd find out eventually. We had to ask the coroner's office in Oak Park. So he's not being cooperative.

"His lawyer talked to me this afternoon and wanted to know in detail what we had against Taylor. Normally we try to be pretty cooperative with lawyers, but I told this one that if his client wasn't going to talk to us we certainly weren't going to say anything to him."

"Have you formally charged Taylor yet?"

"No. We'll do that tomorrow; we daren't keep him longer than that without charging him. We have enough evidence to charge him and hold him for a while. We'll just have to hope that we can get something from him before the first hearing."

"The thing that bothers me," Harry interjected, "is that I still don't understand how he did it. I mean, the evidence is conclusive that there was no poison in Matthew's bloodstream at the time of death. If Matthew was poisoned, then we should have found something. We *would* have found something. But we didn't. It still doesn't make sense. Everything we have points to Felix Taylor, but it's the things we don't have but which would confirm him as the killer that worry me."

"I know what you mean," said Salter. "But that isn't what bothers me most. It's what *was* in his bloodstream: that damned hypnotic. What was that doing there? And why was there an extra capsule left in Chambers' pill bottle?"

Joanna said, "Maybe Taylor's statement is wrong. Maybe he gave Chambers seven capsules, not six. Or maybe Matthew's shoulder stopped hurting and he simply skipped one of them."

"Or maybe" — this from Harry — "Taylor gave him six and somebody else put a seventh one in his bottle."

"No, that still seems farfetched. In the first place, how would one go about taking a pill bottle away from a man, adding a capsule and then replacing the bottle without the man knowing? In the second place, the capsule would have to be identical to the ones already there, and that would be practically impossible."

From Joanna: "How about if Taylor used two different kinds of poison and Matthew just happened to take the other one first?" She thought about that for a moment and then concluded, "No, that's just as farfetched as some third party adding a capsule."

"Wait a minute." Salter sounded excited. "Maybe you're on to something there. If there were capsules with two different types of poison, then that would tend to throw suspicion away from Taylor, wouldn't it? After all, even if he admitted to poisoning one of the capsules, then the jury would conclude that any reasonable, sane, logical man would have no reason to poison a second one with a quite different substance."

"Yes," Harry joined in. "And if he actually gave Matthew one more capsule than he said he did, then at whatever time he took the first poisoned capsule, there would always be one more capsule in the bottle than we would expect, leaving room for reasonable doubt in the mind of the jury that perhaps someone else had added a capsule."

"That's it, that's it, I'm sure of it." Elation filled Salter's voice. "Or if not, it's something like that. It has to be. And maybe the hypnotic is there because it was needed to mask the other poison. I'll check with the coroner, but I bet he'll tell me that the hypnotic could have masked some other drug, something fatal."

"Even if he does confirm it, you still have to prove that that's what happened," cautioned Joanna.

"Not necessarily, although we certainly aren't going to stop trying. We have the motive, the means, the opportunity, and, best of all, we now have a story which shows how cold-blooded and logical Felix Taylor is. The sort of man who would wait four years before committing his crime is exactly the sort of man to concoct a complex scheme like this."

Salter looked at Joanna. "You don't look convinced."

She shook her head. "I don't know. It's a story, but it's not a *good* story." She shrugged. "Maybe you're right, though. I can't think of anything better."

"Of course I am. You'll see. Waiter! A bottle of champagne, if you please."

Chapter 21

It had been a glorious two days. Martin Salisbury could not remember ever being happier.

He and Davina had reveled in each other's company like two teenage lovers. Joanna had maintained a discreet distance. They had seen her at breakfast and occasionally around the house, but she had made a point of being out most of the time, "taking the opportunity to get out and see some of Colorado," she said. Too absorbed with themselves, they had not questioned her, and were unaware that she had been accompanied in her explorings by a young detective from the Pinetree police department who was taking things easy after cracking a tough case.

The third day began much like its antecedents, except that as Joanna and Davina leaned on the railing of the redwood deck sipping coffee, they had goose bumps on their arms. Joanna shivered.

Davina said, "it seems colder today."

Instead of the pellucid cerulean they had come to expect, fluffy clouds dotted the sky. It was not yet eight o'clock, and experience had shown that the sky only became more cloudy as the day progressed.

"I hope you don't have too many plans for today; the weather doesn't look very cooperative," Davina continued.

"I've arranged to meet someone for lunch, that's all. If it's all right with you, maybe I'll stay at home this morning, if you're sure I won't be in the way."

"It's your house as much as it is Martin's. Anyway, you've been off gallivanting so much the past couple of days, you need a morning to relax. Oh, there you are, lazy thing."

Martin stuck his head out of the French window which led on to the deck. He sniffed the air. "Brrr... it's cold this morning." He retreated into the house.

Joanna met Harry as arranged at the foot of the gondola at half past eleven. As always the past few days he was smiling, a contrast to the sky above which was becoming steadily more overcast with clouds that had changed from attractive cotton wool to menacing steel.

Joanna wondered how Harry thought of their burgeoning relationship. More to the point, how did *she* think of it? It would be easy to dismiss the question as silly — or at least premature; after all, all they had done was to spend a couple of days in one another's company. But she couldn't remember two more enjoyable days. Harry made her laugh. Even when she was head-over-heels crazy about Kevin, he had never done that. Twice she had caught herself seriously wondering what it would be like to resign her job in Australia and move to the tranquility of Pinetree.

Today, Harry had returned to work after his two days of vacation. As they settled themselves in the gondola and the town began to fall away below them with what still seemed to Joanna to be incredible speed, she asked him, "So how's progress with Felix Taylor?"

Harry's face became taut. "It's exactly like we thought, just as we suspected that evening in the restaurant — we're making no progress at all. He's decided on his story and he's sticking with it. He admits to poisoning one capsule with cyanide — the one we found — but that's all."

"And what news from the coroner about that hypnotic? Could it have masked something else?"

Harry shook his head. "No. It was a good theory, but unfortunately he says he knows of no poison that would be masked like that."

"Damn! So you can get him on attempted murder, but not murder?"

"Yes. And even then if his lawyer does a good job he'll get a pretty light sentence. After all, the death of his son and then his wife are bound to be viewed as extenuating circumstances."

Joanna did not reply. Her gaze settled on the middle distance; her thoughts were a muddle.

The gondola shivered as they passed a support pylon. Ahead of them the restaurant came into view. The entire journey had passed without her realizing it.

Shaking herself from her reverie, she asked, "So, what next?"

"I don't know. We'll keep questioning him. But he always has his lawyer with him and he's been adamant with his story so far. I don't think he's likely to break."

"So, after all this, Matthew's killer is going to get away with it?"

"I'm afraid so. I'm sorry."

"It's all right. It happens. I've seen it too many times to lose too much sleep over it. Martin won't be happy, though."

Harry looked at Joanna. He freely admitted — to himself — that he found her very attractive, both physically and intellectually. She really was a good policewoman. Her reaction to his discouraging news showed that even when she had every right to lose her objectivity, she remained dispassionate. Not only that but she really was remarkably beautiful.

Chief Salter looked up as he barked, "Enter."

His eyebrows arched in surprise when he saw the man who walked into his office.

Trenton Byers closed the door behind him. Salter looked at the middle-aged, dark-haired, lanky man, and wondered what Felix Taylor's attorney could possibly want with him. He offered the lawyer a seat. The tall man sat, looking slightly ill at ease. His uneasiness was a novel sight. Byers was usually so sure of himself.

"What may I do for you, Mr. Byers?"

John Salter had had dealings with Trenton Byers before. He had found him punctilious, a stickler for the rules, an exasperatingly annoying opponent in the courtroom and someone whose ability to reveal flaws in the prosecution during cross examination was second to none. He wondered what had brought him to his office.

"An off-the-record conversation, Mr. Salter."

Salter let out his breath audibly. Now this *was* a surprise. He leaned back in his chair, taking the opportunity to study Byers. There was definitely something bothering the attorney.

"I really can't do that, Mr. Byers." He nearly added, "And you know it," but he preferred to see if the lawyer would give any clues as to why he wanted a private conversation. If it was sufficiently important, the rules could always be broken, although this was not the place.

The lawyer nodded. "Yes, I know. Well, I'll be going. I think I'll take the rest of the morning off work. I expect I'll be at Eagles' Nest Park in" — he looked at his watch — "about an hour. Good-bye."

The lawyer rose, nodded once, and was gone.

There it was, no clue as to the purpose of the meeting, just a time and place. He'd go, of course, just as Byers had known that he would. He only hoped that he would not regret it.

An isolated valley five miles out of town, Eagles' Nest Park saw few visitors. As Salter drove his personal car into the parking lot, there were only two vehicles in evidence on the gravel: an old yellow Volkswagen bearing California license plates and a blue Mercedes with Pinetree County plates that read: A1 LAW.

He pulled in next to the Volkswagen, got out of his car, and scanned the surroundings. There was no sign of Byers. But he was here somewhere: Byers' Mercedes was unmistakable. Salter locked the car and began to walk down the trail from the parking lot to the meadow at the base of the cliffs that formed the haunt of the eagles for which the park was named.

He had gone about a quarter of a mile, the parking lot now lost to sight behind a grove of aspen, when he saw movement next to a boulder some way ahead and perhaps a couple of hundred feet off the path. Coming closer, he recognized Byers, seated adjacent to the rock, alternating between scanning the sky with binoculars and examining a book that was open in his lap.

Stepping through the tall grass that bordered the path, he approached the lawyer. Byers wordlessly continued with his apparent search. Salter looked around, more concerned about being seen than about what Byers was looking for.

They were close against the eastern wall of a deep spur in the valley. The rock towered high above. In crannies, small evergreens grew. The trees' tenacity and ability to thrive in the most unlikely of circumstances always amazed the policeman. Even where there seemed to be no soil, stunted evergreens challenged the world.

No one else was visible.

"There."

Salter looked up, following the line of Byers' binoculars. A golden eagle had taken flight; somewhere in the scree high on the craggy cliff was an eyrie. The eagle circled, magnificent and regal, its wings outstretched, an enormous, majestic bird whose appearance complemented the rugged contours of the valley.

"Fantastic, isn't she?"

Byers offered the binoculars to Salter. The detective declined. He hadn't come to look at wildlife.

Byers continued, "There used to be five pairs here up until a few years ago. Now there's only two. They say that when this valley was first discovered there were at least twenty nesting pairs. It's sad, isn't it, what humans do to nature even by their mere presence?"

The last thing the police officer wanted was a discussion of the demise of eagles in Pinetree County. He had come out here for a reason, and every second spent in the company of Trenton Byers was a second when they might be seen by a witness — a witness who could later testify to that effect in court. He tried to force the pace of the conversation.

"It's not half as sad as what humans do to one another, Mr. Byers. Now, if we could just get on with it; I have work waiting for me back at the office."

The lawyer turned to face the detective.

"Strictly off the record?"

The policeman nodded.

"Felix Taylor is telling the truth."

"What do you mean?"

"The story that Felix Taylor is giving you, the one that you are so desperately trying to break, it's the truth."

For several seconds, the policeman was surprised into silence. Then he asked, "How do you know?"

"Because he told me."

"And you trust him? He's a cold-blooded killer, Byers. I wouldn't trust him as far as I can see with my eyes closed."

The lawyer nodded.

"I know, I know. Let me tell you what happened. As you know, he insisted on seeing me in private, as is his right. And, as usual, the first thing I told him was that if he wanted me to represent him, he had to tell me the full, unvarnished truth, and if I ever discovered that he had lied to me, I'd walk away and leave him to take his chances.

"He's an intelligent man, Salter, a very intelligent man, but I'm sure you already know that. He understood his position, and he came clean without any prompting from me — the whole thing.

"He told me about his son and his wife and what Mr. Chambers had done. Just as you surmised, he followed Chambers to Pinetree with the aim of killing him when the time was propitious. He was in no hurry, no hurry at all. In fact, he said that he'd have been equally happy for Matthew Chambers to have been run over by a truck or die by any other means. He just wanted to see the man dead and he didn't particularly care how it happened.

"But eventually fate gave him the perfect opportunity to carry out a plan that he had worked out a couple of years ago. He knew that Chambers was something of a fitness fanatic and therefore it was likely that at some time he would come to him with some sort of muscular pain.

"Taylor had put a special bottle of capsules to one side against the day when that happened. It finally happened on the eleventh of this month.

"Taylor gave him the bottle and that, as far as he was concerned, was going to be the end of Matthew Chambers. And it was, but not the way he expected. You see, he insists that he poisoned only one capsule. That was the capsule you found. There really were only six capsules in the bottle, just like he told you. Chambers must simply have skipped taking one, which was why there was one more capsule in the bottle than there should have been. Or possibly someone slipped another capsule into the bottle. Discovering what happened is your problem, not mine.

"What has bothered Taylor about this whole affair was that he has been waiting and waiting for the police to produce the damning evidence — that Matthew Chambers was poisoned, and cyanide was found in his blood. But not only have you not produced that evidence, the lab reports make it quite clear that the evidence doesn't exist. Salter, I felt that I had to warn you: you've got the wrong man."

Salter was silent for ten full seconds while he considered the attorney's story. At last, he spoke.

"And what if you're just telling me this to try to convince me that Taylor is innocent?"

Byers shook his head violently. "No, no, you don't understand. I care very little how you personally feel about Felix Taylor's guilt or innocence. My job is to get him off as lightly as possible, regardless of what you or anyone else thinks. No, Chief Salter, what I want you to understand is not that my client is innocent. Keep trying to prove him guilty. I really don't care about that. But you need to understand that there's a cold-blooded murderer still walking around Pinetree and you've given up looking for him."

Salter looked at Trenton Byers. He was sure the lawyer was telling the truth.

Chapter 22

The massing clouds brooded ominously three thousand feet above the mountain community. The cloud base was peppered with obtrusions: inverted mounds, hundreds of them, black, almost green, pregnant with rain and hail. The obtrusions filled the sky, some extending below the level of the mountain-top restaurant. Harry and Joanna gazed at them.

"Mammatus, that's called," said Harry, "and it's a sure sign that we're in for some real weather this afternoon. It's not uncommon in summer. Actually, I'm surprised we haven't had a decent storm since you've been here."

Joanna shivered. It was not cold inside the restaurant, but even so the glowering beyond the glass made her feel exposed and chill. When the storm broke, it would be spectacular.

Harry continued, "Come on. I should be getting back to work, and we want to be sure of getting down the hill before the lightning starts."

Joanna shot him a querying look.

"We don't want to be on the gondola if the power goes out," he explained.

Privately, Harry thought that that situation might not be all bad, but even so he did not want to risk it.

"I hadn't thought of that."

Joanna finished her coffee in a single unladylike gulp and began to gather her belongings.

They reached the bottom of the mountain only moments before the show began.

Harry had been wondering for the entire downward journey what Joanna would think if he attempted to kiss her good-bye. While he was still trying to make up his mind, the first heavy drops thudded around them. In moments, they were standing in a downpour. Suddenly a kiss seemed impractical.

"See you later," Harry called, running in the direction of his parked car.

Joanna reached her car just as the first flash flickered overhead. Thunder rolled around the valley as she threw herself inside.

The drive back to the house was truly frightening.

It was the kind of deluge that sometimes occurred in the outback; the rain was a gray-black sheet hovering a few feet in front of the car, barely pierced by the twin beams of the headlights. The three-speed windshield wipers even at their fastest were barely able to cope.

She began to climb the track to the house, down which rivulets were already flowing. Lightning flashed intermittently overhead; when it flashed, crashing thunder followed with only a moment's delay.

She braked to a halt in front of the garage, next to Davina's car. For a second, the rain eased slightly. She decided to make a run for it. Throwing open the door, she jumped out, slammed the door closed behind her and hurried up the twisting stone steps to the front door.

It was no more than fifty feet, and she was in the rain for ten seconds at the most. By the time she reached the eaves of the house she looked like she had been standing fully clothed in a shower for a good minute.

She dripped great drops of moisture on to the hardwood floor. Martin and Davina were both in the living room. Davina was reading a book while Martin worked on a crossword puzzle.

"We didn't expect you to be out in this," Martin said, looking at his bedraggled sister. "You look like a drowned rat. You'd better go get changed," he added needlessly.

"I'll go make some coffee, you look like you need it," said Davina.

Leaving a wet trail, Joanna headed for her bedroom. When she reappeared several minutes later, showered and dry, there were three steaming mugs on a table in the middle of the room, and Davina and Martin were standing hand in hand at the window watching the spectacle beyond the glass.

Joanna joined them. The downpour was even more opaque than before. There was a wall of blackness seemingly only a few feet from the house. Every few seconds it was lit with a flash, sometimes white, sometimes blue, sometimes pink, accompanied by the sharp crack of thunder. She could feel the floor tremble with every thunderclap.

The spectacle lasted another ten minutes before the rain finally began to slacken. The black wall became gray; it receded and eventually resolved itself into vertical lines, a forest of parallel pencil strokes reaching across to the other side of the valley, which was now mistily visible. They turned away from the window and seated themselves.

Over coffee, Joanna told them about her lunch. She did not mention her confused feelings for Detective Harry Jones.

The conversation drifted gradually to other topics: life in England, Australia and Pinetree; the house in which they were sheltering from the storm; Matthew himself.

"I've never seen a picture of Matthew. Was he handsome?" asked Davina.

"Oh yes," said Martin. "You'd have fallen for him straight away."

"A much improved version of my brother," added Joanna impishly (although she had never met her cousin).

Martin said, "I don't think there are any photographs, are there? Oh, except that really old one which doesn't really do him justice."

Joanna agreed. "We found one in one of those cardboard boxes" — she waved towards the six boxes that had been rescued from the attic, now neatly stacked in one corner — "with one of his old girlfriends. We can probably dig it out if you like," she added without enthusiasm.

"I'd like to see what he looked like," Davina said.

So the three of them retreated to the corner and started emptying one of the boxes. The photograph and its accompanying letter were near the bottom of the box.

Joanna handed the photograph to Davina.

It was blurred and of rather poor quality. A young couple was standing in some kind of garden, the flowers in bloom but too blurred for certain identification.

The man looked quite tall and rather dignified, but this impression was conveyed more by his posture than his face, which was a blurred fuzziness with no details clearly visible. The girl was shorter, her smile broad and clear, the top of her head level with his eyes. Her hair was dark and, from the tilt of her head, it appeared to be long, flowing out of sight down the back of her head; she wore a dress that was cut low and ended high; there was no mistaking the decade in which the photograph had been taken.

Martin watched Davina as she concentrated on the photograph. How beautiful she was. He wondered if he could stand another rejection. He had not proposed to her since she had suddenly appeared in Pinetree. Whenever he thought of Matthew, though, the shortness and uncertainty of life made themselves felt. He knew he wanted to spend the rest of his life, no matter how long or short, with this woman.

His eyes moved from Davina to the photograph.

Suddenly something struck him about the photograph. It was something to do with the way that the woman was holding her head.

He tried desperately to remember... what?

Time seemed to come to a halt. He was oblivious to everything — Davina; his sister; the rain outside — desperately searching for something which he knew was buried somewhere inside his head. Like solving a difficult crossword clue, seemingly unrelated facts flitted in and out of his consciousness as he tried to fit them together.

Then he remembered.

He stretched his hand out to the cardboard box. To his surprise, his hand was trembling.

At the bottom of the box was one more item: an envelope containing a letter written long ago; a letter telling a distant young officer fighting for his country in the jungles of Vietnam that a young woman had left him for another. He picked up the letter and examined the writing on the outside of the envelope.

It was the same, he was almost sure of it.

Slowly, his hands still shaking, he removed the single sheet of folded paper. Yes. He was right. He was sure of it. There was the simple, idiosyncratically looped "L."

He lowered the letter and stared into space.

Joanna noticed first. She looked at her brother and wondered what had come over him. The color had drained from his face and he was trembling.

"Martin, are you all right?"

There was no response. He was staring into the distance; there was no indication that he had even heard his sister. Davina pushed him playfully.

"Martin?"

Martin returned from wherever he had been. He held out the letter wordlessly.

Joanna took it and glanced at it, but could see nothing new.

"What is it? What's the matter?"

"I know who wrote it."

"You mean you know who 'L' was?"

"Is, not was. The 'L' is for Lucinda."

Joanna's jaw dropped.

"You mean... Lucinda Healy? Bill Healy's wife?"

Martin nodded, his face now grim.

"Yes. It's that signature, the looped 'L'. Something has been niggling me for some time and I just haven't been able to put my finger on it. Then, just now, when Davina was looking at the photograph of Matthew and 'L,' it came to me that I'd seen someone else who held her head that way. Her hair is shorter now, and the features are blurred in the photograph, but just for an instant I had a picture in my head of Lucinda Healy greeting us at her front door. She held her head that same way. And then I realized what had been bothering me.

"Do you remember the cork noticeboard that the Healys have above the telephone near the entrance to the kitchen? The board covered with little memos and notes?"

"Yes."

"Well, it was the writing on some of those notes. In particular, it was the single letter 'L' with its flourish. That's how she signed them. I'd seen that 'L' before, but hadn't realized it until now. But it all suddenly came together. It was the same as the letter Matthew had kept." He pointed to the signature. "There, you see; there's a sort of twisty tail. It's not there any other time she writes a capital 'L', just on her signature. And it's exactly the same as the 'L' she uses on her memos to her husband."

There was silence for fully a minute.

Davina was the first to speak.

"So the person in this photograph, the one who was once going to marry your cousin Matthew, is now Lucinda Healy?"

"Yes, I think so. I'm almost certain of it."

Joanna spoke. "And where did Matthew have his last meal?"

She spoke to the room in general; they all knew the answer. Martin said it.

"At the Healys' house."

The ramifications began to sink in. In a moment Joanna was a professional once more.

"OK. We can either call Harry right away to tell him about this, or we can check it out for ourselves."

The mere fact that she had given them a choice reflected which course she favored. Her eyes strayed to the window. The rain was now only a heavy shower. High above, the sky was a thin gray in which patches of blue were beginning to appear.

Martin lifted himself to his feet. "To the Healys', then?"

They arrived at the house on the opposite side of town thirty minutes later. The rain had ceased and the sun had come out. The air smelled damp and clean.

They got out the car and walked together — quietly, grimly — to the front door. Martin pressed the doorbell. Ten seconds passed before Mrs. Healy opened the door, and when she did so all of them knew with a terrible certainty that Martin had been right. Now they could match the concrete Mrs. Healy in her early forties with the blurred image in Joanna's handbag, they could all see that it was the same person. As if to confirm it, she tilted her head before speaking.

"Hello. I do hope you don't have more bad news for me?"

"May we come in?" Martin asked.

"Yes, of course."

Mrs. Healy swung the door wide and they trooped in. As she led them to the living room, Martin introduced Davina.

Davina said, "I'm sorry, but the altitude makes my throat dry. Could I possibly have a glass of water?"

Joanna remained in the living room while Martin and Davina followed Lucinda Healy to the kitchen, talking about the just-concluded storm. As Mrs. Healy was occupied getting the water, Martin removed from the corkboard a small square of paper which said: "B: Frank called; please call back. L." The "L" was exactly as he had remembered it, the twin of the one in the letter in Joanna's handbag.

He placed it in his pocket, then spoke to Joanna quietly. They looked up as Mrs. Healy and Davina approached.

Martin said, "Excuse me. Could I use your telephone for a minute? I have to make an important call."

"Certainly," said Mrs. Healy. "You may use this one, or there's one in the kitchen."

Martin hurried to the kitchen and punched a number. He faced a corner and spoke quietly so that no one would be able to overhear.

238

Davina kept the conversation flowing in the living room, talking mostly about herself and her work, regaling her audience with anecdotes about her just-completed trip to Kenya. Mrs. Healy listened politely but, quite obviously, without particular interest. She was beginning to feel distinctly discomfited when Martin returned. Martin nodded to Joanna as he took a seat on the sofa next to her. Davina stopped talking and the conversation trailed into nothingness.

Joanna broke the silence. Lucinda Healy ought to be given one last chance to come clean before the evidence was placed in front of her.

"Mrs. Healy, how well did you know Matthew?"

"Oh, as well as anyone I suppose. We had him around for meals quite often, you know. I suppose that in a way we sort of took him under our collective wings, Bill and I. You know, I think he was quite lonely, really, living in the isolated house of his...."

Martin tried something more direct.

"How long had you known him?"

"Oh, he arrived in Pinetree about four years ago, I think it was. We've lived here for about twenty five years, and we always like to welcome newcomers to our little mountain community."

Martin and Joanna looked at one another. Joanna took a deep breath, then asked *the* question.

"How long had you been having an affair with him?"

That stopped Lucinda Healy. She looked from one to the other. Her breathing became tense.

Her voice rising indignantly, she said, "How dare you ask such a question? I think it's time for you to leave. If my husband was here, he'd throw you all out of the house."

Davina said quietly, "We know, Mrs. Healy. Matthew kept a photograph and a letter. The last letter you sent him in Vietnam, breaking it off."

Mrs. Healy looked at them all again. Slowly, she sank back into her chair.

She looked deflated.

Joanna said, "Please, Mrs. Healy. There's no point in keeping it secret any longer. We won't tell your husband. Or does he know?"

"No. I suppose you're right: it doesn't really matter now. Yes, Matthew and I were lovers. Bill would kill me if he ever found out."

"So Matthew came to Pinetree four years ago because of you?"

She nodded as she blinked back tears.

"Yes. He never got over me, you see. We were engaged when he went off to serve in Vietnam. While he was away, my parents moved from Ohio to Connecticut and I met what I thought was a spectacularly handsome and intelligent young man called Bill Healy.

"I thought it was love at first sight. Of course, it was nothing of the kind. It was a lustful infatuation, that was all. But it was returned, you see; Bill felt the same way about me, and I was blinded to everything. I wrote to Matthew breaking the engagement, and within a couple of months Bill and I married. Bill was just finishing his degree. When he graduated he wanted to come back to his home town to set up a business. So after only a few months of marriage, we moved here, to Pinetree.

"I never told Matthew we had moved. I lost track of him. At first, I was happy enough being married to Bill, and then, when things began to go downhill, I really didn't want to be reminded of what might have been.

"When Matthew moved to Pinetree, he told me what had happened. He made no effort to find me when he came back to the States. He completed his degree, went through law school and then took a job with a large law firm in Chicago. After a while something happened there — it isn't important — and he decided to get out of the rat race.

"He had gone to Connecticut and wheedled my address out of my parents several years earlier. And in fact he had already visited Pinetree several times, although we never met. He decided that he liked Pinetree for its own sake, not just because of me, you see. At least, that's what he told me. Anyway, he decided to move here permanently; within two weeks of his arrival he'd purchased a house and within a month he had set up his practice.

"He didn't search me out even then. He was a guest at the Rotary Club a couple of times, and then he was invited to join. He got to know Bill pretty well. The first I knew of any of this was at a Rotary Ladies' Night. I nearly passed out when I walked into the room and there, like a ghost from the past, was Matthew, looking fitter and more handsome than ever. At first, I was sure that I was mistaken, that it couldn't possibly be Matthew, but as I approached, he winked at me.

"Well, I didn't know what to do. Bill and I began to see more of him, but somehow I never got around to telling Bill about our past together. I think things would have been very different if Matthew had actively pursued me, but he didn't. We just found ourselves in one another's company every now and then, and I discovered that I was beginning to look forward to those times.

"I suggested to Bill that Matthew must be lonely and we should perhaps have him around for an occasional meal. He agreed and that's when things began to get serious.

"Matthew came around one evening when Bill had to go out to a meeting of the planning commission. I don't know how it happened, but I don't regret it."

Her voice was firm, resolute, defiant.

"After that first time, we would get together a couple of times a month somehow or other. We were made for each other, you know. He knew that, he said he always had known it. It took me two decades of a very average marriage to come to the same conclusion.

"Bill and I have never talked about divorce. It would be too hard on Bill. Bill loves me, you know. He would have been terribly jealous if he'd found out what was going on. I hate to say it, but I suppose that I am at least grateful that I no longer have to live my life gnawed with guilt for having an affair behind my husband's back...."

Her voice petered out and she stared blankly at the wall.

Davina said, "Mrs. Healy, thank you for sharing that with us. You can be sure that your husband won't find out from us."

They rose to leave. Mrs. Healy pushed herself up out of her chair.

As they crossed the room towards the front door, Joanna asked, "At least you have the comfort of knowing that Matthew ate his last meal in the company of someone he loved. Did he stay behind that night? If I remember correctly, your husband went to a council meeting straight after the meal."

"Yes, there was a council meeting that night and Bill left at about seven. You're right: normally, Matthew would have stayed behind; but he was feeling awfully woozy and decided he'd better get back home."

"Woozy?"

"Yes. He was fine when he arrived for the meal and everything seemed all right when we were eating. Let me see now..., what exactly happened? Oh yes, I was in the kitchen getting the dessert ready. We were having a pavlova, and I wanted to put the whipped cream and kiwi on at the last minute so the meringue wouldn't go soft. Anyway, I heard a noise in the dining room like something heavy falling to the floor. I was in the middle of whipping the cream, so I couldn't leave it to see what had happened."

"An electric mixer?" Martin asked. "Noisy?"

"Yes. Anyway, as soon as I had finished with the cream, I went into the dining room and saw Matthew on the floor, rubbing his head. He had had some sort of a momentary blackout. Bill told me to bring Matthew some ice and something to drink.

"I got them for him and then mopped up Matthew's spilt orange juice. By then he was looking more normal, but he still seemed a bit slow. Bill offered to go to the pharmacy for him, but Matthew said it wasn't necessary.

"So we got through dessert, Matthew insisting that he was all right, but it was obvious that he was not at all himself. Bill went to get changed for the council meeting and Matthew decided that he'd better get home. I was worried about him driving, but he said he'd be fine. He still didn't look very steady on his feet, but I let him go. He could be very forceful once his mind was made up, you know. I think that's all I remember."

She sniffed back a tear. "I still can't believe he's gone."

"I'm sorry. I know that telling us was painful. But we had to know" said Davina.

"It's all right, dear; I understand."

They were standing by the doorway by now. Martin, Davina and Joanna thanked Lucinda for her help and they said their good-byes.

Martin's lips were drawn into a tight line as he drove to the police department.

"What do you think?" Davina asked.

Joanna said, "Healy. He did it. I haven't figured out how yet, but he did it."

"Why? Is his motive better that Felix Taylor's? I don't see that myself," said Martin.

"No, it's not. But it's enough. More than enough. Let me think."

But she had made no progress when she summed up the recent happenings to Harry Jones twenty minutes later as they crowded into the officer's cubicle. Harry marched the three of them to Chief Salter's office and made them repeat the story. One look at the letter written a quarter of a century earlier and the recent note taken from Mrs. Healy's noticeboard convinced the chief.

"So, you surmise that Bill Healy found out about the affair and decided to end it permanently?" he asked Joanna.

"Yes. Mrs. Healy admits that her husband is very jealous. And it's quite understandable, isn't it? Someone whom you've looked on as a friend turns out instead to be a lover from your wife's past and he's taken up where he left off twenty-odd years before. I would say that was more than adequate motive for murder."

"But," the chief pointed out, "we still have one problem. Whoever did it, Felix Taylor or Bill Healy — and let's face it, they both had sufficient reason, at least in their own minds, to do away with Matthew Chambers — we are still faced with the fact that we don't know exactly how it was done. Both of the scenarios point to death by poisoning, but the evidence just doesn't support that. As I am sure none of you has forgotten, there was no poison in Chambers' blood — none. We still don't know how he died."

And the final piece clicked into place in Martin's head.

He flushed with excitement. "I think we do," he said. "And only Bill Healy could have done it."

"Why? Taylor's a doctor. He could get his hands on any number of poisons."

"Not a poison. Far from it; a life saver, in fact."

He looked at Davina.

For a second she stared at him blankly. Then her eyes opened wide.

"Oh!" she exclaimed. "I see."

Chapter 23

Sunday, August 28

Five people were gathered around the table at the *Top of the Mountain*. It was obvious, even to the least discerning of the other diners, that this was a celebration. Cocktails arrived and the first toast was made.

"To a case solved," proposed Harry Jones.

"And to Joanna, Martin and Davina for making this evening possible," added his boss.

They drank the first of innumerable toasts.

"So he confessed, then?" Joanna asked.

Salter nodded.

"Yes. It was just like Martin guessed. He found out about it quite by accident, of course. He says it was a handkerchief, monogrammed 'MC', lying on the bedroom floor that aroused his suspicions about three months ago.

"To make sure, he invented an excuse, a nonexistent meeting one evening when Matthew was visiting. He parked his car a short distance up the hill and walked back to the house. They made love with the curtains open and the lights on. They couldn't've expected anyone to see, of course, the house is too well-screened. But Healy saw. He says that he nearly broke in and killed Matthew then, but instead he decided to be more subtle. And I have to hand it to him, he nearly had us."

"He was helped by a lucky fluke, though."

"Felix Taylor?"

"Yes."

"Yes, it was bad timing on his part to make an attempt on Matthew's life at exactly the same time as Bill Healy was doing the same thing. If it hadn't been for that racquetball injury, Taylor wouldn't have been involved at all."

"And the rest of it happened like Martin speculated?"

"Yes. Bill added 65 milligrams of ground Halcion to Matthew's orange juice when his wife left the room to make the dessert. Matthew drank the juice and passed out within about two minutes. Healy was already carrying the syringe of insulin.

"He injected it into the scalp knowing full well that although the coroner would examine the body for fresh needle pricks he was most unlikely to go to the extent of shaving the scalp to check there as well. He found and removed Matthew's candy. The Halcion was enough to keep Matthew out for a minute or two — Bill was very proud of the accuracy of his timing; he said he had been experimenting on himself — and when he came around, Bill simply explained the soreness away by telling Matthew that he had hit his head on the table leg as he passed out."

"Wait a minute," said Joanna. "There's something here I don't understand. Why did Healy have to inject the insulin into Matthew. Why didn't he just drop that in his orange juice instead of the sleeping drug?"

Davina said, "Because it doesn't work if you take it orally. That's the worst thing about having to take insulin: you have to jab yourself twice a day."

Salter continued, "At this point, Matthew, although he didn't know it, was dosed up to the eyeballs with insulin. There are several varieties of insulin available which can act anywhere from immediately to several hours later. In any case, the dessert turned out to be laden with sugar. The insulin acts to depress the blood sugar, but the sugary dessert raised it for a while. So whether by accident or design the additional insulin didn't kick in immediately.

"Bill urged Matthew to go home because he wasn't feeling well — the after-effects of the Halcion, of course — and Matthew took his advice. If it weren't for the pavlova, Matthew would probably have become unconscious on the way home and we would have had a vehicular accident to deal with. As it was, the sugar in the pavlova staved off the effect of the insulin until after Matthew was home."

"So when he got home and started feeling bad, why didn't Matthew use the phone to call for help?" Joanna asked.

Again Davina explained. "It's too fast. One minute he would have felt fine. Within sixty seconds he would have been unconscious. As he began to lose consciousness, he would have reached for his candy; he probably wasted vital seconds wondering why he couldn't find it in his pockets. There would be no time for him to realize that something was seriously wrong before he lost consciousness. And as soon as consciousness was lost, he was as good as dead. He was found on the steps to the kitchen. He was on his way to get sugar.

"He was dead in minutes. The excess insulin would have been metabolized away as his body died. There's nothing left behind that a lab would find unless it was specifically looking."

They fell silent for several seconds, all contemplating in their various ways what that evening twelve days before must have been like.

Their food arrived.

Davina asked, "How's Lucinda Healy taking it?"

"Badly," Harry answered through a mouthful of filet mignon. "She says she's always hated it here and she's going back to Connecticut. I feel sorry for her in a way. She hasn't had a very happy life, married to someone whom she stopped loving a long time ago."

Davina pondered Harry's words. How awful to live one's life without someone with whom to share a love.

"And Felix Taylor: what's going to become of him?" Martin asked.

"Nothing," Salter said.

"But surely you can get him on something like attempted murder? After all, he's confessed to that much."

"Yes, he has." Chief Salter sighed heavily. "It wasn't an easy decision. The district attorney and I spent nearly two hours together this afternoon, and we're still not certain we're doing the right thing."

"But is the decision yours to make? If the man attempted murder, surely he must be prosecuted?"

The chief shook his head. "No. A DA has tremendous discretion about which cases to prosecute. If he decides not to prosecute a case, then he opens himself to a lawsuit or an investigation by the grand jury if someone feels sufficiently aggrieved by it. But that won't happen. The only people who know about the case against Dr. Taylor are ourselves and his attorney. So the decision is effectively ours."

"And you and the DA decided not to prosecute? Why?"

"Believe me, it wasn't easy, but in the end we both decided it was for the best. Dr. Taylor's not a menace to society, and putting him in prison wouldn't do either him or anyone else any good. He's just a lonely man now. What good would it do to put him away? If he remains free, he'll help a lot of people in Pinetree. He's a good doctor, you know...."

"But even so, if Bill Healy hadn't got in the way, Matthew would have taken that poisoned capsule and Taylor would have been guilty of murder."

"In which case we would have charged him and done our damnedest to put him behind bars. We can't have citizens taking the law into their own hands. But Chambers never took the poison, and as long as it stays out of the papers I think we'll be all right. I had a quiet chat with the editor of the paper and he understands enough that he agreed not to publish any speculation about Felix Taylor that might come his way."

"Still," Martin argued, "it seems unfair. On the one hand, if Taylor succeeds in his objective, he goes to prison for the rest of his life, but if he doesn't succeed, even though he *should* have succeeded, there is no retribution at all. It seems a bit... I don't know... all or nothing to me."

"Yes, I suppose it is. So you think we're making a mistake letting him go?"

Joanna said, "The way I see it, sometimes the most important part of enforcing the law is to do what will help the most, not to unthinkingly apply the law we are supposed to uphold. It's when we forget we're dealing with the lives of real people, not just statistics and cases, that we lose our sense of perspective and become a danger to the very society we're supposed to serve. The greater good is always more important than the law, Martin — although it's a rare officer who has the strength of character to do what Chief Salter has done. I congratulate you, Chief." Joanna raised her glass.

Joanna's toast effectively put an end to the discussion, and they ate for a while in silence.

Eventually, Salter asked, "So what happens now? Martin and Davina go back to England and Joanna returns to Australia? You sell Matthew's house?"

Martin looked at Davina. She was pensive. He wondered what she was thinking. She was also stunningly beautiful. He held his wine glass in front of his face, twirling the liquid and eyeing Davina through the wine. He had put off this moment, purposefully not thinking about it; but now there could be no more procrastination. He wanted desperately to marry her. He had never asked in front of witnesses before. Maybe it would change his luck.

"Davina."

She was deep in thought, looking into the flame of the candle in its glass vase in the middle of the table. She nodded slightly to show that she had heard. He realized that she knew what was coming.

"Will you marry me?"

There was silence around the table. Of the three onlookers, only the chief did not know that this was a frequently-asked question.

Martin gazed at Davina, silently praying that this time would be different.

Davina looked inside herself. For five minutes she had been half praying, half dreading, that this moment would come. Not taking her eyes from the candle, she took a breath.

"Yes," she said, and turned to her fiancé.

Spontaneous applause broke out and the chief called for another bottle of champagne.

Martin and Davina kissed and smiled at one another. Martin decided that there would be time enough later to discover why she had changed her mind. Plenty of time. A lifetime.

Joanna's eyes left her brother and Davina, and rested on Harry. He was looking at her, not at them. She felt uncomfortable, embarrassed that he might take a cue from Martin. She wasn't ready for that. Not yet. Not for a long time.

He asked — but it was not the question that she had feared.

"And what about you? Are you going back to Australia?"

She could not decide if the pleading look she saw in his eyes was her imagination. Her own decision was easy; in fact it had already been made. She shook her head.

"No. At least, not for a while. If Martin and Davina will let me stay on in the house, I think I'd like to stay in Pinetree for a while. I've had enough of city life. I'd like to get to know the people here better. Who knows, I may even find that I'd like to marry and settle down here."

Her lips smiled for everyone; her eyes smiled for Harry.

Colophon

The main body of the text of this book was typeset with the pdfTEX digital typesetting system. The typefaces used are mostly from the Latin Modern family, set at 10·5/12·5.

The paper stock used for the body of the book and for the cover depends on the particular printer that created the book you are holding.

The VEDIT PLUS text editor was used to create the original text.

The cover was created with the Scribus desktop publishing system and the GIMP image manipulation program.

Computer processing for this edition of *All or Nothing* was performed on an Intel quad-core system running the Kubuntu 9.04 64-bit distribution of the GNU/Linux operating system.

www.ingramcontent.com/pod-product-compliance
Lightning Source LLC
Chambersburg PA
CBHW020829260626
47169CB00003B/904